knot gonna give you up

ELIZA JONAS

For all the cuddle monsters out there.
Find your cozy and snuggle in.

contents

about the matchverse

If you haven't read an Omegaverse before, welcome! If you have read one before, welcome back! The next couple pages will give you a few basic pointers on character dynamics and how my Omegaverse is set up.

ALPHA

Providers and caregivers. Overall dominant designation, can "bark" to command, but it's considered taboo to do that. Historically, financial providers to their pack, but in recent years, more Alphas have stayed home to raise kids. This fulfills the caregiver drive in them.

BETA

Part of a complete pack, bonds can't snap into place without one. They balance Alpha and Omega hormones and pheromones, but only when in a pack. In a single mating, they can't provide balance. Don't produce their own extreme pheromones, but do have unique scents.

OMEGA

center and heart of the pack, goes into heats three times per year. *Can get pregnant outside of one, but less than 1% chance.* Require physical touch regularly to avoid overactive pheromones which can lead to other health issues.

TOUCH SICKNESS

Omegas can get Touch Sickness if not touched or cuddled enough. It causes them to pull away from people they don't know and can have physical signs of sickness, such as fatigue and numbness in the skin. Treatable with regular snuggles.

TOUCH LOSS

The ultimate disease from Touch Sickness. Not transmissible. Prevents the Omega from finding their Match via touch. It also causes them to crave comfort more than others, leading to increased nesting and cuddling. However, cuddling with a non-pack member is draining to them, despite the need for comfort. Only someone in their Pack Bond or a Match can provide true comfort.

PACK DYNAMICS

Cannot complete pack bond without each designation. Two designations can bond with each other, but things will always be "off" until a full pack is formed with at least one of each designation. Nature's way of keeping balance between the designations. If the Pack does not complete, it can cause mental instability.

PACK PULL

The feeling that pack members get when they find others meant to be in their pack. It draws you to those people like a magnet but there's no forced bonding.

PACK BOND

Pack Bonds are between three or more people, as long as there is one of each designation. Will not take if a person is unwilling. Pack members are naturally drawn together (Pack Pull) with or without the bond.

MATE BOND

Mate Bonds are between two or more people, and must be consensual. Will not take if one party is unwilling. Does not have to be a Match, can be chosen. Mate Bond is different than a Pack Bond. Mate Bonds will give you insight to a person's emotions.

MATCH

Matches are uncommon. There are two indicators to show that a Match is present. One is scent, meaning the scent of the other person is extremely appealing and you're drawn to it. The other is touch. The first time touching someone's skin, there will be a physical sensation that has been described as tingling, a small zap, and/or a rush of energy. Matches have their own bond, if chosen. Matches do not *have* to solidify the bond. They can walk away from it.

MATED MATCH BOND

When two or more Matched bond together, it is stronger than a typical Mate Bond. Mated Match Bond allows for awareness of other person's location and mental communication in small distances.

one

JOSIE

The Omega in my arms is too young to need my services. She only presented two years ago, so for her to need me feels off. Like there's something wrong, almost. She's sweet, so I don't mind spending time with her. She nestles in a little closer to me, and I oblige her by holding her closer.

"Thanks again for this," she tells me softly.

It's probably the fifth time she's thanked me since I got here.

"Hey, it's no problem. Not only is it what I do, but I understand the need. It's okay."

She sighs and relaxes more into me. We're close to the end of her hour, and that's always the hardest part. Even though they know the session is only an hour, they all give me hopeful eyes that I'll extend their time for just a little more. A little more touch, a little more comfort. However, I'd never leave if I did that, so the hard hour limit is set.

"Tell me about school," I request.

I can feel her smile against my collarbone. I'm a tall Omega, that's for sure. It's not super rare, but the majority of Omegas are usually 5'5" and under. I stand at 5'10", so the smaller ones can easily cuddle in. It would be easy to feel jealous because I'll never be that dainty, but

1

it makes my job easier with the difference. If I can help another Omega, that's good enough for me.

"I think it's going well. My professors are all nice this year, and I'm happy with my Beta bodyguard. Dad insisted, so I couldn't refuse, but it seems like overkill sometimes. He's nice enough, though, and I know he'll chase off any bad Alphas. It doesn't hurt that he's cute."

"Ohhhh, I see where this is going. Has he touched you yet?"

Most people feel a zing of energy, or a zap, when they touch their Match. There can be more than one Match, but it's not necessary for mating. If there's consent from both sides, mate bonds can be formed between any designation. However, it's fun to ask and see if someone has found one of their Matches.

"No." She laughs lightly. "Not skin to skin, at least, he's careful to only touch where my clothing is. And before you ask, he wears blockers so I can't tell how he smells."

I sigh dramatically. "You've been clit blocked. That's some tragic shit right there."

She giggles, and my heart lightens at the sound. If I can make the Omegas I work with laugh, even better. They may require touch to stay healthy, but when I can bring joy, too, that brings some emotional relief to the table, not just physical relief.

"Well, I suppose we'll find out some day. Maybe an Alpha will Match with me and he'll go into a rage of jealousy and demand to join whatever Pack accepts me." Her voice is wistful as she plays out the drama in her head.

"Whatever happens, I hope it's amazing for you," I tell her honestly.

We chat about nothing for the last few minutes, with small, quiet pauses. There aren't many Omegas I'm willing to do regular visits with, but if she asks, I will for her. Most of the time, I get called in for one-off sessions, Omegas whose Pack or family is away for more than a couple of days. My Betas are the ones who take regulars.

With this Omega, though, I want her to have some stability as she moves through her college experience. She doesn't talk about home life much, but I know she has some family who helps her pay for my services. She's softhearted, and if I can give her some solid Omega support, I think she'll really benefit from it.

My timer goes off with a gentle chime, and she sighs. I give her one more squeeze before I remove my arms and move my body a bit away. She sits on her own and looks at me with a small smile.

"Can I thank you now that we're done?"

I chuckle. "Sure, if it will make you feel better."

Her smile is radiant. "Thank you so much. What you do is amazing."

"I'm glad I can help," I reply, my cheeks burning.

I grab my timer and bag, making sure all my things are where I put them. She walks me to the door and we say our goodbyes, no hugs or handshakes. I make sure there are specific rules about when we touch and when we do not. I'm too paranoid not to. We wave goodbye as I head to my compact SUV and turn toward home. My body is tired, and I just want to curl up with some blankets.

I started my company, Touch Helpers, to help Omegas who aren't getting enough touch in their lives. It feels like my own body hates touch, though. Each session leaves me fairly drained, and I find myself retreating further into my introvert lifestyle. Deep down, I recognize it's my own touch issues causing the exhaustion. My Omega side didn't get enough touch as a child, and it caused a more severe version of Touch Sickness. NTS, Non-Touch Syndrome – when Touch Sickness eventually becomes more permanent. Meaning, too much touch actually causes discomfort and drains my energy.

The doctors told me I'll only be comfortable with touches from my Mate Matches, but that I'll likely never recognize my Mate Matches by touch. Pretty dumb, right? There is only one way to be 100% certain of a Match, and it's through touch. If you have a Match, your body feels a zing of energy. So, if I ever do find Matches, I'll have to rely on scent and hope that they're not lying if they say they feel our Match. I could scent to multiple people, but the scents of my Matches should be irresistible. We'll see about that one, but I'm pretty doubtful.

Once I'm back in my small condo, I close all the decorative drapes, letting light into the space, but muted now. I make my way into my nest next, turning on my fairy lights and closing the light-blocking curtains. After a moment of shuffling and burrowing, I feel sufficiently cocooned, and I finally relax. My fingers touch the shirt I stole years ago, and even though his scent is long gone, the fabric still brings me calm and comfort. I pull out my phone from my pocket and lay it on the blanket next to me after dialing his number.

"Josie Girl, how are ya?"

I smile. "Better now. Just got done with a job."

"Oh, do you need me to come over?" he asks.

"Victor, I don't need you to come over after every job. Besides, you live like a million hours away," I tell him.

"As your best friend, it's my duty to ask. Even if coming over is a bit unreasonable."

My smile widens, and I let out a small laugh.

"Tell me about her. Him?"

"A female Omega, she's adorable, just starting college on her own, so when she started noticing some symptoms, she reached out. She's got a supportive family, but they're not nearby. Doesn't have anyone to help her out right now."

"Well, now she has the best," Victor teases.

My fingers rub on his shirt beneath my blankets, and I can't help but think that he's way better than I am. We've been best friends since we were in our early teens. My foster family at the time sent me to the same school he was in, but it didn't last long. They had to move out of state, and I couldn't go, so I was shipped elsewhere. During those six months at the same school, Vic and I bonded as best friends and never lost touch. However, it's probably been a year since I've seen him.

"Pretty sure you're the best," I finally retort.

He laughs, and I find myself laughing along, just out of desire to join him.

"How are you doing?" I divert attention away from me.

"I'm good, but I'm about to be even better."

"Oh? Do tell."

"Well, I just got news," he pauses for dramatic effect, "that I'm being transferred to a new location!"

I'm confused, "I thought you liked where you are."

"I do, it's great here, but where I'm going is going to be even better."

My heart breaks a little. I'm worried he's going to go even further away than he is now. Right now, it's a 20-hour drive to him, so we don't see each other much more than once a year. If he moves any further, it's going to be even harder. I don't want to make him feel bad, though, so I try to mask my fear.

"Wow! That's great. I'm glad you're so excited."

"Want to know where I'm going?" he teases.

No, not really.

"Yeah, tell me!"

"I'm moving to Blackford."

Blackford? As in, my city Blackford? A giddy feeling starts in my chest, but I don't want to get ahead of myself. There are other cities with that name, too.

"Oh, wow! So, like… *my* Blackford?" I ask tentatively.

Vic laughs, "Yes! *Your* Blackford! I'm moving to the same city as you."

My body is exhausted and I'm so damn lonely, and those are the two excuses I'm going to use for the tears that now burst out of me. I start sobbing like an idiot on the phone.

"Oh, Josie, are you okay? Do… do you want me not to move there?" He sounds so unsure.

"No! I mean, I do want you to, I'm just…" I can't finish the sentence, I'm hiccupping and trying to calm my emotions with deep breaths.

"Me too, Josie Girl, me too."

If I didn't know better, I'd say he sounds a little choked up, too. I force a deep breath, working my emotions down so I can have a rational conversation. God, I miss him.

"Do you have a place yet?" I ask him through my final sniffles.

"Soon, I have a couple of leads that I'm sure will pan out. I move in a month."

"I miss you so much, Vic," I confess.

"I miss you, too, Josie Girl. Soon enough you'll wish I was gone, though, I'm gonna bug the shit out of you." He laughs.

My heart feels a bit lighter now that I've calmed down, so we continue our bantering about nothing. We get along so well that I've always wondered if he could be a Match, but I can barely remember what he smells like. Then again, I'm not sure I want us to be. If we are Matches, is he going to want a full Pack? I'm not sure how I would handle that. It's always been just me. Even if we ended up as a Pack of three, who would we find for an Alpha? What Alpha wants an Omega with Touch Sickness?

No, for now it's better to keep my brain firmly in the friend zone, I don't need to get ahead of myself. I can focus on just enjoying our friendship and worry about the rest later. My bestie is going to be here soon, and I can't wait to see him again.

JESSE

The screen in front of me blurs again. I think I've forgotten to blink. What time is it? Leaning back into my chair, I rub my eyes with the heels of my palms, willing moisture back into them. I came in early today to get some extra coding done, and apparently, I haven't moved much. Have I moved at all? Getting in the zone is easy, getting out of it? Not so much. People at work know I'm not a "people person," so I don't go into the office much. I prefer to stay at my condo.

However, today I wanted the extra boost of the company network and servers, so I came here to plug straight in. It was well worth it for the amount of work I got done. There was a particularly tricky piece of code that I needed the extra computer power for. With the speed of my office network, I was able to solve it in half the time. Then I got sucked into other projects.

When I glance at the clock, I note that it's after lunch already. I've been here since four or five this morning, so I decide I'm done for today. I pack up my things and take the back exit of the building, doing my best to avoid people. They always want to talk, and I can't understand why. I don't need to know about every detail of their lives, and they sure don't need to know about mine.

Raking a hand through my hair, I let out a sigh of relief once I'm out of the building. It's short-lived, though, because one of my colleagues is on their way back in. Probably from lunch, like a normal person.

"Hey Jesse! Fancy seeing you here!" he says.

"Yup," I answer.

Do I know his name? Probably. Do I care to remember? Not right now. Maybe I can get through this without admitting that.

"Did you get that code fixed? I know you mentioned it was giving you trouble," the guy goes on.

"Yeah, fixed it this morning. Merged it into the branch, good to test."

"Awesome, I can let our testers know, I know it's something the boss has been chomping at the bit for. Good thing we've got you around."

"Thanks. See ya." I end our conversation with a nod and walk past him, aiming for my car.

"See ya!" he calls after, as if I didn't just awkwardly walk away.

I grimace internally, knowing that I really should open up and talk to people more. But I've got no good reason to. It's exhausting trying to talk to people, to try and remember things about them so they think I actually care. Newsflash, I don't care. At all. I don't wish them ill, but I don't really give a shit about other people. I like my space. I like my quiet.

When I finally pull into my driveway, I feel all the tension finally roll off me. I'm ready to relax in my quiet condo, with nobody nearby. I moved in about a year ago, and I've never had a problem with noise or my neighbors. Most of the neighbors are retired, so it's perfect. Except for the woman I share a wall with. I only see her in passing, but I stare every time.

She's tall, always has her beautiful auburn hair in a ponytail, and seems just as solitary as I am. I never see anyone come to her home. It's only ever her leaving. Just like me. There's never a chance to talk to her, and I'm not about to disrupt her peace just to say hi. No, that sounds like a terrible choice. If she turns out to be horrible, I'm not sure I can take my fantasy being shattered by reality.

I grab my laptop bag and lock my car door before turning and freezing in place. She's just locking up her own door, leaving her condo as I'm just getting in. I've never had the chance to ever talk to her, and I don't know if she's even aware that I exist. Do I approach her? Should I leave well enough alone? The decision is made for me when her purse slips off her shoulder just enough to spill all over her walkway and grass.

"Oh, shit!" I hear as I walk over.

Hiding my smile at the sound of her swearing, I take the final couple of steps toward her and grab a couple of tubes from the ground. She's so effortlessly adorable. I hold the tubes out.

"Here, your... uh... tubes."

Her eyes flash to mine, warm brown eyes wide with surprise. She must not have heard me approaching.

"My *what?*" she asks.

Her voice soothing, not too high-pitched, but still incredibly feminine. I look down at my hand dumbly.

"Uh, tubes," I repeat.

She looks down at what I'm holding, then back up at me, and breaks into a beautiful smile. I swear I almost fall over backward at the impact of it. So far, my dream girl has exceeded every fantasy I've had of her. I don't think she can get any better. I'm officially addicted to her, and I need more. Now I just need to pretend I know how to talk to people. Easy, right?

"Thanks for saving my tubes... It's just gum and some creams and stuff," she says, offering me her purse to drop them into.

"Uh, yeah, no problem. What are neighbors for, right?"

"Oh, you live in the unit next to mine?" she asks, fully standing.

I bring myself to full height as well and am pleased to find I don't have to bend down to meet her eyes. Trying not to feel like a creeper, I nod my head, clearly I've been watching her, but she hasn't noticed me.

"Uh, yeah, right there," I tell her, pointing behind me with my thumb.

She glances between my door and me, clearly still a bit flustered. Does she smell me? Do I smell good to her? Is that why she looks a bit unsure? I don't want to come on too strong, so I've left some space between us. I can't smell her, but maybe I'm upwind of her.

"Well, thank you for helping. I appreciate it," she tells me.

"Anytime! Um, my name is Jesse."

She smiles again. "Jesse. I like that. I'm Josie."

"Josie." A matching smile spreads across my own face. "If you ever need a cup of sugar, feel free to knock on my door."

She bites her lip and looks up at me through her lashes.

"Same for you. I mean, I'm open for you. Uh, no, shit. God, I'm awkward." Her face flushes a beautiful red.

I chuckle, "I got you, don't worry."

She places one of her hands on her forehead, groaning in embarrassment.

"This is why I don't flirt," she mutters.

My grin widens, "You flirtin' with me, pretty girl?"

"Pretty girl?"

"Yeah," I clear my throat, trying not to let on how nervous I am, "One of the prettiest girls I've ever seen. Or met."

She giggles a little, and if I wasn't already smitten, that would have gotten me. I feel all warm and shit when I hear it. Internally, I work myself up, deciding to just shoot my shot.

"I know we're neighbors, but, um, can I give you my number? You know, in case you need that sugar. I can make sure I have some so you don't come over to disappointment."

"I'm not sure I could be disappointed if you're there."

I duck my head with a smile. I'm not used to compliments or being social in general, so I'm not sure what to do with myself. I reach down and rifle through my laptop bag for a piece of paper and a pen. I land on some sticky notes and pull them out, hastily scrawling my number on one.

"Uh, my handwriting isn't great, can you read that?"

She peers over and nods, "Yeah, totally, it's not that bad."

I pull off the sticky note and hold it out for her. She reaches out to take it from me, and as she does, I feel it. A zap, straight from my fingers to my heart, then throughout my body. It's brief, no more than a second, but I recognize what it is. A Match. Everyone hopes to find theirs, but I never had. I didn't want the burden of having to care about another person besides myself. Now, though? Now my entire world has shifted.

My soul feels like it was never whole until this moment. Maybe it's dramatic, but I wouldn't be surprised if a beam of light came from the sky to focus solely on her. Everything revolves around her now, just from that one feeling. It's not something we can solidify until we bond, but just feeling that zap is unlike anything I've heard. People talk about a zing, or a zap, but it's also a sudden clarity of what's important. Which is this person you Match with. The woman in front of me. I have to hope that she's happy about this and not horrified.

My eyes fly up to her, needing to see her reaction, but she's not looking at me; she's busy putting the note into her wallet. Once it's secure, she looks up brightly at me, seemingly unaware of the shift that just occurred in my soul. Fuck, did I imagine it? She's completely unaware of what just happened, while my fingers still tingle. How?

"Well, thanks again for the help! I'll, uh, text you later if that's okay?" she says with a small smile.

"Please do," I tell her, forcing a smile on my face.

I have to believe that she was too distracted to feel it. Next time we see each other, I'll make sure I'm close enough for her to smell. She'll have to notice the Match then. Yeah, definitely, that will work. Resolve settles in me as I watch her get into her car and drive away from me. We'll figure this out.

three

JOSIE

Finally, certain that I have everything, I put on my shoes to leave my place. This is a first-time visit, so we're doing a short session to relieve some of her needs, but not a full session. I'm not sure I have the capacity for a full session today, plus her scent card wasn't something I enjoyed, so I'll have to use a nasal scent block to avoid taking her scent in. If we get along well enough, I can ask her to wear a scent-block perfume to dampen her scent.

As soon as my shoes are on, I apply some of the scent blocker to my upper lip, effectively preventing me from smelling anyone. I have no idea how scientists do it, but I can still smell normal things, just not other people. Walking down my pathway, I feel my purse start to slip off my shoulder. I scramble to catch it, but half of its contents dump out anyway.

In a whirlwind of activity, I finally get to meet my elusive neighbor. I knew someone moved in there a little while back, but I've not gotten a chance to meet them. Now I know it's a him. A very tall, sexy, masculine him. All I could think was controlling my body's reaction to him. I could feel my arousal ramp up, but I have a stronger will than most and I lock that shit down. Of course, he has to make it hard with his gorgeous blue eyes and flirty smile, but I make it through without perfuming.

He's all I can think of as I drive away, my mind spinning on the entire encounter. There's something about him that draws me in, even though I couldn't smell him. The way he looked at me in the end, though, like I'm his entire world? That was enough to make me want to jump his bones. Shit, could he smell me? Is that why? Pretty sure we didn't touch, so I'm not sure why he was staring at me. I definitely will be texting him later, there's no way I can resist. Once I arrive at my appointment, I take a moment to enter his number into my phone and decide to bite the bullet.

ME

> Hey! This is Josie. I can't text much, but I thought I'd say hi.

THERE'S NO IMMEDIATE REPLY, which I'm honestly not surprised about. I'm sure he's got things to do today. I take a deep breath, gather my things, and step out of my car. As I close it, I hear my phone ding. My mouth starts creeping into a smile, and I bite my lower lip to try and stop it. When I glance at the screen, there's no holding the smile back.

JESSE

> Hey, pretty girl! Glad you texted, good luck with whatever you're doing right now.

IT TAKES every ounce of professionalism in me not to squeal and jump up and down in front of this client's house. There may be nothing that comes from it, but it's hard to deny the excitement of talking to my hot neighbor. Slipping my phone into my purse, I take a deep breath and make my way to the front door. We're in a nice neighborhood, thankfully not mansion territory, though. Mansions make me nervous, and they're always too clean. It creates too much pressure over not making a mess.

The door opens, and I'm not sure what higher power is smiling down on me, but I get my second super-hot guy interaction today. Where my neighbor had light hair, this guy has hair as black as night, an un-styled, slightly too long mohawk. His blue eyes pierce me, and his eyes flare wide when he sees me. We stand there, staring at each other for a moment before I remember myself.

"Hello, I'm Josie from Touch Helpers. I'm here for an introductory appointment," I explain, and try to subtly ensure I didn't start drooling.

He startles and seems to shake himself, "Hi, I'm Henry, please come in."

I step into the house, and I'm impressed with the level of welcome it exudes. A small smile comes to me as I look around, my eyes sweeping from warm family photos to casual throws lining the couch, and small clutter sitting out on surfaces. It seems like a home with plenty of love, so I'm curious and a little concerned as to why an Omega needs touch here. One should get plenty from what this environment presents.

"Where's the Omega?" I ask the man, who is still staring at me.

His mouth is slightly open, and his eyes are riveted on me. The fuck is wrong with this dude? He may be hot, but I'm not into creepers.

I clear my throat, "Excuse me? Henry, was it? Are you okay?"

He comes back to himself and apologizes.

"Yeah, sorry, I'll go get her. Or, do you need to come with me to her nest? I don't know how this works."

I give him a soft smile. "Why don't I follow you, and we can ask what she's most comfortable with?"

"Yeah, right, of course."

I follow him up the stairs, where there are several rooms, and we stop outside the door furthest from the stairs. Henry knocks, and we wait in the quiet for a moment. A small voice speaks, but I can't quite hear what she's saying. Henry must be used to it because he seems to understand her just fine.

"Ray, it's me. Your Touch Helper is here," he calls gently.

There's some shuffling from behind the door, and it opens a crack to reveal a shorter woman with shoulder-length blonde hair, pulled half back. I can see her distrust of me, but I'm happy to see that she looks at Henry with plenty of trust. It's a good sign, even if she's not getting what she needs from him.

"Hey, I'm Josie, you're Ray?" I introduce myself gently.

She nods, but doesn't verbalize anything.

"I'd love to talk for a few minutes and see how you feel about some touch therapy. Would you like to do this in your nest, or is there another place in the house that would be better? It's totally up to you, whatever you are most comfortable with."

Ray looks at Henry, and he nods with a smile, reinforcing what I've said.

"Umm, I guess the living room couch, I don't want you in my nest yet." She looks incredibly nervous as she says it.

I respond with my gentle smile, "No problem at all, I want you to be comfortable over anything else."

She gives a small smile back and closes her door before coming out a moment later, dressed in lounge pants and a hoodie, most of her skin covered. I make a mental note of that; it's an indication that she's not comfortable with skin-to-skin touch quite yet. It's something we can try to work up to, if this ends up being a good arrangement. If we don't mesh, I can refer her to one of the two Betas I use for touch therapy.

Letting her lead, we make our way down to a comfortable seating area on the first floor. The couches are plush and soft. Ray grabs a spot and burrows herself into the corner of a couch with some blankets around her. I indicate the spot next to her, and she nods, so I take that as permission to sit next to her.

"Do you want Henry to stay or leave?" I ask, looking only at her.

Her eyes jump between us, and she bites down on her lip as she thinks. It's pretty clear that she's trying not to upset anyone.

Henry walks a little closer and kneels down. "How about I stay until you tell me you're okay without me here?"

She nods, "Yes, please."

Henry smiles and makes his way to the other side of the room and settles himself into a chair. We sit in the quiet for a moment, Henry scrolling on his phone while Ray and I take each other in. I make a point to settle in a bit more, and I can see Ray relax just a bit more.

"How about I tell you about me?" I ask.

I get a small smile in response, "Sure, I'm not good at small talk."

"I totally get it," I tell her, leaning in slightly, "It's so awkward, am I right?"

That one gets me a full smile, and a warm feeling fills my chest. I love making other people smile. It gives me a sense of accomplishment to see their eyes light up, chasing away any tension or negativity, even if it's just for a moment.

"Well, you might know, but my name is Josie. I started Touch Helpers, oh, maybe five years ago now. I had a job as a secretary, and when I overheard someone at the office talking about a friend they knew who had touch sickness, I offered to help. Being able to help gave me a sense of purpose, and I started Touch Helpers. I have two others who help with touch, both Betas. I'm hoping one day I'll find another Omega to help too, but for now it's me and two Betas who live together."

"Live together? Are they mated to each other?" she asks softly.

"No, they're siblings. They'd both like to find their own Pack someday, but they're happy with supporting each other for now. They're both incredibly warm and understanding, so even if you and I don't work out, you could try one of them."

She nods thoughtfully. I let her process my words for a few moments to see if she has any questions or further thoughts.

"Can I ask if you're mated?"

Most Omegas don't ask me this, so I'm a little thrown, but I don't mind the question. "People don't usually ask me that, but I don't mind telling you. I'm not mated right now. I've been happy enough being single, so I'm not looking either."

"Oh, that's good." She seems almost relieved.

"Do you prefer someone unmated?"

"I don't want someone to use this as an excuse to try and mate me. Does that make sense?"

"Completely. We have a policy in place that if it does ever happen where a Match is found or even just interest in being Pack, we re-evaluate the contract. You make all the decisions on whether you want anything to happen. If you choose to leave my service, I can recommend another one if needed. There aren't many of us, so we try to work together as much as possible."

She smiles. "Sounds like you have all the bases covered."

"I try to, but I'm always up to learn something new if a new situation comes up."

Ray looks over at Henry, "I'm good if you want to go to another room."

I look over in time to see him looking at me before catching himself and turning back to Ray. "Okay, I'll just be a few rooms away if you need me. Just shout."

"What should we shout?" I ask, waiting to see if either of them takes the bait for some levity.

"Henry, you're the best and we can't live without you!" he exclaims.

Ray snorts, "Or we could just say 'Get your ass in here.'"

Poor Henry slumps in mock sorrow, "Someday you'll admit I'm the best."

"Keep trying."

I can't help but giggle at them. There's definitely sibling affection here, but they look nothing alike, so I'm very curious how they know each other. The application didn't list any relatives, just that she was living in town and needed help. Henry grins at us before winking and walking out of the room.

"He clearly cares about you," I mention.

A happy expression appears on her face, "Yeah, he's been a good big brother-not brother."

"Do you want to talk about what's happening in your life? Or we can just spend a few minutes cuddling to see if we're comfortable with it."

"I could go for some snuggles."

I nod and grab a couple more blankets before peeling hers back and sliding under them. I arrange the new ones around us so we're completely cocooned, only a hole at the top to let air in. Reaching out to her, I pull her in close, and she slides in without complaint, resting her head on my shoulder. That's how we exist for the next fifteen minutes, and I can feel her slowly relax and calm the longer we go. She absolutely needed this.

VIC

Simon places our last cardboard box on the moving truck as I sign the final agreement with our moving company. My eyes can't help but be drawn to him. He's got all the Alpha swagger and confidence but none of the arrogance. He and I have been dancing around each other for a while now when it comes to full commitment. There's no Match between us, and we're acquainted with each other's bodies enough to have ruled that out. We don't want to separate either, though. Pretty sure we have a Pack Pull, but it's a subject we haven't brought up yet.

I hand the clipboard back to the driver, and he nods before making sure his associate locks the back door of the truck. It's reassuring to know that our stuff won't fly out of the back and scatter everywhere. I've heard some moving nightmares, so I appreciate the detail these guys display. The truck leaves our driveway, and I look at our rental house with nostalgia.

"We had some good times here," I say to Simon.

He places an arm on my shoulder, leaning against me lightly. "Yeah, it was a good place. Especially the sofa."

"Good thing we're bringing it with us," I tell him, eyebrow arched.

Simon grins, "Are you excited about the new house?"

"I'm looking forward to trying somewhere new. Having Josie there helps."

"Ah, the elusive Josie," Simon chuckles, "I'll finally get to meet her."

"She'll like you, don't worry," I reassure him.

"Who *doesn't* like me? I'm very likable."

I turn and give him a skeptical look. He acts impervious to everyone's opinions, but he struggles to feel like he's enough. Add on that he's an Alpha, and it creates more pressure for him to be a certain way, increasing his insecurities. He's never a disappointment to me, and, if I'm being honest with myself, I'm pretty sure I love him. I need to talk to him soon about the Pack Pull, maybe once we're settled in Blackford.

"Let's go," he says, but before he can take a step, I pull him close and kiss him softly.

"Anywhere with you," I tell him.

He flushes, and a small smile comes to his face, but that's all the reaction I get from him. His nerves are riding him too hard. We hop in our cars and start the twenty-hour drive to our new city. Thankfully, the drive is smooth without any problems. We even stopped at the same hotel as the movers, so I know they didn't get lost. Having all our stuff in just one truck makes me nervous because if it goes wrong, then we have nothing. Next time, maybe I'll split things up so we have two trucks. Maybe we just won't move again for a long time. I'm okay with that.

The next day, Simon pulls into our new digs ahead of me, parking his car on the street. I pull up behind him so the moving truck can park in the driveway, and we walk to the door of the rental house. It's nice, quite spacious, and even comes with a small Omega Suite. Nothing like what you find in the rich people districts, but still cozy and separate from the other rooms. I walk through the first few rooms, finding a note from the rental agency on the kitchen counter.

"Hey, look, we have a welcome note!"

Simon ambles over and steps up behind me, looking over my shoulder at the paper. There's nothing exciting about the note, just a standard "welcome" message with some directions on where to find local restaurants if needed. A spare key sits with it, and I grab it for my own key ring. They mailed us one to our old space, so Simon got us in with that one.

"That's nice of them," Simon comments. His head snaps up when the rumbling of the large moving truck fills the air. "I'll go direct them. Can you grab our clothes from the cars?"

"Sure thing!" I tell him.

I go to my car and grab my first box, taking it up the stairs to the bedrooms. I find the master bedroom, which is next to the Omega Suite, and dump the box in there. It's got plenty of room, the king-size bed will be perfect here. We have a full-size bed as well, which Simon uses most of the time, but I'm hoping he'll use the king-size more and more. I want to spend every night with him, like an official Pack.

I survey the room across the hall and decide it will be perfect for the full-size bed, so when I pass the movers, I tell them which rooms to put the beds in. After two hours of hauling things into the house, we finally wave to our movers as they pull out of the driveway.

"Home sweet home," I say, hands on my hips.

"Do we want to unpack more or get a late pizza dinner? I vote pizza and more unpacking tomorrow."

"Sounds good, how about you order and I'll make sure the beds are made up at least so we can sleep tonight."

"Just do the king size, less work and big enough for both of us," Simon suggests.

I try to contain my grin, but based on Simon's smirk, he sees right through me as I huff it up the stairs. Digging through a few boxes, it takes me a minute to find the bedding and shake out a set of sheets. I'm about to throw the blankets and pillows on when my phone rings, and when I see the Caller ID, I pause what I'm doing.

"Hey Josie Girl!"

"Hey, Vic, are you in town yet? Or did you get distracted on the way and decide to settle somewhere else?"

I give her a slight chuckle, "No, we just got here. Movers left about twenty minutes ago, so Simon and I are ordering a pizza now."

"Simon?"

"Yeah, you remember my roommate, right?"

"Uh, yeah, I just didn't realize he was coming too," she says, sounding nervous.

"Oh, sorry, I thought I told you. I didn't mean to spring that on you."

"No, no, it's okay, I know you've lived with him a long time, so it's logical he would come with you."

"You're still my Josie Girl, don't forget that," I tease her, hoping to reassure her that this changes nothing for me.

"Such a charmer," she teases back.

I look up as she says that and see Simon leaning in the doorframe, looking a little lost. My hand reaches out for him, wanting him to be part of things, and he takes it for a moment, giving it a soft squeeze before mouthing "pizza" to me.

"Well, this charmer has some pizza to devour. Can we make plans soon? Once Simon and I are a little more settled? I'm excited to introduce you guys to each other." My eyes are glued to Simon as I ask.

"Definitely, go eat and we'll make plans later," she tells me.

"See you soon, Josie Girl."

"See you soon, Charmer."

I follow Simon down the stairs and we dig out some paper towels before settling in on the floor of the kitchen, pizza boxes sitting open in front of us. We each grab a slice of pizza and eat in silence. It's nice to take in the ambiance of the house, but we're also both starving. Long trips will do that to a person. Especially an Alpha like Simon. He looks over at me and quirks a brow.

"You're drooling."

Startled, I wipe my hand across my chin, but it's perfectly dry. Asshole. I narrow my eyes at him, but Simon just laughs at me.

"I couldn't help it, you've been staring for a good minute." He laughs.

"Well played, Simon, well played. I'll have you know that I *wasn't* staring. I was admiring."

He laughs harder, and we settle back into a comfortable silence. When we're done eating, we pack up the leftovers and settle in on the couch. The sight of boxes all around feels like possibility, like the future is just waiting for us to step into it. Simon clears his throat.

"So, you start in a couple of days, right?"

I nod, "Yeah, I'll have tomorrow and the weekend to get us fully settled in."

"You mean *we* will get settled in."

"Yeah, yeah, I know you'll be helping. Just wandering along behind me and fixing what I've done," I tease with a smile.

"If you did it right the first time, I wouldn't have to," he smiles back.

"I'm just trying to include you in my creative process."

He nudges my knee with his, "Sure, whatever you say."

I flush with pleasure, savoring the flirtation. Simon isn't overly affectionate when he's unsure about something, so this display warms my heart. I know he can be affectionate, between the two of us, and in his interactions with his family. He's sure of them, so he openly hugs and teases them. Normally it's the same with us, but something's been riding him, has been for the last week or so. It's probably the big move. Everything feels uncertain and up in the air. I know we'll land in the right spot, though. I have faith in that.

"Are you doing okay?" I blurt out.

Simon raises his eyebrows, "Yeah, why?"

"It feels like you've been a little distant," I shrug, "I figured you'd feel more settled after the move, but you're still distant. Like you won't let yourself relax."

"We only finished the trip today," he says, a soft smile on his face.

Needing the connection with him, I turn my body and make sure I can see him fully. I meet his brown eyes that remind me so much of Josie, and that pull hits me again. We're Pack, I just know it. Simon's been hard to convince of that, so I don't bring it up much.

"Please don't hold back from me, Simon. You're one of the most important people to me, and I don't want to say or do anything to lose you."

"Oh, Vic, you won't, but I promise I'll talk to you. You're special to me," he reaches out and grabs my hand, "You know that, right?"

"I might need reminding," I smirk at him.

He chuckles and pulls me close, gently taking my lips with his. His lips caress mine, our tongues languidly stroking each other. Slowly, my pants get tighter and I groan at the building pressure between my fly and my dick. Simon rumbles in that way only an Alpha can, and I swear I melt like an Omega. I'm a confirmed Beta, but this man makes me melt.

Guilt eats at me, so I end our kiss gently. He likes to play around, and yeah, we're special to each other, but I think my feelings go deeper than that. Of course, I'm too scared to confess that and scare him away. So I'll keep my feelings close, and if we ever get the chance, maybe I'll tell him. I stand and hold out my hand.

"We should head upstairs, and an early bedtime is definitely called for after all that work."

Simon quirks a brow, "Is it now? Are you ready to sleep already?"

"I said *bed*time, not sleep time."

He grins and follows me to the bedroom, hands touching me wherever he can. Some teasing, some to spur me on faster, and when I finally turn to look at him in the bedroom, his eyes sparkle with anticipation and joy. I grin at him. It's going to be a good night.

five

JOSIE

I fidget again with my hair, trying to decide if I should bring a coffee cup or just get a paper one at the shop. I know bringing my own is more responsible, but it feels silly to carry an empty travel mug. Grabbing my mug, I shake my head at myself. I need to stop overthinking everything. Jesse has been really wonderful via text, so I'm sure today will go just fine. My phone is in my hand, so I take a second to re-read our messages for today. Not that I haven't done this several times already.

JESSE
I still can't believe you're an 80s music fan.

ME

Better believe it! So many of the best songs written are from the 80s!

JESSE
Okay, so what's your favorite song?

Me

How can I even pick? That's just cruel asking for only one favorite.

JESSE

Okay, okay, how about one of your favorites? I will hereby attest to the fact that you have multiple, and this in no way reflects your absolute favorite.

Me

LOL

You're too funny. Ok, one of my favorite songs is "We Didn't Start the Fire."

Jesse

It's been burnin' since the world's been turnin'.

ME

Is it too soon to say I love you?

JESSE

Well, I need to take you on a date first.

ME

I could be persuaded into a date...

JESSE

Do you like coffee?

There's a shop downtown that I've heard good things about.

ME

Sounds like we better check it out.

JESSE

Indeed. Our opinion is very valuable.

I SMILE AT THE EXCHANGE, and my stomach gives a little flutter. He clearly likes me, or he wouldn't flirt and text so much, right? I'm pretty sure he wouldn't. From what I remember, men don't put in the work if they're not interested. Granted, I haven't dated in probably eight years, but it can't change that much, right? Right.

Stepping out of my house, I turn my face up to the sun, enjoying the warmth on my skin. My ears catch the sound of Jesse's door closing, and he walks over to me, cutting across our shared grass. My body instinctively turns toward him, and my smile is wide and excited. Then his scent hits me, and I almost buckle and fall to the ground. I have never smelled something so wonderful in my entire life.

His eyes widen, and I wonder if he's caught my scent as well. It's been a while since I've paid attention to it, but my scent is like a cinnamon dessert. Sweet, decadent, and swirled with cinnamon. Jesse, though, smells like fresh rain. Full of new opportunities, a fresh start, the underlying scent of petrichor lacing it to build a beautiful scene in my mind.

There are scents that call to each other when you Match with someone, but there are also scents that are just wonderful to smell. So, the key to finding a Match is touch. Something that I'll never be able to experience. My past means I can't feel the zing of a Match. I stopped dating when I realized guys would tell me they felt the zing after realizing I couldn't. It soured things for a few years, but I thought I was ready to jump back in.

Now, as we stare at each other in awe, I wonder if I'm not quite ready. Maybe I should head back inside my condo and wrap myself up in my nest and hide. There's something that keeps me here, though, the hope dancing in his eyes. Jesse told me that he's an introvert, and considering I hadn't seen him before my purse incident, that supports that. He keeps to himself. So, if he's hopeful for this, maybe I should give it a shot.

He clears his throat, finally breaking the silence that cocooned us for a minute.

"You look great," he tells me with a smile.

"You smell fantastic," I breathe.

His smile grows, and I realize what I said, my cheeks heating with mortification.

"I mean, you look nice too, I didn't mean—I don't want—"

"It's fine," he cuts me off before leaning in like he has a secret, "you smell fantastic too."

We grin at each other before moving to Jesse's car and hopping in. Normally, I'd drive separately, but we already know where each other lives, so it seems silly to drive separately to protect that. Jesse finds street parking, and we pay the meter to get us through a couple of hours while we wander and enjoy each other's company. As we walk into the coffee shop, Jesse puts his hand gently on my lower back, and I almost swoon.

It makes me feel dainty and cared for, two things I don't feel very often. I turn my face to grin at him. "So, do you drink your coffee black or do you get super fancy drinks?"

He chuckles, "I like cream and sugar, but sometimes I'll get a super fancy one, just because."

"What's today calling for?"

"Today feels like a special day." He grins at me.

"I agree."

We put our orders in and move to the side to wait.

"So, um, tell me about your family," I say, wanting to avoid awkward pauses.

He goes quiet for a moment, and I worry that I've now created an awkward pause. So, like the smooth Omega that I am, I try to fix it. "I mean, only if you want to tell me, you don't have to, it's not like everybody has a good one, or even likes their good ones! Sometimes what's good isn't, and sometimes what can seem bad is good... and I'm rambling."

Jesse just grins at me. "It's adorable."

My face flushes from equal parts embarrassment and pleasure. "Sorry, I just wanted to avoid any awkward topics."

Our drinks get set on the counter in front of us, and Jesse grabs them before we leave the cafe. Belatedly, I realize I left my travel mug in the car, but it's too late now to worry about it. I take mine from

Jesse, and we stroll down the street, doing some window shopping as we do.

"I suppose family is never an easy topic," Jesse comments.

"True. Okay. What if we ask simple questions? No details."

"Can we pass if we're uncomfortable?"

Thinking of my own family history, I nod. "Absolutely, I want to get to know you, not make you feel bad."

"Same. So, do you have siblings?"

"I don't. What about you?"

"I have two extremely social sisters." He sticks to minimal details, and as much as I wish I could ask for more, I want to respect his boundaries.

"Do you have lots of extended family?" I ask.

"Not a ton, maybe 40 people on both sides of the family. I don't go to family reunions much. I don't like dealing with a lot of people. Do you? Have extended family, I mean?"

Pausing, I kick myself mentally for my original question. I wanted to learn about Jesse's family, not talk about mine. Or lack thereof.

"Uh, nope, no family for me."

Instead of replying, Jesse cautiously takes my hand, and my fingers eagerly thread through his. Belatedly, I realize we're touching, but he hasn't reacted at all. Before I can remove my hand out of panic, he starts talking again.

"Favorite kind of music?" he asks, glossing over my family comment.

"The 80s, duh!" I say with a grin.

He turns and gives me a furrowed brow. "Really? I mean, I knew you liked the 80s, but that's your favorite?"

"We just texted about it! It's only the best music decade ever!"

He chuckles and leads me to a bench nearby and we sit down to continue the conversation. "I don't know about the *best* music decade…"

"How can you not agree? Your name is Jesse, and there is a literal song about your girl."

"If you knew how many jokes I heard growing up, maybe you wouldn't love the song quite so much," he tells me with a small smile.

I groan in acquiescence, "Ugh, fine, you have a point there."

We continue back and forth, and I find out that he actually prefers movies and TV that avoid overly technical things. He hasn't met a food he doesn't like, and he struggles to talk about himself. Listening to him talk, I can tell he feels a lot more than he lets on, and it's clear he does care about other people, even if he doesn't like being around them. He talks about some of his family on occasion with a smile, and even admits he doesn't mind his co-workers, he just doesn't know how to talk to them.

Coffee cup empty, I stand and toss mine in the nearby public disposal, grabbing Jesse's to toss for him. We stand next to each other for a moment before I grab his hand again and pull him down the street.

"I heard about this new coffee shop going in and I feel like we need to do a walk-by," I tell him as we go.

"Oh? What are we evaluating on this walk-by?"

I tap my finger to my chin as I think. "I don't think it's open yet, so I say we evaluate the general vibe."

"General vibe, huh? Not sure how we can do that if it's not done, but I'm up for a challenge."

I turn and grin at him as we walk. On the next block, we almost pass the shop. It's fairly unassuming, no sign up yet to tell the world what it's becoming. Through the window, we can see construction tools strewn about the edges of the room, and it's easy to find the customer counter, plus a few tables placed around the room. Almost like someone is trying to block the space and see how things will look. There are even boxes placed around as if they are benches that could be installed.

"Wow, it looks really open," I say as we peer in the windows.

"Yeah, not bad. Too social for me, but if the coffee's good, I would venture in. It's not too close-spaced."

"What colors do you think they'll use?"

He hums for a moment, thinking. "Definitely dark greys and blacks. Full emo vibe."

I can't help but laugh at the idea. There's no way this place is going to be an emo hangout.

"I vote bright neon colors. Well, bright if not neon. Put some weird squiggly lines on the walls and it's perfection."

Jesse chuckles, "I doubt it's going to be an 80s lounge either."

"We're actually going to go with wood floors, a medium gray wall, and pops of color with art and plants."

I squeak and spin at the deep voice behind us. Jesse turns, sans squeak, and holds his hand out in front of me. The fact that he's trying to protect me makes my inner Omega swoon. Talk about a worthy Alpha. We're on a first date, and he's already showing he'd protect me.

The newcomer holds his hands up, "Sorry, didn't mean to scare you. I'm renovating this joint and overheard you talk about the interior, so I wanted to hear what you thought."

My eyes take in this new Alpha, and I can't deny that my interest is piqued. His curly black hair is long enough for the half knot that sits on his head, but the other half of his hair brushes the tops of his shoulders. He's got caramel brown eyes that I could easily stare at all day. The small scar on his right eyebrow makes me curious to know how he got it.

Jesse relaxes a tad when he realizes this new guy isn't going to attack us, but he still stands close to me just in case. I can tell his Alpha instincts are riding him to protect, so I rest my hand on his upper back to reassure him that I'm okay. My hand may or may not have checked my chin for drool as I moved it to Jesse's back. I admit to nothing.

The new guy is just standing there, staring, and even though I've already checked myself for drool, I make a point to ensure my mouth is closed. He is a cool drink of water on a hot day, and I feel guilty feeling like that while I'm already out on a date with Jesse. I know there's going to be multiple men if I end up in a Pack, but these two aren't Packed up. Something about this guy tugs at me, but I can't put my finger on it, and I'm not sure I want to try while I'm on this date.

"So, when do you open?" Jesse asks, and the awkward moment breaks.

"Oh! Uh, hoping to open next month," the guy says.

"It looks great," I add.

He smiles and I'm ready to swoon, "Thanks. It's my first satellite shop, so sometimes it feels like things are under a lot of pressure."

"Oh wow, I bet. Maybe we'll have to stop by and grab a coffee once you're open."

He nods, "Absolutely, I don't have any business cards on me, but I'm Simon. Mention me and I'll make sure your first drink is on me. For both of you."

Jesse nods back at Simon, a look of appreciation on his face. Looking at Jesse's face, I can tell he's really uncomfortable, so I make excuses to leave. I promise Simon that we'll come back to try the coffee and turn us to walk back the way we came. One glance over my shoulder shows Simon still watching us walk away, a stunned look on his face.

Biting my lip, I look forward again, wondering how to navigate this. I've never had this problem before—being attracted to two people, I mean. It's almost like the start of a Pack, but I've never really considered that I'd have one. Jesse hasn't ever mentioned one, and it seems like it's way too early to broach that subject. Especially since they're strangers.

"Looks like we're VIP," Jesse comments.

I look up at him, startled, "What do you mean?"

"We know the owner now, and we're gonna get free coffee. We should demand an entourage follow us around to signal how important we are." Jesse's face is set in a mischievous smirk, and I can't help but giggle and play along.

"Oh yes, we may even need to hire security. Only if they wear sunglasses and talk into their wrists, though, no walkie talkies for us."

"Exactly."

I could definitely handle more time with this man.

JOSIE

Ray and I are having our second session, and while she's not ready for us to go to her nest, there is a plethora of pillows and blankets in a small room that looks like it's typically used as a den of sorts. It's dark in here, the furniture is dark wood, and the drapes are closed, giving it a cozy feeling. Subtly sniffing the air, there's a lingering scent of cedar and a touch of eucalyptus that calls to me. I want to bury myself in the smell, but then I might get kicked out for lack of professionalism.

Even though my original scent sample of Ray didn't sit great, I decided to give it another shot today. She's sweet, and I don't want to pass up time with her for something as silly as my nose. I'm hopeful that since it will be in person instead of a scent card, I'll be able to handle it better. So far, things have been fine. She doesn't have my favorite scent, but in person, it isn't as harsh and meshes well with the other scents around us, so I can ignore it.

Once the blankets are how she likes them, I look to her for permission before settling in and opening my arms for her. Carefully, she steps closer and gently lowers herself, resting her head on my shoulder, her body tucked tight almost in a ball. Resting my arm around her, I use the other to cover us so we're nice and toasty. At first, the quiet of sitting together feels a bit strained, but eventually I feel her body relax against me.

"How are you today?" I ask her softly.

She shrugs, but doesn't answer verbally. It almost feels like square one again, but maybe she's just slow to open up to people. That's something I can definitely relate to. I don't push her for an answer, I can respect her space.

"Yeah, I get that," I tell her.

We snuggle in the quiet, but after only a moment, I can't help but start to hum. I get through the first chorus before I feel her start to shake in my arms. Glancing down, worried that she's crying, I see she's actually biting her lip to keep from laughing.

"What?" I ask with my own smile.

"Are you humming 'Jesse's Girl'?"

Oh my goodness, I totally was. The realization sets me to giggling.

"I hadn't even realized what I was humming! I just do it sometimes when I'm relaxing." I laugh.

"Why 'Jesse's Girl'? There are a lot more relaxing songs you could hum."

"Well, I absolutely love 80s music. I don't know why, but it just makes me happy. I, uh, also went out with a guy named Jesse recently, so that might play into it," I tell her.

"Tell me about your date?" she asks.

"Sure. He's actually my neighbor, but we only met the other day. When I was on my way here for our first session, actually, he was coming home from work, and we finally crossed paths. He's a bit anti-social, but super nice. We went and got coffee together, and it was nice just getting to know each other."

"Did he kiss you?"

I laugh. "No, no kissing yet. I, uh, I actually don't date much."

"Oh, I can understand that. Dating is the worst. Do you want to date more?" she asks softly.

"It sounds nice to do that, to find a person I can be with, but I have my own problems that make it hard for me to meet new people," I admit.

She goes quiet at that, and we embrace the quiet for a few more moments. Ray shifts and snuggles closer before talking again.

"Henry isn't really my brother," she says quietly. "But he may as well be. He took me in a few months back with the support of his family, and they're super nice."

"I'm glad to hear that," I match her volume and speak quietly as well.

"My mom died a while back. She wasn't bad, but I'm not sure she ever really wanted me. When she passed, I stayed with my stepdad, who used touch withholding as punishment. If he thought I was bad, I didn't get any kind of touch. He always found a reason for me to go without."

I hum in understanding, knowing there aren't any words that I can offer her. Sometimes words aren't enough. Sometimes the only way to feel understood and seen is to have someone sit in silence with you. Knowing that they understand your pain enough to endure it with you in silence is comforting in a way words can never be. A few moments later, there's a light knock at the door. My eyes go to Ray to see how she wants to handle the knock.

"I think Henry was planning to bring some snacks in, if you're okay with it?" she tells me as though it's a question.

"Sure, I don't mind if you don't."

"You can come in, Henry!" she calls out, more confident talking to Henry than she has been to me.

The door opens, and before I can see his face, Henry's scent slams into me. Cedar and eucalyptus hit me full-force and tell me whose den we've been using. It's almost physically difficult for me to stay in this mini blanket nest with Ray. All I want to do is put my nose to his neck and smell him. As soon as that thought crosses my mind, I check myself.

I've never had a reaction to someone's smell so strongly, except maybe Jesse. His scent was a similar overwhelming experience. The thought of Jesse immediately shames me. Not only did I drool over another man during our coffee date, but now I'm comparing him to another Alpha. I'm a terrible person. Jesse might not be *my* Alpha, but it feels like a betrayal anyway. Who drools over multiple Alphas when they're not in a Pack already?

Henry steps through the door with a wide smile on his face. His hair flops on his forehead as he tosses it out of his eyes. He sets the tray of food and drinks on a nearby table.

"Hey, sorry to interrupt, just delivering some snacks for you guys if you want any. I won't stay, but let me know if you need anything."

I smile at him in gratitude, and I'm pretty sure I swoon inside when he winks at me on his way out. Warmth infuses my cheeks, telling me I'm blushing like crazy. The door finally clicks closed, and my eyes linger on it for a few moments more.

"See somethin' you like?" Ray quips, a playful tone I haven't heard from her yet.

"Uh, no, I mean, yeah, but no, I mean... ugh."

Ray laughs, delighted with my discomfort. I can't help but smile along through my embarrassment, hearing her joy. She pulls away for only a moment to grab each of us a cookie and a bottle of water.

"It's okay, he really is good-looking. If I were older, I'd be interested. Well, if I were older and he wasn't like a brother to me."

"Good to know," I chuckle.

We adjust ourselves so that Ray is sitting between my legs, her back resting comfortably against my front. It's a position that could easily be sexual, but with her, it's not. It's just soothing, even for me. Ray's scent may not be something that I particularly like, but I find myself accepting her touch more easily than most.

The two of us spend the rest of our time oscillating between comfortable silence and chatting. Ray is bright and easy to talk with, and I'm finding myself happier to have her as a client than I would have originally anticipated. Experiencing her opening up to me is beautiful, and I'm grateful that she's comfortable showing me this side of herself.

She chooses to stay and snuggle in the blankets when we're done, so I wave goodbye from the doorway with a smile. Closing it softly, I jump when I realize Henry is right behind me. He holds his hands up with a sheepish grin.

"Sorry, didn't mean to creep up on you. I was coming to check in, and you were closing the door, so I waited. Probably should have said something." He apologizes.

I exhale and put my hand on my chest, "It's no problem, really, I was just startled."

"Things go okay in there?"

"Yeah, Ray really is lovely. I'm grateful to have her as a client."

"I'm glad. She has a hard time opening up to people sometimes, so it's good to hear she likes you enough to show her warm side," Henry comments as we amble toward the front door.

"She mentioned some past weaponizing of touch, and that you helped her get out of the situation. Thank you for that."

Henry's face flushes, and I melt a little at how cute it is. He catches me watching him, and it's my turn to flush as I glance away. He smells so damn good, I don't think I can handle making eye contact with him when he's that cute and smells that good.

"It's nothing, really. She's a good kid. My younger cousin is friends with her, and when she mentioned the situation and we found out she's over eighteen, it seemed like a no-brainer to have her live here. She can finish high school here and then do what she wants. My whole family was supportive of the decision."

"It takes a lot to house a new person. Don't short-change yourself."

"I'll try not to, I promise. I might need you to remind me, though."

"Oh?" I give him what I hope is a flirtatious smile.

His mouth twitches in a smile before he puts a serious face on and nods, "Definitely. Sometimes I just don't know how good I am. You might have to remind me. Maybe over dinner or drinks."

Grinning now, I bite my lip before responding, "That does sound nice. I don't really date, though."

"We could call it a confidence-boosting seminar." His smile is full of mischief.

I chuckle, "Not sure I'm qualified for such a prestigious event. Perhaps we'll have to try and see if I can live up to the reputation you've given me."

"Definitely."

He moves slowly, giving me a chance to pull away, but I'm curious about what he's planning to do. Slowly, his fingers reach out to brush my hair back, not touching my skin at all. My scent must be strong right now, because I see his nostrils flare as he leans close to breathe me in. A small purr rumbles through me, startling me out of the moment. I can't remember the last time I purred; it's normally associated with touch, so it's not something I'm used to doing.

I step back from Henry, and he respectfully leans back and takes his own space, silently giving me what I need. A grateful smile comes to my face, and now I'm looking forward to more time with him. His instincts are spot on, and I really appreciate that. Although I'm grateful for his instinctual need to give me space, I'm still supremely embarrassed by my response to his closeness.

"Sorry, um, I didn't mean to..."

Henry holds up one hand, palm toward me. "Hey, no need for explanation. I want to respect your space, and if you need more of it, then you need more of it."

"Just like that?" My voice is small as I ask.

He nods. "Just like that."

Unsure of what motivates me, I blurt out a thought to him. "I didn't get much touch as a kid. Um, it's why I started Touch Helpers."

Henry's face is a mix of sorrow and pride. "I'm sorry you had to go through that, but I'm grateful you started this business as a result. Something about you draws me in, and I hope that's not too forward of me."

"Thank you," I reply, unsure of what else to say.

Placing his hands in his pockets, Henry takes another step back before speaking again. "See you next time?"

I open the door and give him a smirk. "Not if I see you first."

His chuckle follows me out the door, and I find myself very pleased that I made him laugh.

seven

SIMON

Nerves are riding me hard as I make the final touches on the cafe. I'm pretty sure I've adjusted this fake plant twenty times, and I'm still not satisfied with it. Letting myself make one more adjustment, I abandon it to check in with my new staff. It looks like the two baristas are ready to go, the manager is here doing final checks, and the bakery case is fully stocked. I managed to get a deal with a local baker as a way to draw people in. This cafe is my first satellite location, and I want to make sure it has this city's presence in it. The bakery is a local favorite, so it was a no-brainer for me.

"Everything looks good, boss," my Beta manager, Tyler, tells me.

I take a deep breath, "I don't know if we'll get slammed or not today, but I did note down two customers who get a free drink if they stop in. Did you see that?"

He chuckles at me, "I did. Like I said, everything looks good. We're ready to go."

"Let's do this."

My feet carry me to the door of the shop, and I'm not surprised to see Victor standing there, a large grin on his face. I pull the chain on our neon "open" sign and unlock the door. Pulling it open, I can't help but laugh at Vic's excited smile.

39

"Fancy seeing you here," I tell him.

"Hey, it's basically required for me to be your first customer. I couldn't resist!"

Waving him in, I direct him to where the ordering counter is. A few people follow behind him while I hold the door, and I make a point to greet all of them. When the last customer comes in, I let the door fall closed and go behind the counter to make sure things are running smoothly. My manager is taking orders while the baristas fill the first orders.

As business flows, a few customers breeze right out of the door, but a few stay and sit for a little bit. I make a point to greet those who stay and let them know they're welcome to provide their thoughts in the designated feedback box. The day is a steady stream of customers, and I've had to empty the feedback box so people can fill it right back up. I try not to look at them before filing them away to be reviewed later. My goal is to look at them weekly instead of daily, so that I can see if there are recurring patterns of suggestions to act on.

When I finally turn the "open" sign off and lock the door, I'm completely exhausted and completely elated. Upon hearing the click of the lock, I turn and raise my arms over my head.

"Wooo!! We did it!" I shout into the space.

The two baristas on duty and my floor manager join in the cheering, and I move closer to them to share high-fives. My manager is grinning, and even the young baristas are smiling widely.

"Well done on a great first day, you guys! I'm so proud to have you here with me," I tell them honestly.

"Thanks for being someone great to work for." My manager pats me on the back and moves on to closing duties.

I finish my own end-of-day tasks, including emptying our feedback box and downloading our transaction records. I opted to use a system that records the information automatically on a cloud server so I can easily download my copies and get daily reports. It's the same one I have at the main location, so while I was worried it might be too much for this smaller site, I'm glad I got it. Wrapping up my closing tasks, I'm grateful to be headed home.

The dynamic I have with Vic has been a little charged lately. We've been friends since college, and while he suspects there's a Pack Pull there, neither of us has commented on that. I only know he feels it because I overheard him on the phone with his parents once. However, I'm too chickenshit to address it, and I think he doesn't want to push me into anything. Maybe I should ask, but the last time I thought there was a pull, I was wrong and now I have a scar through my eyebrow to remind me.

Deep down, I know Vic isn't like that, but old fears are hard to erase. I feel a pull to him, but it's entirely possible that's just because of his body. We enjoy each other on occasion, but I know he wants a Pack someday, so I'm not holding my breath for commitment beyond friendship. For now, I'm enjoying our time together, and I'll take the rest as it comes. Hopefully, whatever comes includes me, but I'm also not going to stand in his way. I know he loves his friend Josie, and there's no guarantee that she'll like me.

When I finally walk through the door, delicious smells of food assault me. I take a deep breath, enjoying the smell of whatever Vic's been cooking.

"Honey, I'm home!" I call out, my bass voice carrying toward the kitchen.

Kicking off my shoes, I follow my nose to the kitchen, where Vic is moving food from the pans he used onto plates. His eyes glance up at me, and he grins before finishing his task.

"Hey! Welcome home! Figured I would cook a nice dinner to celebrate today."

Smiling back at him, I move to get out the silverware as he places the plates on the table. "Beer?"

He nods. "Sounds great, thanks."

I grab one for each of us and place the silverware and beers on the table. We crack open our drinks and raise them in the air.

"To a successful launch," I declare.

"To new beginnings," Vic adds.

We drink before eating, and the food is delicious. I groan in appreciation.

"This is so good, man."

He blushes, "Thanks, it's just chicken."

"Mine's always dry when I try to cook it, take the compliment." I smile at him.

We finish the meal with some light chatting about the cafe, Vic's work, and life in general before washing dishes together. Vic's hip bumps mine as we finish up, and I can't help but bump him back. He's an inch or two taller than me, so I take the towel I was using to dry and loop it around his neck, gently pulling him toward me.

Vic's eyes light up, and he drags them down to my feet and back up my body. He raises one eyebrow, and when I pull him even closer, his lips land gently on mine. It's been a bit since we were intimate, and I'm eager to reconnect. Celebrating the opening is an excuse for me. The real reason is just because I crave the connection we have. The kiss is gentle, neither of us taking charge.

His hands rest on my hips, holding my body against his. My tongue darts out against his lips, savoring the taste of him mixed with the lingering flavors of the spices he cooked with. Vic growls teasingly and nips my lower lip before pulling back to look at me. Our eyes lock for a moment before I drop the towel and pull him closer with just my hands. We pull each other so our bodies are flush against the other, and I can feel the bulge getting bigger in his pants.

My hips press against him, seeking that delicious friction. Vic responds in kind, and I can feel my dick straining against my zipper. My hands move from his neck and drag down his body to the button and zipper of his jeans. Now that I have access to him, my hand reaches into his jeans to touch him over his boxers. Vic's breathing hitches as I do, and he cants his hips into my touch, seeking more. Neither of us wants to give at the moment, so we're torn between pressing against each other and giving enough space to touch as well.

Usually, one of us would give and lean against the counter, but it seems today neither of us is willing to bend, and it fires up my blood even more. My hand leaves Vic's shaft, and I use both hands to pull his jeans and boxers down entirely. I follow them down until I'm on my knees and spit on his tip before taking him in my mouth. Vic's head falls backward with a loud groan of pleasure.

"Fuck, that mouth, Simon," he rumbles.

Humming around him, I take him deeper, bobbing my head leisurely, enjoying the weight and feel of him in my mouth and throat. Each pass I take him a little deeper until I start to gag, but I don't let it stop me. I've only lost to my gag reflex one time, and that was early on while still learning my limits. I pull my mouth to the end of him and place my hands on my thighs, giving him permission to take over. Vic growls and grabs my head before pushing himself into my throat and back out again.

As he pumps in and out, I make it a point to slacken my mouth a bit so everything is nice and messy. Vic always loses it when it gets sloppy. He said it's something about the primal feel of it that spurs him on. When he sees drool running down the sides of my mouth, he literally growls and speeds up.

"Do you understand what you do to me, Simon? Do you feel how hard I am? I'm going to come down your throat, and you won't be able to swallow all of it. It'll run down your chin and get this new kitchen dirty like it should be. Fuck I'm gonna..."

He tapers off, and his hips stutter as he keeps his promise to come down my throat. It's as much as he warned me it would be, over-flowing in my mouth, running down my chin, but I still manage to swallow some. He pulls out watching in fascination as strings of spit and cum trail from his cock, breaking and leaving the floor a mess. Vic crashes to his knees with me and slams his mouth against mine.

"I love the flavor of me on your tongue," he murmurs.

I almost come in my pants hearing that, and the way his hand moves to my dick tells me he understands. His hand moves gently, but firmly, increasing my pleasure and driving me wild. I press against his hand with my hips, hoping to get more from him. Vic chuckles darkly and moves his hands to my pants, unfastening them so he can reach in to touch me. A harsh breath leaves me at his touch, and my eyes are locked in where his hand disappears into my clothes.

I need his bare hands on me, it's a drive I don't understand, but I'm not about to question. I've never felt the zip of energy that comes with a Match, so I know that's not it, but something draws me to him like he's the one thing I need. So I start to shimmy out of my pants when he stops me. Vic kicks his pants off all the way before using his own hands to slowly pull mine off. His mouth licks and nips at my skin, taking a moment to swallow my cock down his throat before moving off and giving the tip a kiss.

Once my jeans are off, he leans back against the cabinets, legs splayed out, and beckons me over. I settle on his lap, my ass on the cool tile, but our balls, dicks, and thighs touching. Vic's hand slowly drags up and down my dick, and we both watch as he begins to harden again. His other hand moves to bring our cocks together and he moves up and down them at the same pace.

"Spit," he commands.

So I spit on our tips and feel my dick twitch when he commands it again. After several more spits, I stop and grab onto the counter behind him. Using it for leverage, I move my hips, rubbing our shafts together as he strokes, doubling the sensation for both of us. Vic takes the liberty of adding his own spit to the mix, and my head tips back in a moan of pleasure. I can feel my knot inflating, adding extra sensation as it drags against Vic's smooth skin.

"Shit, you feel so good Vic. I love when you let me rub my knot on you," I confess.

Vic growls again, "I can't get enough of you Simon, fuck! I'm so fucking close, harder, please!"

I lean my body into it now, pressing myself closer to increase the friction and pick up my pace. I'm right on the edge, my legs starting to shake, and a tingle building in the back of my spine.

"God, Vic, I'm gonna—"

I can't even get the words out before my balls draw up and I spray cum all over our bellies before Vic does the same. Once we're spent, I place my forehead against his, resting against him while he places his sticky hands on my face, holding me close. I turn and lick a few of his fingers, causing him to twitch against me.

"We're going to be here all night if you do that," he admonishes without sounding angry at all.

I grin at him and raise an eyebrow. "Maybe that's what I want."

HENRY

My nose has been tingling for days, dying to get another whiff of Josie. She was close enough to smell the last time she came for Ray's appointment, and I almost buckled at the knees when it hit me. I've never liked any cinnamon-based desserts, but that's all I want now. I've eaten several cinnamon rolls this week just to try and re-create her scent in my mind. None of them measure up.

That's how I found myself standing at the kitchen island, hands braced on either side of the coffee cake that I'm glaring at. It's not the coffee cake's fault that it doesn't smell quite the same, but I'm glaring anyway. My ears pick up on footsteps, and I debate trying to hide the dessert, but I don't think I'll get away with it. Ray walks into the room and bends over the cake, inhaling deeply.

"Not quite right, is it?" she says, taunting me.

I stand up straight, "I have no idea what you're talking about."

All that does is make Ray cackle.

"Sure, big bro, whatever you tell me."

"As the big bro, you're supposed to believe anything I say," I inform her.

She looks at me, her face solemn and her eyes large. "I'm a poor, touch-starved Omega... are you saying I don't know things?"

I raise an eyebrow at her, noting the slight twitch in her lips.

"Nice try, you should take acting classes," I tell her.

She latches on to the idea, her concentration broken. "Oh! That could be fun! Maybe I'll be a famous actress! Can you imagine? Ray: Hollywood Sweetheart."

A smile takes over my face as she continues to fawn over the idea of being famous. She would absolutely hate it, and I'm pretty sure she knows that deep down. If she wanted to really go for it, though, I'd support her one hundred percent. When Jon told me about his friend being purposely touch-starved by her stepfather, I knew I had to intervene. Jon's been my best friend for years, and we'd do anything for each other. Then we found out Ray and one of my younger cousins were friends as well, so that pretty much sealed the deal.

Since he didn't have the space for her, I offered my house—even though it technically belongs to my parents. He got her out, and we both worked to get her settled with some financial help from my family. He takes on way more guilt than he should over it. He thinks he should have figured things out sooner, but I try to remind him hindsight is 20/20. Sometimes you just don't know until you look back. Besides, my cousin hadn't noticed either. It's not an easy problem to see.

I grab an apple before walking to get my shoes on. Smelling cinnamon has increased my desire to see Josie, so to mitigate that, I'm going to go buy her something nice. Maybe a soft blanket.

"Ray, do you need anything from outside the house?"

She hums, "Where you goin'?"

"Grabbing a present for Josie, then a coffee maybe."

"Bring me back a hot chocolate?"

"You got it, princess," I say with a shit eating grin.

She bristles at the nickname, like always. "I swear one of these days I'm going to actually punch you in the face, Henry!"

"That means you'd have to touch me," I point out.

"Oh, it's gonna happen," she says, shaking her fist exaggeratedly.

We both laugh as I walk out the door, and I hop in my car, heading toward downtown to find an Omega store. There are a few big-box stores in the area I could go to, but I find that the smaller, local stores are better for presents. If I ever need to supply a nest, then I would go to a big store. There's an open spot in front of one of the local shops, so I parallel park and head in.

I meander through the small shop, enjoying the different displays that have clearly been created with care. I'm not sure if Omegas are big on scents, but there is a space near the back with scented soaps and lotions, sealed up so the Omegas won't get overwhelmed. Each one has a scent sample, though, which is smart if you ask me. Finding myself in the pajama section, I see an oversized fluffy robe.

My hand reaches out to feel it, and I almost purr at the texture. Keeping my instincts firmly reined in, I make sure that the inside is as soft as the outside. I'm a little disappointed that it's not quite as soft. As I glance around the shop, I see an extremely fluffy, oversized blanket. There are a few sizes, so I make sure I get the largest size they have. Josie's tall, and she's no stick figure, which honestly turns me on more. Having a large blanket will hopefully satisfy her Omega desire to be snug and small.

Snatching it off the rack, I take my prize to the checkout desk and accept the offer of wrapping it in a box. The box is gently placed in a bag, and I swipe my card before heading back to my car. I'm not sure when Ray's next appointment is, so I'll keep it in my room until I look it up. Next time I see her, she's getting this gift. My inner Alpha puffs his chest up, loving the idea of providing something to her.

It's a nice day today, so I drop the box in my car, make sure it's locked, and start walking down the sidewalk toward a new cafe that opened. There have been good reviews online, and it's nice to try new things sometimes. I have a favorite shop already, but if these guys are better, I'll have a new favorite. Never know until you try. Once I'm in front of the café, I peer in the windows before opening the door and walking in. It's decently busy in here, not a huge line, but it looks like they have a steady flow of customers.

The baristas are smiling but busy and have an air of concentration about them. Customers who are seated chat with each other comfortably, and everyone seems at ease here. Other coffee shops have customers who tend to be quiet and keep to themselves, but the socialization is almost encouraged here. Nobody is sitting with a book or a computer and avoiding the crowd. When I reach the employee taking orders, I put in for my latte and a hot chocolate, extra hot.

"You don't need to check the feedback boxes every ten minutes," I hear a deep voice near me say.

A sigh comes next, "I just want to know if people are enjoying themselves."

"Clearly they are, Vic," the first voice chuckles.

"Sorry, I'm just so excited!" Vic, as the first voice named him, says.

Something about their voices intrigues me enough that I turn to them. Both of them are tall with black hair like me, which almost makes me chuckle. Their combined scents of vanilla, orange, and sandalwood call to me. I'm not sure which of them carries each scent, but the combination is delicious. Typically, men don't do it for me, but there's something about their combined scents that piques my interest.

One of them looks over my way and pauses for a moment, his slicked-back hair falling around his face, refusing to cooperate with his style. A smile appears on his face, and his eyes flick from his companion, then back to me. The other guy turns a bit more, so I can see his face, and there's a small scar running through his right eyebrow. It gives him an almost roguish look. I lift my hand in a small wave, accepting that I've been caught looking.

The guy with the scar gives me a tight smile and a nod, but the other one comes over to me and offers his hand. His subtle Sandalwood scent reaches me and helps me identify who owns each scent, and that he's a Beta. His scent is too soft to be anything else. I take his hand in mine, noting he's not a Match. There's still something that draws me in, though.

"Hey, I'm Victor, Vic for short."

"Henry, no nickname," I reply with a grin.

Vic grins back at me, seemingly pleased with my response.

"First time here?" he asks.

"Yup, saw an ad for it and figured I'd stop by. Just got done at a local store, and my little sister wanted a hot chocolate, so here I am."

"You went all this way for your sister? That's nice."

I chuckle, "It wasn't far out of the way and I got myself a caffeine boost, so it's not an entirely altruistic visit."

Vic turns to look at the other guy and signals him to come over. To his credit, he obliges while looking unhappy, but not rudely so. Mentally, I peg him as a guy who likes his space and only opens up for his people.

"Simon, this is Henry, no nickname," Vic says.

"Hey," I greet Simon, holding a hand out for a shake.

Simon looks at my hand, then back up to my face, before grasping it. "Nice to meet you."

"Nice place you built." I take a stab in the dark.

When they were talking about the feedback, it signaled that one of them owned the joint, and my bet is on Simon. He seems to observe everything, telling me he's invested in what's happening around him.

"How'd you know?" he asks.

I shrug, "Somewhat lucky guess. Overheard you guys talking about a feedback box or something, and you seem more invested in what's happening around you. You're continuously surveying the room."

He smirks in response and nods his head.

"It's obvious you put a lot of thought and effort into it. I'll definitely be telling people to visit if the coffee's as good as the ambiance," I continue.

Vic chuckles, "Oh, just wait. Simon makes the best coffee you've ever had. We live together and I'm *spoiled* by it."

When he mentions living together, that's when this feeling clicks, and I realize it's a Pack Pull that I'm feeling. These guys are Pack, and now I feel frozen in place with the knowledge. Vic's eyes light up when he sees me freeze, and Simon looks like he just got indigestion.

"You feel it!" Vic states, excitedly.

I rub at my chest. "Yeah, shit, I didn't think I'd ever feel that."

Simon clears his throat, "I need to go check something in the back."

My name is called for my drinks as Simon walks away, so I turn and grab the two cups before stepping back with Vic. We stand by the wall, a bit away from where people are waiting for their drinks. Taking a sip of my coffee, I hum in appreciation.

"You're right, this coffee is fantastic."

"Right? He's got a thing for beans. They have to be just right and have to help small farmers," Vic explains.

"How long have you two known each other?" I ask.

"We met in college, been roommates ever since."

"Oh, when you said you live together, I assumed you were together or part of a Pack. You seem tight enough to be Pack."

He sighs, "I think we are Pack, but Simon walks away any time I mention it. He got burned pretty badly before we met in college, so I try to be careful in approaching the topic. You don't seem to be bothered by it, though."

"I wasn't sure if I would ever find the pull, so yeah, I'm definitely interested in talking about it. If we want to pursue it, there are lots of details to start thinking about. Of course, I don't want to make problems for either of you, so please tell me if I overstep." I realize I'm rambling a little by the end of that thought.

Vic just smiles, and I'm impressed with how easy-going he seems in general. It will be nice to have someone in the Pack like that. Assuming we become Pack. I don't even know if there are others, but it's not something I want to push. Yet.

"Maybe we can catch dinner sometime soon?" Vic suggests.

"Yeah, for sure, I'd be up for that. Can I give you my number? My hands are full at the moment." I hold up the drinks.

Vic grabs his phone, and I recite my number to him. Not a moment later, I feel my pants buzz with a text message. We part ways with a smile, and by the time I get home, I'm glad I ordered the hot chocolate extra hot. Normally, it's not something I do, but it just felt right today. I guess my instincts were on point because it was still hot when I got home.

"What's got you all smiley?" Ray asks after taking a sip.

"I think I have a Pack."

nine

JOSIE

I'm buried in my nest, and I don't want to leave. Today I need to do a video call with the Betas I work with, but it sounds like a lot of effort. I've been feeling extra fatigued lately, and I just need time buried in my cozy nest of cushions, blankets, and pillows. My nest is the spare room of the condo, something I've had to cobble together. Not every house or housing unit has a built-in nest, so I never expected to have one in a designated room.

Since this room isn't circular and it has multiple windows, I've had to modify it a bit. Typically, I would want only one window, something small to let in just a little light. A circular room also gives more of a "nest" feel, allowing an Omega to really go wild with blankets. As it is, I've had to drape additional fabric on the walls to mute the daytime light, and I have light-blocking shades to help during my heat. Thankfully, I'm not due for that for another two months.

Rolling over, I sigh and snuggle in deeper with my blankets. My need for comfort has been high lately, which is a bit unusual. Maybe I'm in for a doozy heat. Normally, I take a mild suppressant to just take the edge off and ride it out myself, so we'll see how this next one goes. If my body has found someone with a scent I like, I'm not sure how that will play into my heat. Now that I've found two scents I like, it could be my body telling me to go find them. Or maybe I've been working too much, it's hard to tell sometimes.

Trying not to worry so much, I call out to my smart speaker and put some music on. The smooth tone of the Beach Boys fills my nest and I smile with relief. Letting myself get into the music, I close my eyes and sing along under my breath. This song, Kokomo, always soothes my frayed edges. It's smooth and has a nice beat to it.

Heaving a sigh, I repeat the song two times before feeling soothed enough to face my Betas. I shuffle to my couch and find my laptop still on its stand, ready to be used. Snuggling into my favorite spot, I pull the coffee table flush with the couch so I don't have to reach, then unlock it and dial up my Betas.

Georgie and James pick up after two rings. The siblings are almost inseparable and currently live together. I grin and wave at both of them. While it can take a lot out of me to interact with people, these two are almost always a joy. It makes things a little easier to deal with.

"Hey Jojo!" Georgie says.

"Hey Gigi! Hey James," I reply.

"Why do you sound happier to see her?" James tries to grumble. Unfortunately, he's too friendly to pull it off well.

"Must be a girl thing," I tell him, shrugging.

He sighs, long-suffering, "I suppose I'll just press on. Only for you two, though."

"*So* generous," Georgie tells him.

I chuckle at the antics before reining them back in, "Okay guys, let's get down to business. First things first, how are both of you? Are there any signs of burnout?"

We discuss how each of us is doing, making sure that all three of us are okay. Being a touch helper can be draining sometimes, especially if you have a lot of people you have to physically touch for hours. There was one month a while back that Georgie had to take a few weeks off due to burnout, so we've all been better about workload since then.

James and Georgie have more clients than I do, as Betas, they can naturally handle more touch, but I'm limited due to my Touch Loss. My tolerance level for touching outside of my bonded Pack is very low. I'm able to find ways to cope between sessions, but it's easy for me to get burned out. If I ever find a Pack, they would be able to touch me constantly without it draining me, and it sounds amazing. I'm not hanging my hat on that idea, though. Most people want Omegas who aren't damaged in some way.

Focusing on the task at hand, I find we have about ten new applications for Omegas who need the help we can provide. Looking at workloads, I'm not sure if we can make it work. Maybe we need to start a waitlist. The three of us discuss the intake process, potential need for new employees, and other various details of their visits and the progress of our current clients. We review financials at the end, and I'm surprised to see our profits are increasing. We'll need to really consider how we want to leverage that profit since we all currently take home a salary.

We hang up the call with a confirmation of next week for our next official meeting. During the week, we'll check in with each other if needed, but the only official meeting is this one. I stretch on the couch and resist the temptation to curl back up into my soft blankets. They're my kryptonite: soft blankets. Having one wrapped around me is one of my favorite things. My phone pings before I can stand to grab some food.

VIC

Hey Josie Girl, been thinkin' about ya. Can we get together soon?

Me

Hey yourself! It would be nice to see you, it's been a few weeks since you've been here. I'm surprised you haven't knocked my door down.

VIC

🦢 Well, I figured I'd give it some time to settle, and then I just chickened out.

OKAY, this is getting a phone call now. I hit his name, and it only rings twice before he answers.

"Hey, got tired of texting?" He chuckles.

"Uh, excuse me, sir, did you tell me that you chickened out over *me*?"

"Ah, yeah, I kind of did."

I frown, "Why is that? I mean, I thought you were excited to be here. Did that change? It's okay if it did."

I'm not about to be the jealous bitch here and demand his time. But my heart breaks at the thought that he's changed his mind. Maybe it's been too long for him. I force myself to listen to him before jumping to conclusions.

"No! Definitely not, I mean it when I say you're my Josie Girl. I think... hang on a second."

There's shuffling in the background now, as if he's looking for someone or something.

"Okay, I wanted to say something, but I don't want to upset Simon, so I was checking for his car, and he's not home yet." he clears his throat. "I think that I'm really nervous that you and Simon won't like each other. Whenever you've visited us, he hasn't been around, so I'm not really sure how it will go. I don't want to lose either of you, you know?"

"Oh, Vic, I'm sure it will be fine. Maybe we'll get along, but maybe we won't; it's hard to know until it happens. One thing I do know is that even if he ends up being a giant asshole, you're still my Vic and I won't pull away from you. Okay?"

I can hear the small smile in his voice as he agrees, "Okay."

"So, when do you want to get together? What works for you?"

"I mean, I always want to get together."

"Well, do you want to come over now?" I ask tentatively. I'm not sure if it's too fast or not to have him over. Maybe he's busy.

"Do you mean it?"

"Yeah, I'm home for the night, maybe I'll treat you and make you some food," I joke.

"Maybe I'll take over that part of things," Vic laughs.

"Hey, I can boil spaghetti just fine!" I protest.

We giggle together, knowing that I'm really not half bad at cooking. However, the one time I tried to cook for him, I burnt everything. He was distracting me with his beautiful ass, it wasn't my fault.

"If you're serious, I'll come over now," he offers.

I nod even though he can't see me, "I'd really love that."

"Done!"

We hang up, and I look around my condo, realizing it needs a good tidy. So I turn on my 80s mix and get to picking up. Mail, extra blankets, socks, all kinds of little things that just pile up over time. Thankfully, I haven't started my dishwasher yet, so I add a few dishes to it and run it. Feeling satisfied with the way things look, I crack a couple of windows to get some fresh air moving. Only a few minutes later, I hear a car pull into my driveway and I bite my lip with excitement.

Scampering over to the front door, I open it to watch Vic step out of his car. He's so gorgeous, tall with plenty of muscles and hair that never stays fully slicked back. I love the little tendrils that frame his face. My body starts bouncing in excitement, and despite my typical behavior, I decide I want a hug. Vic closes his car door and meets my eyes with a wide smile. Grinning in response, I hustle over to where he's standing, and he moves to meet me halfway.

My arms wrap around his waist, and I lay my head on his chest. I can hear his rumbling hum of contentment as he holds me close, his nose pressed into my hair. We pull apart, both of us still grinning like crazy.

"Well, come in, stranger! I'm glad you took the bait to come over!"

Vic laughs, his eyes crinkling at the edges as he does, "You're irresistible, Josie Girl. I'll always come see you if you want."

I let Vic walk into the condo ahead of me, and as I move to follow, my eyes catch on Jesse's window. He's standing there, watching with the quiet intensity he has, and I feel my cheeks heat. I continue to smile and give him a happy wave. He sends back half a smile and a small wave before walking off. Oh, shit, is he mad? I suppose he doesn't really know about Vic. I'll have to text him. I don't want to ruin things with him before we've even started something.

"Who was that?" Vic asks as I close the door.

I squeak in response because he hasn't moved more than six inches into the house, and our noses are almost touching.

"You startled me!"

"Sorry, Josie Girl, I was just curious who your neighbor is. Seems awfully intense." Vic takes a step back.

"He's quiet, but he's so nice. We, uh, went on a date a bit ago and haven't been able to find time again. It's a bummer because I really like him, so we'll just see what happens."

Vic just hums under his breath. I frown at him.

"Why are you being weird about it?" I ask him, but Vic shakes himself out of it and smiles.

"Sorry, just got lost in thought. Show me around your joint again, it's been too long," he tells me.

I give him the short tour of my living room and bathroom, vaguely gesturing to my room and nest, then we plop down on the couch. For a minute, we just look at each other.

"I missed you," I blurt out, then hold my hands to my cheeks in embarrassment.

"Hey," Vic moves closer, "I missed you too. Don't be embarrassed."

I pull my hands from my face, which is now flushed with pleasure instead of embarrassment. I'm destined to just have a red face, apparently. I set my hand down, not paying attention to where it lands, and then realize I've landed directly onto Vic's hand. Fuck. I didn't want to touch him, I don't want to know if we Match or not. I won't be able to tell, and while I don't think Vic would lie, what if he doesn't want me like that?

Panic starts to overtake me as my thoughts spiral. This is the end, isn't it? Even if we're not a Match, he's going to see me panicking and want nothing to do with me. He already knows I'm broken, then add in random panic? My breathing picks up with the irrational thoughts, and I look up to meet Vic's blue eyes. His eyes bore into me, and I need to know how he's going to respond to my touch. I take my hand off his in an attempt to avoid further awkwardness.

ten

VIC

Josie's hand lands on top of mine, and my world freezes. She's always extremely careful not to have skin-to-skin contact since she can't feel when a Match is found. In the past, I never pushed it, wanting to respect her boundaries. Now thought? I absolutely feel it, and it's almost like time stops as the realization sinks in.

I was right.

I've thought we are a Match for years, but with how careful Josie is, I've been respectful not to touch her skin to skin. The closest we come is when I put my nose in her hair to smell her, even then I'm careful not to touch her scalp. When she touches my hand, though? A rush of energy zips through me, lighting my nerve endings up and bringing an awareness of her that I didn't have before. It's almost like seeing color for the first time. Everything's the same, but there's more depth to it now.

Her eyes shoot up to lock on mine, and I can see the panic running through her. She didn't mean to touch me, and I'm sure she's having an internal meltdown over the "what ifs" now. When she lifts her hand from mine, I have my own panic moment and quickly grab it back. I thread our fingers together, and she responds exactly the way I'd hoped, by accepting the touch.

"Josie," I whisper, needing to clear my throat before I can go on.

"It's fine, Victor, really, um, we can just pretend I didn't touch you and... and just..."

"Listen," I tell her more sharply than intended. She stills and focuses on me. "I have suspected we are Matches for a long time. However, you are more important to me than having a Match is. I am fucking *elated* to tell you I feel the Match, but I also know you. I know you're not really ready for it, and that's okay. I'm not leaving you. Okay? You're still my Josie Girl, and I'm still your Vic."

"Do you promise?" she whispers.

"Yeah, sweetheart, I promise."

I see her breathe out and relax her body, and the tension she was carrying starts to drift away. This girl needs to be touched and cuddled by someone, and now that she knows we're Matches, maybe she'll let me. My touch will actually help, rather than drain her. Not as much as a full Bond with a Pack, but it will help a little.

"Can... Can we snuggle?" I ask, "It might help since the Match is there. I'm not asking to solidify anything tonight."

Josie smiles, "I think I would really like that."

I shift on the couch, using its L shape to move into the corner where I can prop myself up and stretch out my legs. Holding my arms out, Josie takes the bait and wedges herself between my body and the couch. Her hand darts out to grab a fuzzy blanket, so I help her pull it over us so we're cozy and toasty.

Her cheek rubs into my chest where she's getting comfortable, and I wonder if she's aware that she just scent-marked me. I haven't had a chance to see this side of Josie before, so I'm curious to see what else she's going to surprise me with. I can't wait to find out.

JOSIE and I snuggled for hours before I realized how late it was getting. So, I left and now I'm walking into my house, still feeling like I'm on cloud nine. It'll be a slow process courting Josie, but it'll be well worth it. I know Simon will love her, and everything is going to be fine. Even if he doesn't Match, he'll be happy to be Pack with her.

I find Simon on the couch, watching a reality baking show. Taking a moment to admire him, I stand quietly, leaning against the wall. He can't quite see me from this angle, but I can see him, and I love watching all the microexpressions that cross his face. Grinning, I take a seat on the couch next to him.

"I thought you'd never sit down," he comments in that deep bass of his.

"How'd you know I was standing there?" I pout.

He's still looking at the TV as he speaks, "Your scent. It's stronger than usual, and you smell like someone else."

Frowning, I look between the TV and him. "Are you upset with me?"

He sighs and pauses his show. We sit in silence for a moment while he gathers his thoughts.

"I'm worried about whose smell you have on you. You're super happy, I can tell that much, so either you've finally met an Omega you want or your Match. I'm not mad, just... well, I don't know how to put it into words."

"Josie. You smell Josie. She's my Match, her hand accidentally touched mine, and that confirmed it for me," I tell him softly.

He finally turns to look at me, and I can see the confusion and heartbreak on his face. Does this asshole really think I'm going to leave him? God, why do the two people I love seem to think I'm going to leave at any moment? I refuse to lose either of them. I reach a hand out to him.

"Come here, please?"

Simon hesitates for a moment before taking my hand and moving closer to me.

"At least take a good smell, tell me what you think," I suggest softly.

He leans in close, first taking a deep inhale at my neck, greedily taking in my own scent first. Then he moves down to my shirt and chest, taking his time to savor Josie's smell. It's not the same need that he had smelling me, but I can tell he doesn't hate it. I can tell his dick doesn't hate it either.

"Fuck," he groans softly.

Hook, line, and sinker.

"Amazing, right?"

"I've never smelled something that feels like a slap in the face before. It's amazing, so full of cinnamon and sweetness. I almost want to lick your shirt," he says with a small smile.

"So what's your hesitation?" I ask. "I can see your brain working through some shit, and while I know you and Mr. Happy down there like the smell, you're not as pleased as I had hoped."

He sits back in his own space, licking his lips as if the scent is tangible to his tongue. Closing his eyes, he heaves a deep sigh, putting his words together as best he can.

"There's no guarantee that a Match is there for me, or that she'll even like me. If one is there, she can reject me as a Match. If one isn't there, she might just reject me to get you all to herself. If she wants a full Pack, I don't know if I can do it." He shrugs.

I reach out and take his chin gently, holding his face so he's looking at me.

"I don't want to lose either of you. I refuse to do it. We'll find a way to make it work even if Josie doesn't like you. If, for whatever reason, you guys don't get along, we'll find a way to make it work. I swear it."

"I want to believe you, but it's really hard when everything feels so off-kilter."

Using my hand, I pull his face to mine and kiss him gently, trying to convey to him that he matters without being pushy. I may not be an Alpha, but I can be just as pushy as one. Knowing the situation is delicate, I try to handle it as such. There's something Simon isn't telling me, and I bet it's about what happened to him. He's never told me the full story of his bad experience, and I've never asked. It might be time to have some serious discussions.

We pull apart and look at each other for a moment before my mouth starts running again. "I think there's some other shit that we need to talk through as well."

Simon sighs and leans against the back of the couch. "Okay, give it to me."

"Did you feel the Pack Pull to the guy from the coffee shop the other day?" I ask.

I'm not sure if Simon will admit to it one way or the other, but his reaction to the guy makes me think the pull was there. I know he's generally uninterested in Pack, but he's not cold or stand-offish as a rule. So, why the hesitance? I brace myself, telling my brain that I need to remain calm for Simon so he doesn't feel attacked.

He sighs, "I'm not sure, but maybe?"

"Have you felt it before?" I ask.

"Yeah," Simon murmurs. I almost don't hear him because he's talking so quietly.

"You don't have to tell me until you're ready, but I'm curious why you're so hesitant. Do you think I'm going to abandon you?"

Simon's hands cover his face, muffling his answer, "Yeah, I'm afraid of that."

My eyebrows shoot sky high. I hadn't actually thought he'd feel that way. It makes sense, though, now that I think about it. He's happy enough to be physical, and when it's just me, everything is great, but his insecurity skyrockets when others come into play. He doesn't play games or push anyone away, but he does get really quiet and keeps to himself. I reach out hesitantly and put my hand on his knee.

"Simon, I'm never going to abandon you."

I hear a sigh filter between his hands. "That's what they said, too."

Frowning, I turn my body fully toward his, making sure I keep contact with him.

"Tell me, Si, please."

Hands falling from his face, he looks at me with watery eyes, and I gaze back steadily at him. Trying to show him, without words, that I'm here for him. I always will be, even if he decides to reject the Pack Pull and go his own way. If he does, it'll hurt like hell, but I want him happy.

"In college, before I met you, there was this group of people. A few Betas, two Alphas, and they were hoping to find an Omega," he clears his throat, "Honestly, the idea of an Omega terrifies me, but only because I'm worried I'll never be enough for one. So, after a few months of hanging around with them, they started talking about Packing up and being serious about courting an Omega. Even though I wasn't bonded in, they swore we'd all stay together. When it came time to start making dates, I tried to be a part of it, but they shut me out.

"One night, I saw them out on a date with someone new, and just knew it was an Omega. So I walked over to them and asked what was happening, wanting to know why they had gone out without me. All they would say is that I was a joke, and they were surprised I hung around as long as I had without any kind of commitment from them. The Omega looked sympathetic, but she hadn't ever met me, so she didn't interfere. When I tried to introduce myself, one of the Alphas clocked me and told me to stay away. The Alpha had a class ring on and split my eyebrow. Thus, my charming scar."

My heart is frozen, and my lungs are screaming for air. I'm pretty sure I stopped breathing as he told me about his past. For someone to string along another with the promise of a future Pack is awful. Add in how they treated him when he saw their date, and I hope like hell they never found their Omega. They don't deserve one. The anger washes through my body, and I feel my heart go into overdrive, rage taking over my body, making me shake.

"Those motherfuck—" I stand and pace angrily around the room. "Who the hell do they think they are? Who treats someone that way? Especially *you*, you're amazing! What are their names? I'm gonna go beat the shit out of every single one of them!"

Simon stands and puts his hands on my shoulders. I look down slightly at him, the anger making my hands shake. One of his hands lifts to my face, cupping my cheek as he searches my eyes for something. I have no idea what he's looking for, but he must see it because he pulls me tight to him. I grasp him hard, my arms banding around him protectively as he buries his face in my neck.

"We're Pack, aren't we?" Simon whispers into my neck.

"Yeah, Si, we are."

"I don't... I don't know if I can handle a full Pack, Vic."

"One day at a time, okay? I'm not leaving you, but I'm not going to force a bond on you either."

He nods, and his hair tickles me a little as he does so. I understand why he pulls away now, and I'm so grateful he opened up to me like this. I only hope that I can be his rock the way he needs me to be.

eleven

JOSIE

Jesse is sitting on my couch, and I have to pinch myself a few times to make sure this is really happening. We were texting, and I told him it's silly to text when he can come over, so now he's here. In my space. With his amazing smell and smile. My inner Omega is bursting with happiness. And horniness, let's be honest. He's so gorgeous and I can't help but sit right next to him, with my legs tucked under me and body facing him.

"Okay, so let me get this straight," he says, a smile on his face, "You touch other people for a living, but you don't touch other people?"

"Not generally, no, but it does sound silly now that you say it that way." I smile back.

"No, not silly, it sounds like you're careful about your boundaries, and it's something I know nothing about. It's pretty cool, even if it sounds a bit like an oxymoron."

"Thanks." I'm sure I'm blushing as I glance down at my hands. "It's, um, it's personal for me."

Jesse shifts so he's facing me directly.

"I'd love to hear about your reasons if you want to tell me, but don't feel pressured, okay? I'm happy getting to know you at whatever pace you choose."

66

My heart melts as he reaches out to gently put a hand on my knee. My leggings prevent skin contact, but it reminds me about when we held hands on our date. Should I ask him about that? I found a Match in Vic, is it possible I have another? Would Jesse even want to share? There's no way I'm rejecting Vic even if I'm not ready to bond yet. Deciding that worrying about the future won't help, I take a calming breath.

"Can I ask you a question first?"

He smiles, "Of course. I'm an open book for you."

"I... Um... We... Are we a Match?" I blurt out.

Jesse's eyes widen in surprise. He suddenly looks insecure, and I want to beat myself up for asking that question. I can't apologize for asking, so I wait to see what he'll say. My inner Omega wants to soothe my Alpha because he looks so unsure, but I remind myself he's not *my* Alpha until he tells me he is, so I need to be calm. I gaze steadily at him, needing this information.

He clears his throat a couple of times before replying, "Um, yeah, we are. I figured you knew. I'm sorry that I didn't bring it up before."

"No, don't be sorry. I'll explain it." I take a deep breath and blow it out slowly with my eyes closed.

"My parents died when I was young. Four or five, something like that. I don't remember them, really. They were both only children, so I ended up in the foster care system. None of the families that I was with were *bad*, really, but I got a lot of families who changed their minds after they got me. At first, it was because I was so young, they wanted older kids. Then I did have one good family, but they moved to a new state and I couldn't join them. Once I presented as an Omega, it was worse. Nobody wanted to keep me for very long.

"I never lived in a place where physical touch was a thing, so I went the majority of my life without touch. I developed Touch Sickness in High School, but by then, I had presented as an Omega, so nobody wanted me around long enough to treat it. They avoided touching me even more at that point. Touch Sickness was pretty painful, my skin felt raw all the time, my emotions were out of control, and I was absolutely exhausted. All the time. When it turned into Touch Loss, the pain went away, but it means I can't feel a Match. There's no fixing it."

Jesse just stares at me, his face a mask of sorrow. "I'm so sorry, Josie."

"It's not your fault. I can tell scents that pull me to people, and I was almost knocked over by yours, but when we held hands, you didn't react at all, so I thought maybe we weren't Matches."

Jesse reaches out to gently take my hand. I can feel tears building behind my eyes, realizing that he's knowingly touching me because I'm his Match. I can feel a tear fall as I look at him.

"You're killing me, babe, can I hold you?"

I nod and help him arrange our bodies so he's surrounding me with his arms and scent.

"When you dropped your purse that day we met, our fingers brushed when I handed you my number. That's when I knew. You didn't react that day, so I avoided bringing it up, but when I took your hand on our date, it just felt *right,* and that solidified it for me. I assumed you felt it."

I shake my head and try to bury my face in his neck, inhaling his fresh rain scent. Between his scent and how gorgeous he is, I'm a complete goner. My mind is in disbelief that I have *two* Matches, but I'm so happy I do. We snuggle and talk about shallow things until I have to go to work. He gives me a hug before I hop into my car, and when I look in the rearview mirror, he's watching as I drive away.

When I pull up to Ray's house, I still feel a little giddy, but I try to calm myself before going to knock on the door. My time with Ray should be focused on her, not me. Henry greets me at the door, and even though I'm still happy about my time with Jesse, my Omega is greedy and wants Henry, too. Telling my inner hussy to knock it off, I follow him to where Ray and I spend our time.

The session goes by as well as it usually does. In two more sessions, we'll do a re-evaluation of her symptoms to see how she's progressing. She's looking a bit better each time we meet, so I'm encouraged by her progress. Hopefully she's opened up to some friends her age and is getting touch time in that way as well. It's good to have some variety, assuming you know the person.

Henry meets me at the door to the room I was in with Ray, and I can't help but smile at him.

"Are you my personal attendant today?" I sass him.

He laughs, "I suppose I am. I was actually hoping I could walk you to your car?"

"I'd like that."

He nods, and we start toward the main door, and I notice a bag in his hand. Wonder what that's for.

"How have you been?" he asks.

"Good. An old friend of mine moved back into town, and we were able to spend some time together, so that was amazing. Normally we see each other once a year at the most due to the distance."

"That's awesome! I'm glad that she was able to be closer to you."

I giggle, "I'll tell him that."

"Oh! I'm sorry, I didn't mean to assume. It just popped out." He runs his hand through his hair, sheepishly.

"It's no problem, I didn't exactly give you any clues," I giggle.

He grins as he opens the door for me. It's a gorgeous day today, and there's a light breeze that feels good flowing through my hair. I take a deep breath, appreciating the smell of nature, and the hit of Henry's scent makes my knees weak. The scent alone makes me gone for this man.

"I realize, we never made plans for your confidence-boosting seminar," he tells me.

I frown at him, trying to remember what he's talking about, before I remember what he called our potential date. I start chuckling as I recall.

"We should fix that then," I tell him.

He grins and pulls out his phone. "My calendar is pretty open, honestly, just making sure here. Is there something that works better for you?"

"I think the weekend. I'm usually pretty wiped out during the week in the evening after my touch sessions," I hum, tapping my finger on my chin.

"Okay, I'll pick you up this weekend, and we can grab dinner or drinks. Maybe both if we're lucky," he waggles his eyebrows.

Another laugh escapes me, and I lean against my car now that we've arrived here. I'm not sure what else to say, but I don't want to give up my time with him. So, we stare at each other for a moment, just smiling.

"Oh!" he startles and holds the bag in front of him. "I got you something."

Honestly, I don't remember the last time someone got me something just because. Excitement and disbelief flood me, but then my greedy Omega comes out, and my hands itch to get into that bag. My eyes go wide, and I look at him with awe.

"For me?"

His smile is blindingly bright. "Yes, for you. I hope you like it. If you don't, I can get you something else."

I snatch the bag out of his hand, "No! It's mine!"

"You're such a cute Omega."

I preen at his words before opening the bag to look inside. There's a gift-wrapped box that I tear into, and I gasp. The fluffiest, most gorgeous green blanket I've ever seen is nestled inside the box. My hand reaches in to touch it, and I gasp at how soft it is. It's a chunky knit blanket, so incredibly soft, and looks cozy and warm. I can't help but pull it out and rub my face against it, purring a little.

"You like it?" Henry asks with a smile.

My eyes meet his, and I feel incredibly special from the gift.

"Thank you," I whisper, "Thank you so much!"

He just smiles, and my Omega instincts take over before I can think about it. I shove the blanket at him and rub it over his chest, around his neck, and under his arms. Fussing to make sure I get the right amount of scent on it from where he's pumping it out for me. When I bring it to my nose, I whimper at how it smells exactly the way he does. Just like I'd hoped it would.

"Fuck, I want to kiss you. Can I do that? Or is that too fast for my adorable Omega?" Henry's words are so unexpectedly dirty that I can feel a small rush of slick hit my panties.

"Um, I don't know… I… Usually don't like touch," I admit, even as I step closer to him.

Henry grasps my waist and makes a point of bringing his nose close to my neck, inhaling deeply. Another whimper escapes me, and I bare my neck for him to explore. His skin doesn't touch mine once, and I think that turns me on even more. He's respecting my boundaries even when I'm not sure if I want to hold them. A rumble sounds deep in his chest when he pulls away to look into my eyes.

"You smell like heaven itself, and I want to keep you. Tell me I can keep you, at least for a little while," he begs.

I nod wordlessly, I'm sure my mouth is open and drooling as I gaze at him.

He chuckles, "Good Omega. I'll call you."

When he steps back, the spell is broken and I begin to breathe normally again instead of massive inhales of his scent. Grinning, I nod at him before turning to climb into my car. I keep the blanket on my lap, not wanting to part with it. It's truly one of the first "just because" gifts I've gotten. It's now one of my favorite possessions. Sometimes, Vic would send me things, and always for my birthday, but that feels different because I've known him longer.

A full giggle escapes me as I drive back to my condo, and I can feel that my cheeks are flushed with delight. I have two Matches and an Alpha courting me. How lucky can one girl get?

twelve

HENRY

The look on Josie's face when I gave her that blanket will live in my mind for the rest of my life. She looked at me like I was the most special Alpha on the planet. I felt ten feet tall for making her so happy. Then we had that charged moment, and I had to lock down tight on my instincts. My Alpha was pushing for me to take her, then and there, and bond her as ours. I'm pretty sure we're at Match, but I don't really know who else she might have. She might already have a full Pack courting her. Plus, I have a Pack Pull to a couple of other guys that I need to work through.

So that's what I'm doing today. I've been texting with Victor and Simon a bit, and we made plans to go get some beers at a local brewery. They have a nice outdoor space, so we can talk without yelling to be heard. I arrive first, which gives me the chance to pick seats that I prefer. I order a beer at the bar and take it to a round table, a little bit set apart from the rest of the outdoor area. I position myself so I can see the entrance and enjoy the sunshine while I wait.

I get the sense that Simon is a little twitchy about all of this, so I make sure that there's plenty of open space, hoping it will help him feel at ease. I'm looking forward to getting to know him better, and I hope that he's willing to open up more. I'm not sure if today is the

72

right time to bring up my interest in Josie, but I'll play it by ear and see.

Maybe they're not even ready for an Omega. Shit, what if they have their own Omega? Vic said they aren't Pack, but that doesn't mean they're without an Omega they want. About five minutes after I sit, I see them heading my way, a beer each in their hands. I grin and stand up to greet them.

I extend my hand out to Victor first, "Hey, glad you guys could make it."

"Us too, I'm excited to talk through this Pack Pull with you," Victor replies.

Simon gives me a "Hey" as he shakes my hand briefly.

When we sit, he chooses the spot where he can see the rest of the outdoor area but isn't caged in by the fence, and I'm pleased with myself for getting that right. My instincts haven't failed me yet. I settle back in and we each take a few sips of our beers, letting the atmosphere settle a bit. I can still feel that tug in my chest, drawing me to these two. Their scents smell *right* like I was always meant to smell them.

"So, anyone want to volunteer to go first? Bare all our secrets?" Vic says in a teasing tone.

"I don't think you have any secrets," Simon teases back quietly, a small smile on his face.

"Well, not from you at least," Vic quips back.

"Tell me more about you two. You seem really tight," I throw out to keep the conversation moving.

Vic raises an eyebrow at Simon, who gestures for him to take point.

"Well, we met in college. I needed a roommate for my rental house, and Simon needed to find off-campus housing. When he walked in the door of the small home I was renting, I knew he was meant to be there."

A smile appears on my face. "Sounds like destiny."

Simon huffs a small laugh, "Yeah, I think it was."

"Since then, we've been pretty inseparable. He's the Alpha to my

Beta. The wind to my sails. The chocolate to my peanut butter." Vic waxes on poetically.

"Oh my god, stop." Simon grins at him.

"Well, you know the basics about us, how about you? What are your basics?" Vic turns to me.

I shrug, "Not much to tell, honestly. I'm the youngest sibling in my family, and I live farthest away from them. I needed to be able to go out on my own, so when my parents declared they were moving across the country to be closer to my scattered siblings, they said I could keep the house and stay here. So, I did. My siblings are all Alphas and Betas, but my mom is an Omega, so I know a little about their designation. She did have a Pack and seemed incredibly happy. I'm excited to talk with you guys about being Pack, hopefully we feel like a cohesive group, you know?"

Vic nods, "Well, it sounds like we just need time to get to know each other then."

"Yeah, don't want to Pack up with a serial killer," Simon mutters with a small smirk.

"Is that the standard? I think I should be okay then. Unless you count tastebuds because I can't cook," I quip.

Simon chuckles, and we talk about our adult lives, what we each do for a living, and touch on families. Turns out that they just moved to town a month or two ago, and Simon opened the coffee shop where I met them. He's the owner of a really successful shop back where they moved from, so he decided to open another one here in Blackford. I love hearing about his passion for coffee and his vision for the new cafe.

Victor works for a business with several buildings in the country. So when an opening came up to move here, he jumped at it. He's been enjoying the city so far, even if his job isn't his passion. He's just happy it pays the bills. I work as a CEO for a larger corporation, and while I don't always love my job, I do enjoy working with people on business needs. Being the CEO enabled me to be able to take Ray in. I hired another person to help with in-person office needs while I work mostly remotely.

"Why did you jump at the chance to move here? There had to be better locations offered," I ask.

Victor blushes a little, and a smile comes over his face. "Uh, my other best friend lives in the city. We met in high school, and even though she moved around a lot, we kept in touch. The opportunity to move here, where she is, came up and I grabbed it immediately."

My mind latches onto what Victor's saying and connects a dot. I'm not sure if it's right, but what if... "What's your friend's name?"

"Josie," Vic says, looking a bit confused.

I smile a little, "I just had an Omega, I'm interested in, tell me her friend moved to town. Her name is also Josie."

Vic looks excited, "What are the odds? Does she have red hair, tall, smells like a cinnamon dessert?"

"Man, I have spent weeks hunting for cinnamon desserts just to try and recreate that scent," I confess.

Vic and Simon look at each other for a moment. Vic is smiling and hopeful, but Simon seems doubtful. Vic bites his lip and looks back at me.

"She's actually my Match."

That was the last thing I expected him to say. My mind grinds to a halt for a moment before it gets moving again, and I laugh loudly, causing other tables to look at us. My hands slap down on the table, giddiness running through me.

"Are you *serious?*" I ask.

Vic and Simon just look at me as if I've lost my mind. I'm pretty sure I have. This significantly increases my chances with Josie. My suspicion that she could be my Match is all but confirmed now. Clearly, I'd need to touch her to confirm, but it's like a weight is off my shoulders.

"Sorry," I say, calming myself, "Sorry, I just... I'm so fucking relieved to hear that."

Simon frowns, "What do you mean?"

"Do you remember when we met? I told you I had been shopping? I was buying her a blanket from a local Omega store. I've been hoping we were a Match, her scent almost brings me to my knees. If you're a

Match and we have a Pack Pull, then that just increases my chances with her," I explain.

"What do you mean by that?" Simon asks, surprisingly aggressive.

I hold my hands up, "Just that I hope she takes a chance on me, and accepts me. If she's Matched to you guys and we're Pack, she could be my Match as well."

Simon eyes me up and down for a moment before relaxing back in his seat, satisfied that I'm not planning anything creepy or nefarious.

"How do you even know her?" Vic asks.

"She comes to my home for work, I have a friend of a friend who needs her and lives with me."

"You just took in some random Omega?" Simon asks, his deep voice full of confusion.

"She needed help," I answer.

His eyes study me, almost calculating in their intensity. Like he's trying to put puzzle pieces together so he can understand me. I find myself wondering what he's thinking, and I want to ask, but I can tell he's not ready to be that open with me. I'll just have to wait and be patient.

"Okay, I think this is good," Vic says, taking a thoughtful sip of his drink. "If you and Josie have met, she seems to like you, I assume? Right, so I think we should tell her and see what she says. If she's not ready to find out if you two are Matches, then at least the three of us can get to know each other. Hopefully, she is at least willing to get to know you two."

"I think she will be, she was happy with my gift and was interested in talking more. She seems really sweet, I can't imagine she'll say 'no' if we do it on her terms." I add.

Simon is quiet, but sips at his beer as he listens to the conversation. I quietly observe him from my peripheral, noting that he's not shutting us out, he's just not engaging either. It tugs at my chest, and I'm finding that I want his input more and more. Something about him just draws me in. I've always been a sucker for curly hair, and his is gorgeous. Down the road, I'd be interested in a romantic relationship, but we need to get to the friendship stage before anything else.

We spend another hour or two drinking beers and chatting, deciding that the three of us will get together again soon. Vic will also work on scheduling a group dinner, so we can subtly figure out how our dynamics will work together. I notice that both Vic and Simon are deferring to me, but I don't want to be Lead Alpha unless everyone is good with it. While I can be dominant, I don't enjoy using that to call the shots on my own. I'm sure we'll talk about it next time. I can't just assume they're okay with it.

We stand to leave after we pay our tabs, and I hold out my hand again. Vic takes it and we move for a quick hug, one pat on the back, and separate. My hand goes out again for Simon, and he shakes it but doesn't move for a hug, so I don't push.

"I just want you guys to know that I'm really excited to get to know you. I've always wanted a Pack, and now there's a chance. I'm grateful for it." I tell them before we part ways.

The guys both give a nod of acknowledgement, Vic with a nice smile in addition. Back in my car, I let my head flop back on the headrest for a moment. A massive smile spreads across my face, and my heart feels settled for the first time in a long time.

thirteen

SIMON

My mind has been buzzing for a couple of weeks, thinking through all the changes that are happening around me. Maybe they aren't earth-shattering things, but it's so much more than I'm used to. Insecurity plagues me in every situation, and the only thing that keeps me steady and grounded is my time with Vic. It's enough to make me forgetful at work, and I'm sure my manager today is ready to kick me out. I was able to quickly hire a second manager, since the cafe is open more than 40 hours a week. The last thing I need is my staff burning out.

Currently, I'm in my office, pretending that I'm doing financials and important paperwork. In reality, I'm thinking through the interaction Vic and I had with Henry. He seems like a nice enough guy, but he's already implying he wants to Pack up, and I don't know if I'm ready for that. I'm finally comfortable with the idea of a Pack Pull to Vic, now I have one for an Alpha that I barely know. Who else is going to show up with one? A random customer in my store? I don't want to be ambushed, but it's not like I can control when the pull shows up.

A face comes unbidden to mind, and my eyes go wide, realizing that I did meet another Pack Pull and didn't recognize the feeling. Before I opened, that couple was peeking in, and the blonde guy was in it. The woman he was with had an amazing cinnamon scent, and I played it cool, but I was ready to drool over her. Wiping my mouth to ensure I haven't started drooling over her memory, I stand and head out to the floor to check on things.

My baristas are still working at top speed, which makes me happy to know we're doing a lot of business. I'll make sure they're getting their breaks, too; I'm sure they're tired from all the movement. Seeing some orders sitting on the counter, I pick them up and begin calling names. There's not a huge wait queue, so maybe someone was in the bathroom or has earbuds in. A few people come when I call their names, and a few don't. My fears of a new Pack Pull are realized as I call out for "Jesse" and see the tall blonde walking toward me. Same guy from my memory.

"You called for Jesse?" he asks.

"Uh, yeah, looks like this is yours," I tell him, still a bit dumbstruck.

"Thanks, had my headphones in. You... you okay there?"

"Yeah, fine, totally fine, all good."

There's a moment of awkward staring between us before I snap out of it first.

"Have a great day," I tell him, before turning around and walking back to my office like my ass is on fire.

I just had to manifest that shit, didn't I? Pushing thoughts of this guy, Jesse, to the back of my mind, I focus on my job. When the day ends, I head home, looking forward to some time with Vic. I need that stability right now with all this shit stirring in my head. Should I be okay with being potentially Pack with two strangers? What about cinnamon girl?

Vic said that Josie smells like cinnamon dessert, but it couldn't be the same girl. The chances are just too slim. Henry honestly seems like a decent guy, but there's no way to know if it's a facade or not. For all I know, the moment we go to bond, I'll get kicked to the curb. Again. My mind turns to Vic's words of "one day at a time", and I try to repeat them in my head.

Once I'm home, I kick off my shoes and stride into the house, looking for Vic. I need him more than I'm willing to admit to myself, or him. When I finally get eyes on him, Vic's sitting on the bed we've been sharing and talking on the phone. He's got *that* look on his face, telling me that he's talking to Josie. I walk around the bed and flop on my back, my face near Vic's thighs and my feet hanging off the other end of the bed.

"Wow, I can't believe it. Are you sure?" Vic says. He looks down at me and smiles softly, gently running his hand through my hair as he speaks.

I can faintly hear Josie, so I settle in to eavesdrop in plain sight.

"Yeah, I trust that he's telling the truth. I'm sorry to tell you this over the phone. It's just so much, having two Matches. If I end up with more, I would be happy to experience that, but it's also a lot of pressure."

"There's gotta be a reason for you to have the Matches you do. I believe it's a good thing. Speaking of good things..." Vic teases.

After a big pause, she starts begging, "What? What? What? You can't leave me hanging like that!"

Vic chuckles, alternating between running his hands through my hair and caressing my face. I close my eyes in pleasure, basking in the feel of his touch as I listen.

"I found another Pack Pull. You'll never guess who it is."

She scoffs, "How would I know? We don't have anyone who overlaps with the two of us. At some point, I hope to meet Simon, but I know he's hesitant."

"He's got some shit to work though, don't take it personally," Vic says gently.

"I know, he just means so much to you that I hope he and I can get along. So tell me your Pack Pull!"

"So... it's this guy named Henry." Vic teases one tidbit of information at a time.

"Henry?"

"Yup. Apparently, he knows you."

There's a pause before Josie all but screams, "Oh my God, you met Henry!!"

Vic chuckles, "Yeah, he came into the coffee shop while Simon and I were there, and it hit me. So we all met up the other day."

"This is so wild! Ah! I'm excited and terrified!" Josie lets out a high-pitched, nervous giggle that comes through quite clearly on Vic's cell.

"What do you think about having dinner with us? Simon, Henry, and I. Henry offered to host one if you're interested."

I miss the rest of the conversation because I immediately realize that Vic didn't ask me first. Is he just expecting me to follow along like a good little Packmate? There's no way I'm going, I can't just do whatever Henry and Vic say. Vic is my rock. Is this the first sign of him abandoning me? He promised he wouldn't do that. Why would he invite Josie before telling me about it? I suppose since she's his Match, she comes first now. That's going to be hard to get used to.

"Want to talk about it?" Vic says, sounding way closer than he did before.

I open my eyes to see him lying down, his head right next to mine, surprising me since I never felt him move. We stare at each other for a moment before I gather my thoughts.

"It's going to sound really petulant," I confess.

Vic just smiles and grabs one of my hands in his, holding them just under our chins.

"Why didn't you tell me about Henry inviting us for dinner?" I ask, my eyes darting away as I speak.

Vic waits for me to look at him again before speaking. "I had just finished texting with Henry when Josie called. I didn't have time to let you know. I'm sorry that you heard about the dinner in a way that made you feel badly."

I huff with a small smile, "Could you please stop being so mature and wise?"

"Okay, poopyhead," Vic grins at me.

We both laugh through the tension I was holding and enjoy the silly moment.

"There is going to be uncertainty," Vic says, his thumb rubbing back and forth on my knuckles, "but promise me that you'll try to give me the benefit of the doubt? I'll do my best to make sure I communicate with you."

"Okay, I promise… I do have another thing," I say to Vic. He nods to show he's listening. "I think I met another Pack Pull. I'd seen him once before but forgot until I saw him again today. I didn't get his number or anything, I ran pretty fast."

"If it's meant to be, we'll get another shot. Don't worry about it for now, just focus on us. Maybe Josie and Henry, too," Vic replies with a wink.

IT'S FINALLY DINNER NIGHT, and while I'm trying to be optimistic, I'm actually incredibly nervous. I still don't feel like I deserve any kind of Pack, nor do I trust the idea of a Pack. Are they really that special if one group can kick me out the way they did? I know we were dumb college kids, but the Pack is supposed to be a serious thing. Will Henry kick me out? I know Vic said he'll always be here for me, but I can't deny him the chance at happiness with a Pack.

Steeling myself, I try to remember that it doesn't help to worry about the future. If I say it enough, it's got to stick. My head is so fucked up. Vic knocks at the door as I stand next to him, my eyes all but glued to his ass. He really has a great one, and his dark wash jeans display it well. His casual long-sleeved shirt suits him well, and when he catches me looking, I give him a wink. Henry opens the door right as Vic is about to say something, and smiles widely at the two of us.

"Come on in! I'm glad you guys were able to make it."

"Thanks, looking forward to spending some time together," Vic answers.

I give a non-committal grunt.

Henry shows us to their living room and grabs drinks for the three of us. We chit-chat lightly and sip at our drinks until the doorbell rings again.

"That'll be the rest of them," Henry says, still smiling, before getting up.

I lean over to Vic, "He smiles too much."

"He does *not*, you just don't smile enough around other people," Vic rolls his eyes.

"If you could not be right about things, it would make my world a whole lot easier."

"Tough luck, babe," Vic lands a quick kiss on me.

I can't help but smile at him. He's just… him. It makes me all gooey inside. Footsteps draw my attention, and I see Henry coming back to the room with two people in tow. Holy shit, these two *are* the ones I saw looking at the cafe before we opened. The guy is tall, like an Alpha is, with blonde, messy hair. He looks somewhat open but incredibly aloof. He'll probably answer questions, but won't engage on his own. I can relate.

The girl, though, the girl is who gets me. I knew Josie was coming and it would be our first time meeting, but I didn't expect her to floor me like this. She's tall, with long auburn hair and a friendly, open face. Her scent wraps around me, and I stifle a groan. It's so much better up close than it was outside. Belatedly, I realize this is Josie, and I almost laugh at the absurdity of all this. How is it possible that we've all met before? It feels insane. It also feels so right that I'm terrified.

"In case you guys haven't met, this is Josie and Jesse," Henry introduces the two.

"Hey Josie Girl, Jesse it's nice to meet you," Vic has manners and actually stands to shake Jesse's hand.

I give a small wave because I'm a chicken-shit and don't want to find out if Josie is a Match on accident. Jesse gives a knowing smile when he sees my wave and does it back. I'm glad he understands that I'm not trying to be a dick. Josie stares at me for a moment, her jaw slightly slackened. Maybe she remembers me? The moment passes, and she gives a small wave in return.

"Nice to officially meet you, Simon," she says.

Whelp, I'm a goner. The way my name sounds in her mouth is just too good to pass up. I'm not sure I'll be able to stay away from her just from that one word. Small talk takes over while we sip on drinks and talk about basic topics, like the weather. Before we head to the dining room, Henry decides he's going to bring up the whole Pack idea.

"So, I would like to take a moment and talk through how our group is forming and functioning," he says.

"I don't think we're quite functioning yet," Josie says with a teasing smile.

"We can fix that," Vic chimes in.

Henry chuckles, "What I meant was we should start the conversation to see how everyone is feeling about any Pack Pulls or potential Matches. Josie, I remember saying you struggle to let others touch you, so before we go any further, I want to acknowledge that we only know of two Matches so far."

Josie blushes, "Sorry for springing Jesse on you last minute, but I couldn't leave him behind."

Jesse gives her a soft smile and a kiss on her temple. Lucky bastard.

"It's no problem," Henry says gently, "It's nice to have him here. I am actually feeling a Pack Pull, but I don't want to speak for Jesse. Vic, Simon, and I have already discussed the Pull between the three of us."

Clearing his throat, Jesse has a very soft-spoken tone, "I think we can all be honest enough to say that the four of us have a Pack Pull, and Josie is our Match, or at least an Omega we'd want to pursue."

I like that Jesse doesn't mince words. There's an awkward moment after his comment as we try to get situated in the dining room. It's hard to figure out who is going to sit where, which it really shouldn't be. I just make sure I'm sitting next to Vic and call it good. Another moment of quiet settles in when Henry steps out to grab the food from the kitchen.

"Um, Simon, right? You own the coffee shop?" Jesse asks.

I look up in surprise, "Yeah, I do. Just opened it."

"Right on. It's great coffee. I'm not sure if you source it locally or what, but it's really good. I think a lot of places it all tastes the same, but not yours," he says.

"Thanks, man." A smile spreads across my face at the high praise.

Before I can ask anything about him, his cheeks flare red as though he said something embarrassing, and he looks away. Huh, must be really shy. I give him the reprieve and stay quiet.

Once Henry comes back with food, we dish it out and spend a few minutes confirming Pack Pulls and interests in Josie. I do my best not to sound over-eager and freak her out, because honestly, I'm freaked out enough on my own. Deciding to try some Pack outings that also include courting Josie, we wrap up our meal and go our separate ways. Secretly, I'm already counting down the minutes until I get to see her again.

JOSIE

Did I win the hottie jackpot? Is that something that you can do? I don't know what I did to deserve this, but I do know I'm grabbing on with both hands. Am I still scared to fully open up? For sure. There's that little voice in my head nagging me, saying they could just be pretending this entire time, but I'm trying to shove it into a sound-proof room. I don't need that little voice.

Jesse pulls up to his condo, and we exit his car at the same time. I'm glad I got to spend more time with him today, and I really don't want to have to say goodbye. He lives right next door, it seems silly to be so close but not, doesn't it? Jessie walks me to my door, and when I turn to try to invite him in, I'm ambushed by his hands. One hand sneaks around to the back of my head, and the other grabs my waist. Then his lips meet mine, and all thought leaves my mind.

I drop my purse on the ground, not wanting it in the way, and wrap my arms around his neck, trying to hold him close. Our lips tangle together, teeth nipping and tongues darting out to explore. I suck his lower lip into my mouth and pull it back, letting it rebound with a small snap. Jesse growls and brings me flush against him. Judging by the sizeable bulk in his pants that presses against me, he's

86

enjoying this as much as I am. Slick is slowly soaking my underwear, and I perfume for him. He pulls back with a groan.

"You smell fucking incredible. I could kiss you all night," he says against my mouth.

"So do it." I challenge him.

Jesse pulls back and looks into my eyes.

"Are you sure? I know I said I could kiss you all night, but I'm worried I won't hold back."

"I don't want you to," I whisper in a moment of bravery.

"Condoms?"

"Birth control, I'm clean."

"It's been years for me. I'm clean. Get this damn door open," he all but growls.

A giggle escapes me as I reach down for my purse, quickly finding my keys before I open the door and lead him inside. He closes and locks the door behind him, and the move is so protective I perfume again for him. I can't help it at this point. Sitting near him all evening, smelling how good all four guys' scents are, I'm borderline needy at this point. I grab his hand and start for my nest before stopping outside the door.

"Um, is my nest okay, or would you be more comfortable in a bed?" I ask.

Some people make a huge deal of others being in their nests, and while normally I wouldn't invite him in so soon, we're a Match. It seems natural to bring him in as long as he's comfortable with it. He might not be ready, maybe he just wants a quick night together. I'd be okay with that if it's what he wants, but I want so badly for him to hold me all night.

Jesse looks at me with awe on his face. "I'd be honored to be in your nest, Josie."

I almost attack him with my mouth, but I refrain so we can at least get into the room together. We step in, and Jesse takes a moment to look around the room. It has a large round mattress in the middle of the room, flat on the ground but with a rounded headboard on one side. Makes it easier to fully nest during a heat or a rut when you have one section that will stay in place despite the movement.

While he looks at the fabric drapes and other decorations I have, I pull my shirt off my body and flip on the fairy lights. His eyes go from awe as he looks at the room, to hunger as he looks at me. I bite my lip and grab his shirt, urging him to take it off. Instead of pulling it off, he does the one-arm removal, and I'm pretty sure my panties are now ruined. I reach out and run my fingers over his skin, watching his nipples pebble and his muscles flex. He's no bodybuilder, but I can see the strength in his chest, arms, and abs. His breathing picks up as I explore before he grabs my hand.

"We're both wearing too much clothing," he rumbles.

"We should fix that," my voice sounds breathier than I thought it could be.

Jesse grabs my pants, unbuttons them, then pulls them down to my thighs. He drops to his knees and looks at how wet my panties are. Before he goes any further, he buries his nose between my legs and inhales deeply. Not one guy I've been with has done that, let alone *any* oral. I can feel my knees shaking with anticipation as Jesse removes my pants and pulls my underwear off, licking his lips at the slickness sticking to my skin.

Hands grasping my hips, he pulls them forward and buries his mouth between my legs. He encourages me to widen my legs with his hands before placing them on my hips again. The smooth glide of his tongue across my skin is heaven, and I can feel the area getting more sensitive as he feasts. My clit is begging for attention as I moan in delight at the feelings he's pulling from me. It doesn't beg for long, when Jesse finally gets to it, he nips gently at it before sucking it into his mouth.

I come with a rush, "Jesse!"

He chuckles as I come down, unfastening his pants as he advances on me. I feel like he's a predator that has me in his sights, so I instinctively back up a step. We move like this for a couple of steps before my feet touch the round mattress. Jesse pulls his pants off, and I step back on the mattress to make sure there's room for him. My Omega switches away from playing prey and is full force nesting, making sure the space is presentable for our Alpha.

Jesse waits patiently, leisurely stroking his cock, eyes riveted on me. When I finally have the space how I want it, I turn to him, staying on my knees.

"You can come in," I say softly.

Wasting no time, he steps in and slams his mouth to mine. He pushes me backward, and I happily change my position so I'm on my back, legs wide to accept him. As he kisses and nips at my lip and neck, his hips are pumping toward me, sliding his cock through my slick, but not into me. I scramble to remove my bra, wanting him to pay attention to my nipples. Jesse helps before tossing it across the room and bringing one nipple into his mouth.

He hums as he licks it, back and forth, around in circles, and sucks like he can pull life from it. One of his hands moves to the other breast to flick and pull gently at my nipple. My cries are incoherent, the sensations overwhelming, but not enough at the same time. Jesse pulls back, but continues moving his dick through my lower lips.

"Are you ready, sweets? I can't wait to push my cock inside you and fuck you until you know well and good who you belong to."

"Yessss..." I moan, arching my hips to try and encourage him along. Remembering one detail, I mumble, "No bites."

"Not tonight, but someday. Someday I'll be sure to mark up that gorgeous throat of yours," he agrees as he lines himself up.

I'm relieved that he won't bond with me tonight. He's wonderful and I'm so glad that he's here and mine, but I'm not ready for a Match Bond yet. He doesn't seem to be either, but it sounds like he wants to, which is enough for me.

Pushing in slowly, we both groan at the pleasure of our bodies coming together. He's stretching my cunt perfectly and I don't think I've ever felt so satisfied from just the size of someone's cock. When he's fully in, he starts a steady pumping, his knot still soft. He takes advantage of it before it starts to inflate, pushing himself in far enough that his public bone grinds on my clit as he goes.

"You feel like heaven, I want to live inside your cunt," he moans as he starts to pick up the tempo of his hips.

"God, yes," I agree, lost to the pleasure he's wringing from me.

He's going fast now, and his knot is inflating, which means he can't get in quite as far yet, not until he wants to lock us together. One thumb is on my clit, making tiny circles and driving me higher and higher.

"Let me see you come, baby, before I shove my big knot into you. I can't wait to see you stretched around it, unable to get away from the pleasure it brings. *Fuck*, you feel so good!"

His dirty words do me in, and I feel my walls twitch twice before the orgasm hits me. My eyes are screwed shut, focusing on the pleasure as I scream into the room. My body is full of tingles and I can feel the liquid pumping from my cunt and soaking his cock. He slams into me once, twice, then pops his knot into me, and I lose all semblance of reality.

I can hear both of us screaming out our pleasure, but it feels distant. My inner walls clench rapidly around him, squeezing every last drop that they can. Tingles run up and down my legs, and I can feel the pleasure racing through my body. Jesse is swearing with a deep rumble in his voice. His body falls over mine, but he catches his weight with his arms, his face buried in my neck. My head turns to rest on the top of his as we both breathe heavily, coming down from our highs.

Jesse starts to move us after a moment, and holds me close as he flips us over so I'm lying on him, then grabs a blanket and throws it over us haphazardly. It doesn't fully cover us, even though it should, and he grumbles under his breath, sounding annoyed. Giggling, I look up at him to see a small smile on his face.

"They make it sound so easy to just immediately be covered in the books," he says.

Laughing, I try to give him a hand, even though his poor Alpha may be offended by the help. He's taken care of me just fine, so if he gets annoyed, I'll just have to purr for him. Remind him that he's done wonderfully.

Finally, we're covered and enjoying the warmth of the blanket and each other. Every now and again, Jesse will softly pump his hips into me, nudging his knot back and forth, and we both relish the subtle pleasure we get from it. I hum, wondering if I should tell him what I'm thinking. This was the best sex I've ever had, but is it okay to tell him that? Will he be receptive to it? Jesse can be so reserved that it's hard to tell sometimes. Biting the bullet, I decide to take the leap of vulnerability.

"That was the best sex I've ever had," I tell him softly.

His lips kiss the top of my head, "Me too, baby girl. I didn't know it could be that good."

"Do you think it's because we're a Match?"

"Might be. We didn't bond, so *that's* definitely not the reason. Maybe amazing sex is a sign of a Match, too. Or it's just a sign of how amazing I am at this," he teases.

I giggle at his silly answer and let myself snuggle in fully. Not a moment after I do, I feel his dick release and a rush of fluids escape my body. Apparently, his knot has gone down. I groan in embarrassment at all the fluid leaking out around his dick, but Jesse grabs my chin gently.

"Don't be embarrassed, it's fucking hot," he says.

"If you say so," I reply somewhat skeptically.

Jesse gently separates us and tells me to wait in the nest. He darts out and comes back with a warm washcloth. Gently, he cleans between my legs and my thighs, getting all the sticky off. He disappears again and comes back with two cups of water. I greedily take one and drink half of it down. Jesse only drinks his once I'm satisfied. Silly Alpha.

We tangle in the nest together, making sure the covers surround us fully. Jese spoons me from behind, my head resting on his strong bicep. As relaxed as I am, when he starts purring, I relax even further. I'm basically a puddle of goo at this point. I feel safe and content in his arms. Slowly, I drift into sleep, secure in Jesse's arms and dreaming about adding three more people into this nest.

VIC

I think all four of us are starting to go a bit stir crazy at this point. It's been about an hour now, and we've gotten through most of the clues, but still haven't found the final answer. Internally, I'm trying to figure out how Henry sold this idea to all of us. I'm impressed, to be honest. Simon is helping a bit, but he's more interested in goofing off than getting out of here. Jesse is a true loner, only interacting when he finds a clue. Henry's pushing everyone to just enjoy it. My ridiculous self is overly invested in the whole endeavor.

When Henry suggested going to an escape room for a Pack Bonding activity, I never thought Simon or Jesse would go with it. Simon, because I know him, and Jesse, because I could tell at dinner he's a bit of a loner. Nice enough guy, but he paves his own path, goes his own way, takes the other road, well, whatever analogy I can think of, it fits. Henry and I are working on the current clue while Simon and Jesse wander around the room.

"Jesse, come look at this," Simon calls out.

Jesse walks over to peer at whatever Simon's looking at. "What?"

"Do you think the skull is from a real person?"

"Probably. I can just imagine someone leaving it in their will to donate their skull for an escape room." Jesse's dry humor makes me smirk as I finally work out the next clue.

"Stones, jewels… rubies!" I exclaim.

Henry looks up at me, "The stolen pirate treasure."

The two of us turn to head over to where the prop is sitting, only to find Simon standing in front of it with his arms crossed.

"Arr mateys! Ye be tryna pilfer me treasure? Ye'll ne'er get it while I be livin'!" he declares.

"Not bad on the pirate speak," Jesse comments idly as he watches.

I dance a little on my toes, anxious to get this last clue figured out. "Simon! This is the last clue, move!"

"Come closer 'n I'll skewer ye wit' me cutlass!" he proclaims.

Henry leans in close, "I'll distract him, you get the clue."

"Deal," I say, amusement filling me and a smile coming to my face.

It's fun to see Henry playing along with Simon. There may be hope yet for both of them. Simon especially, with his hesitance around Packs. Maybe Henry will change his mind.

"Avast! I challenge ye for the treasure!" Henry challenges, standing as though he's holding a sword.

Simon eyes him for a moment before trying to hide his smile.

"Have at ye!" Simon declares, and takes up his own invisible arms.

The two of them start a fake sword battle, and Henry manages to maneuver them away from the treasure just enough that I can slip in. I start digging in the treasure chest, looking for the ruby that I think will open the door. I feel more than see Jesse walk closer and look over my shoulder.

"Try the sides," he says, still sounding uninvested in the outcome.

He cares more than he lets on, I can tell, but he's not used to interacting with people. I take his advice and slide my hand down the sides of the chest, feeling for a large gem. My hand knocks against something with a lot of edges, and I grasp with an excited smile. Pulling it out, I can see the giant ruby is cut the way one would expect, but the crown of the gem has small nicks that look like a pattern.

I walk over to the door and see the handle, but nowhere to put the gem. Thinking through the last clue, this gem is what will get us out.

The nicks on top tell me it fits in like a key somehow. Jesse is quiet next to me, but I can see him analyzing the door and its frame, trying to find the spot. In the background, Henry and Simon are still dueling it out, but it doesn't sound like they're making any progress. Silently, Jesse reaches around me and pushes at a piece of the doorframe, and it slides back, revealing an impression that matches the gem in my hand.

"Good eyes," I tell him.

He shrugs with a slight blush but also smiles at the compliment. I put the ruby into the impression, and it takes a moment to orient it correctly, but then it slides into place, and the door pops open. I turn back to look at Simon and Henry, but they're still locked in battle.

"Hey, Blackbeard and Jack Sparrow, we're free!" I call out.

The two of them stop their battle and see the door propped open.

"Huzzah!" Simon cheers as Henry laughs.

"Wait, which of us is Jack Sparrow?" Henry asks.

I shrug, "Pretty sure Simon is Jack Sparrow with all that hair."

Henry and Simon eye each other, then shrug and agree. We exit the room with smiles and laughter, and it feels perfect. As we go, we take the obligatory "we made it" picture and thank the employees for their time. I look at the others as we exit the building and decide I'm not done yet.

"Drinks?" I ask.

"I'm up for that," Henry says.

Simon smirks, "I'm at your mercy, you drove us."

Jesse's quiet, but I can see some tension in his shoulders.

"You don't have to if you don't want to, man, it's okay," I tell him.

He loses a sigh and glances over at me. "No, I should spend more time getting to know you guys. Especially you, since we're both Matched to Josie. I just... don't like people."

I nod and hold out my knuckles for him. He raps them gently, and we head to our cars and drive as a small procession to a nearby pub. Simon rides with me, and his energy is actually really positive. It makes me happy to see him enjoying time with our future Pack. I'm sure we're all going to bond, even if he isn't.

We find a nearby pub and grab a table, none of us having been here before. The atmosphere seems chill, but there's also a fun energy while people move around to play pool and darts. Having both vibes going makes it easier to enjoy ourselves. Once we're all seated and drinks ordered, we sit in a beat of awkward silence until Henry speaks up.

"I want to make a point and say that I'm really glad you all came today. I'm excited to get to know you all more, and I hope you guys enjoy it too. It's definitely a lot, I mean I never expected to find my Pack *and* a beautiful Omega in the same year, let alone the same month. So, thank you guys."

Jesse's reply is a nod and a shoulder shrug, which seems to be standard for him. Simon rubs the back of his head, and I think he's uncomfortable with so much candor so quickly. I guess it's up to me.

"I know we all have our hang-ups or issues, but I'm really glad we found each other and that we're getting to know each other. So, here's to group bonding activities!"

Simon puts his hand on his face. "Vic, we don't have drinks yet."

"I was on a roll, we'll just pretend," I insist.

Small talk overtakes us as we wait for drinks, and even for a bit after. I learn little tidbits about Henry, like he's the youngest in his family, he hates the color beige (who doesn't?), and he's always wanted his own. Simon shares superficial things, favorite colors, and foods, while Jesse shares that he's used to being alone and usually works remotely in his condo. Alone. That actually explains his earlier comment about not liking people. It's fitting based on what interactions we've had so far. Anyone can tell he's crazy about Josie, but beyond that, he struggles.

Even though the interactions we're having are superficial, I can feel our tenuous bonds building as we chat. There's a way to go yet, but it's a feeling of contentment that grows in my chest. It feels *right* to be here with these guys. I just hope the rest of them feel it. I can easily see Jesse or Simon dragging their feet. Simon is a little easier to persuade since I've known him so long, but Jesse is a complete unknown. He's a Match for Josie, so that has to mean something, right?

"I have an idea!" I announce in a lull of conversation.

Everyone looks at me silently, waiting for me to continue.

Pitching my voice high, I say, "What's your idea, Vic?"

"Oh, I'm glad you asked!" I say with a smile, "I think we should each share one big thing with each other, just to rip off the proverbial band-aid."

"I'm game, but I don't want to force anyone," Henry chimes in.

Simon hums thoughtfully, "I guess I'm okay with it."

We look at Jesse, who just shrugs, so we take that as acquiescence.

"I can go first," Henry volunteers.

So far, he seems to be the de facto Lead Alpha for us, which I don't particularly mind. Considering I'm not an Alpha, and neither Simon nor Jesse are stepping up, it makes sense. Henry takes a deep breath, thinking.

"I haven't had close contact with my direct family in years. It's like we just drifted apart. No bad feelings, we still talk on occasion, but it's fuckin' lonely." His eyes drift between all of us as he speaks.

Reaching out, I put my hand on his shoulder and squeeze before talking.

"I've been in love with Josie since I met her in high school, and we used to have a pact that we'd marry each other by a certain age. I don't know if she even remembers that, but she's it for me." I say, showing how deeply attached to Josie I am.

Nervously, I peek over at Simon, terrified I've hurt his feelings by not sharing how deeply I feel about Josie, but he gives me a soft smile. A gentle nod tells me without words that he already knew all this and is glad I've said it out loud. A small smile comes to my face in response.

Simon clears his throat, "Uh, I'm not sure how big we're going here, but I should probably share that I've never expected or desired to end up in a Pack since I was in college."

Henry looks shocked while Jesse looks intrigued. I reach my foot out under the table to bump his foot, trying to convey that I'm here for him. Logically, I know he's aware of that, but sometimes it's easy to forget when emotions are involved.

"Wow, I never thought anyone would feel that way," Henry confesses softly, "Thank you for telling us that."

Simon nods, clearing his throat again. Jesse looks up at us before turning his attention back to the drink cradled between his hands. He blows out a breath of air but doesn't speak for a moment. We give him the space he needs before he starts speaking. The silence stretches for another minute as Jesse continues in his internal battle. He doesn't give us any indication that he's paying attention to us other than the occasional glances up. Finally, he stands and grabs his wallet, dropping five dollars on the table.

Then he turns and walks out of the pub.

sixteen

JESSE

Fresh air hits me as I exit the pub, leaving the three men I was with stunned. To be honest, I'm just as stunned. I really thought I could do it. I thought I could open up and talk with them. When I tried, though, it was like my vocal cords stopped working. I could feel the anxiety churning in my gut, so I left. Now, I'm speed walking to my car, trying not to give in to a panic attack.

As I drive home, I do deep breathing. Deep breaths in, hold, let it out. It keeps things under the surface for now, and when I get home, I can just let loose and collapse until it's over. I can see my goal as I park my car in my driveway. The front door is right there, calling to me. My feet carry me to the door, but before I can unlock it, I hear a delighted yell behind me.

Oh shit, I don't want Josie to see me like this.

My nose senses her first, her comforting scent of cinnamon desserts curling around me like a weighted blanket. My shoulders drop a fraction as I take it in, but when I turn to look at her, it's almost like everything comes crumbling down. She's so beautiful and amazing, how in the world is she a Match for someone like me? I've been alone for so long, and the anxiety that I thought was long gone has roared to the surface at my first attempt to interact with more than one person. For some reason, with just Josie, it's easier.

Her expression drops as she sees my face, and I close my eyes, not wanting to see the pity in them. Instead of pulling away, she wraps her arms around me. She's tall, but not quite tall enough to really comfort me while standing, so she rests her head on my chest, just below my shoulder, and squeezes her arms around my chest. Instinctively, I circle my own arms around her, and we stand like that for a few moments. She doesn't speak and she doesn't ask me to, she just holds me and exists with me for a few moments. I can tell the moment her Omega instincts override her normal reactions when she pulls back and holds my face so I have to look at her.

"My nest or your place?" she asks fiercely, and I know she won't leave me by myself for a while.

"Your nest," I tell her, wanting to be surrounded by her.

She grabs my hand and marches me back to her condo, locking the door behind us before pulling me further to her nest. Before I can step in, she indicates for me to wait and spends a moment adjusting everything just so. This is the second time I've seen her Omega instincts take over, and it's a beautiful sight. She knows exactly what she wants and how to do it. Her confidence is breathtaking.

"No shirt, no pants, lie down," she commands before departing the room.

A low laugh escapes me at her commands, but I do what she says, and I'm only in my boxers when I enter the nest and lie down in a cozy spot. She returns with a box of cookies and two bottles of water. Her eyes soften at the sight of me in her nest, and she sets the snacks down out of the way, but close enough to grab later. Josie strips out of her shirt and pants and clambers in next to me in a sports bra and panties. My dick tries to rise to the occasion but I tell it not to get its hopes up. My dick gets up anyway.

Josie lies down on her back and yanks me to her, bringing my head to her chest and letting me sprawl over her. My skin touching hers brings a wave of serotonin, and I relax into the happy hormones. After some creative wiggling on my part, I manage to bring a blanket up and ensure we're both covered, increasing the cozy feeling. Josie purrs and runs her fingers through my hair.

"I haven't had anyone comfort me like this in a long time," I rasp out.

"You better get used to it, mister. You're mine, and I'm going to be here to comfort you when you need it." Her voice is teasing but firm.

I turn my head and kiss her where her cleavage starts, giving it a small lick for good measure. A small giggle escapes her, and she wiggles underneath me. I grin against her skin and lay my head back down, relaxing once again into her purr.

"You don't have to tell me what's going on," she says softly, "Just know that I'm always here if you do want to tell me, okay?"

I nod against her skin, "I want to tell you, but I'm nervous to do it. Let me try, though."

"Whatever you want, babe," she assures me.

I give myself a moment to build up my courage and start speaking slowly.

"The guys and I went out today... It was an escape room, so just the four of us, you know?"

She gives an affirmative noise but doesn't rush me. How is she so perfect?

"It was fine, kind of fun really, but I've been on my own for probably 15 years now. I don't talk to people much, only when I'm forced to for work. I think... I think I forgot how to. Talk to people, I mean."

Josie continues her steady stream of purring and running fingers through my hair. My words don't feel like they're making sense, but she hasn't asked me to clarify yet, so maybe she does understand.

"You're easy to talk to for me. It's natural, like breathing air. It takes more effort with the guys. Vic and Henry are so outgoing, and even Simon gets social once he's comfortable. I just can't seem to. I mean, I can't get comfortable. I can't socialize. I tried, honestly, I tried. They all shared, and I wanted to. I couldn't. It was like my body froze."

Josie just holds me tighter, letting me get the words out.

"I never expected a Pack. Maybe I wanted one at some point, but I couldn't tell you when. The longer I'm alone, the more I crave solitude. Maybe I can't do it. What if I can't? I'll ruin everything for you. I want you, Jojo, more than anything, but if I can't handle Pack, then how can it work? I know you want a Pack, and you deserve it. Me? I don't know. Everything feels so jumbled. It's easier when it's just me."

I finally go quiet as the last few words leave my lips. I feel a bit better, like a cleansing of my emotions. Josie waits another moment before speaking.

"First of all, you called me 'Jojo', and I insist on that always now."

I chuckle, but let her continue.

"Second of all, you are *mine*, my Omega has declared it. So we will figure it out," she says, before tipping my head back and looking into my eyes, "*together*. Understand?"

My smile feels wide as I respond. "Yeah, Jojo, I understand."

"Good!" she says firmly before pushing me so I fall back before pouncing.

Her lips latch onto mine, and a moan escapes me as I sink into the feel of her. Her lips are so damn soft and her tongue teases as much as mine does, playing a small game of cat and mouse. My hands start to roam her body before she puts a stop to it.

"As much as I love your body," she pants, "We need a snack first."

I relent, laughing a bit at her insistence, and sit up with her. We each crack open a water bottle, and she opens the cookie container between us. It's one of those peel-top boxes, so you can just grab from the top of the container. Way easier than the old style of tearing open the package and trying to fit the plastic holder back in. She settles in next to me, our bodies touching as we sit side by side, the cookie package balanced between our legs.

"Jesse?" she says timidly after a couple of cookies.

I look over at her, my mouth full of cookie.

"I really like you. I don't care if you need space, I'll give it to you. I just want *you* okay?"

I swallow the cookie, and it feels like there's an extra lump in my throat when I swallow. Leaning forward, I drop a small kiss on her forehead.

"Thanks, Jojo. Sometimes it's too easy for me to close in on myself."

"It's too easy for me to stop trusting people. So I promise to always be here and pull you back out if you promise to always be here and remind me to trust you."

"I can do that," I tell her.

When I'm full of cookies, I offer the package to Josie before putting it away. We both take another sip of our waters before snuggling back down into the nest. This time, I've turned her on her side so I can hold her from behind. Her ass fits perfectly in my pelvis, so I make sure to hold her hips firmly to mine. Her head rests on my other bicep as I curl that arm around her body. She grabs my arms in response, and we let ourselves sit in the quiet of her nest.

Eventually, we must have fallen asleep because the next thing I know, there's muted sunshine filtering through the fabric she has covering her windows. My hand pats around for my phone, and when I find it, the time tells me it's 8 a.m. Time to get up, I suppose. At some point in the night, Josie turned to face me, and her body was sprawled on top of mine, her nose buried in my neck. I decide that being here is too heavenly to get up just yet, so I set a new alarm and let myself doze with my Omega in my arms.

seventeen

JOSIE

Vic has been bugging me for weeks to come and visit his rental house. Now that I've met Simon, I feel a little more comfortable doing it, but I'm still pretty nervous. Simon seems great, and I can understand why Vic likes him so much, but I'm not sure Simon likes *me* very much. The last thing I want is to get between him and Vic. Vic may be my Match, but if Simon is uncomfortable with me, I will do my best to keep the peace.

Do I want Simon to be comfortable with me? Absolutely I do. I want him to assume that I'm always going to be there, and to be happy about it. I want him to look at me the same way Vic, Henry, and Jesse do. I want to explore every inch of his body. If I'm being honest with myself, I want a night with him, Vic, and myself enjoying each other's bodies. My Omega perks up at that, ready to tangle with both men at the first opportunity. I tell her to simmer down and take a few cleansing breaths. I can't show up there smelling like slick, I need to at least pretend I'm not secretly super needy.

I grab the container of pre-made brownies I bought and hop into my car. It's not a terribly long drive, but I haven't been to this side of town before, so I take in the scenery as I go, wanting to remember the route. Hopefully, it becomes second nature to me quickly. My anticipation grows as I get closer, and I swear, I can almost smell Vic and Simon. I was surprised this time around with Vic when his scent hit me so hard. I don't remember noticing it before, but I got so caught up in the excitement of seeing him, then the panic of touching him, that I didn't register his scent. In the past, I've been so focused on maintaining distance that I never entertained the idea of us having Match potential. His scent absolutely draws me more than any of the previous assholes who faked a Match.

Maybe... just maybe the other guys are Matches, too. Henry and Simon both have amazing scents, but I'm not sure Simon is even interested in me, so I remind myself to curb that line of thinking. I don't need to be a clingy Omega when a hot Alpha comes around. I need to make sure to stay strong since I'm at a disadvantage where touch is concerned. It's been magical to snuggle with Jesse and Vic without feeling drained, and I won't take that for granted by throwing myself at the others. Unless Henry buys me another blanket, I might throw myself at him for that. That blanket is heaven.

Pulling into the driveway of their adorable rental house. It's not huge like Henry's mansion, and I'm okay with that. I assume it has two or three rooms, and plenty spacious to have people over. My hands grab the brownie container before opening my door, and I take a steadying breath. Hopefully, Simon will be welcoming tonight. It was hard to tell with him at the dinner Henry hosted, and I'm so nervous about coming between him and Vic, even with the Match between Vic and me. Well, nervous about one kind of coming and excited about the other kind. The door opens almost immediately after I knock, and Vic's face takes up all my focus.

"Josie Girl!" he exclaims and pulls me into a hug.

My natural reaction is to tense, but I quickly relax into him and wrap my arms around his torso. I'll never be able to feel the electrifying Match Touch, but his scent wraps around me, and his arms feel like home. It's enough.

We part, and he pulls me into the house, where I promptly remove my shoes and hand off the brownies.

"I wanted to bring dessert, but wasn't up to baking today. I know for a *fact* that the brownies from this store are delicious," I promise.

My eyes roam the house as I follow Vic into the kitchen. Their decor is minimal, which is what I would expect from a male Beta and Alpha, but there's this sense of home as well. They've well saturated the place with their scent, and there are small knick-knacks and pieces of trash that got forgotten lying around. I pick up a rubber band from the floor as I walk.

Holding it in front of me, I raise an eyebrow, "Gettin' kinky in here?"

Vic turns to see the rubber band and laughs.

"Nah, my hands are too big for this little thing," he boasts.

I give him my best placating agreement and shoot the rubber band at him. He ducks and chuckles as it flies over his head by centimeters. Grabbing the rubber band, he aims and fires back at me. I move out of the way quickly, and hear a masculine "Ow! What the fuck?" sound from behind me. Turning, I look in semi-horror as Simon holds the rubber band in one hand, his other touching his cheek to check for bleeding. Of course, my now-playful brain decides to egg Vic on.

"Vic! How could you? Poor Simon is minding his own business, and you just fling a rubber band at him?"

My eyes flit from Vic over to Simon, and when I raise an eyebrow at him, I can see the mischief appear in his eyes. He sees my game, and from the look I get from him, he's in. Almost instantly, his face transforms into sorrow, a little hurt thrown in there as well.

"Seriously, Vic? What the hell did you do that for? I can't believe you'd ambush me like that!" Simon laments.

Vic smiles for a moment, then slowly starts to frown, trying to decide if Simon's playing around or if he's being serious. I straighten up and walk over to Simon, trying to look concerned for him.

"Are you okay? Looks like it hit you hard. Can you show me?" I ask him, my voice dripping with concern.

Simon turns his face to the side, and I gasp as if his skin has completely fallen off. The mark isn't even that big or that red, just a small splotch that indicates something irritated the skin.

"Is it bad?" Simon asks me, voice wavering

"I'm sure it will heal up just fine!" I assure him.

My voice is wavering with contained laughter, so I try to push out a few tears to make it sound more like I'm crying. Hopefully it's convincing. Simon rolls his lips in, and I suspect he has the same problem I do at the moment.

"Is it bleeding?" Simon asks, a little panic infused into his question.

"Only a little!" I assure him.

Vic moves closer, his face now full of worry for his friend.

"Shit, Simon, I'm so sorry, I didn't realize I snapped it so hard. I didn't see where you were standing!"

I look up to see if Simon wants to try to keep it going, and he shrugs ever so slightly. Apparently, it's up to me. Poor Vic has suffered enough, and I'm not sure how we'd even keep this up. Without thinking, I grab Simon's chin and turn his head so Vic can see the rubber band mark.

"He will *never* heal!" I exclaim.

Vic frowns, looking at Simon's perfectly fine cheek, then looks at me. I can see it dawning on him that I started the whole shebang, and a teasing smile comes over his face.

"Oh, I'm gonna get you for that one!"

I let out a very undignified shriek and dart away from him, scrambling to put their dining room table between us, hoping for a buffer. Vic braces himself on the other side of the table, and we scuttle back and forth, each trying to outmaneuver the other. I hold my hands up in surrender quickly.

"Okay, okay! I'm sorry! You win, you can tickle-torture me later after we eat. I'm so hungry," I tell him, panting.

Vic smiles in triumph and agrees before turning to Simon. I follow his gaze and realize Simon hasn't moved from his spot since I showed Vic his face. The blood in my face drains as I realize what I did. Oh my god, I grabbed his face. Fuck, I touched him without asking. I freeze in horror, unsure what I may have inadvertently done. If he didn't want to touch me to discover if we're a Match, I completely violated that right. What if he's mad at me? What if I just fucked things up between them? My breathing starts to speed up, my eyes glued to Simon, and his eyes snap to mine.

The edge of my vision starts to get fuzzy as I breathe faster, trying to get some oxygen in. My vision goes unfocused as I try to figure out what's happening. Why can't I get oxygen in? Why is it so hard to breathe right now? Is this my punishment for touching him? The inability to breathe. Fuck I think I'm gonna pass out, but I can't stop trying to breathe. Suddenly, there are hands holding my face and a pair of bottomless brown eyes looking straight into mine.

"Breathe!" the eyes command.

Funny joke, eyes, I can't! Brown eyes continue to fill my vision, and I notice that my hand has been moved to something that's slowly rising up and down. It feels nice, I can focus on the feel of the movement while I drown in the brown eyes. So slowly that it's almost painful, my breathing slows, and I finally feel like I'm getting oxygen again.

"That's it, baby, slow and steady," the eyes tell me.

My vision starts to expand beyond the brown eyes, and I realize they're attached to a face I wasn't expecting. That's right, I'm at Simon and Vic's. Oh. Simon. What did I do?

"You didn't do anything wrong," he assures me.

"Oh, did I say that out loud?" I ask.

His smile almost knocks me off my feet. It's bright and beautiful, and it should always be on his face.

"I'm so sorry," I whisper.

"For what?"

A tear rolls down my face, "I didn't ask before I touched you. I *always* ask first, and now you might have felt a Match, but I can't feel that, and I'm scared I've trapped you into something you didn't ask for. Maybe I didn't, but the possibility that I might have is killing me."

A small part of me withers at the idea that we might not be Matches. His scent is something I've been dying to experience again, but it's not like I've had a chance to get to know him. Why am I so nervous that he might not be a Match? Shit, I need to focus and stop thinking. Simon has been quiet for a good minute now, but I wait for him to talk.

"I... I never thought I wanted a Match. I've not wanted a Pack in a long time, so I never thought about a Match. Now, though? I don't think I can go a day without you. Feeling the Match is... life-changing. I'd like to hang around a little longer, if you'll have me," he says, conviction laced throughout his tone.

I feel the smile take over my face before nodding at him.

"I would really love that," I confess.

We stand like that, my hand still on his chest, and my face still held in his hands, both of us smiling. His eyes flit between my lips and my eyes, so I try to make it easier for him by leaning closer. Simon takes the bait and claims my lips, caressing them slowly, softly, savoring how our mouths move together. It's slow and sensual, and over way too soon. A separate pair of arms wrap around us both, and I remember Vic is still in the room. Oops.

"Fuck, this makes me so relieved," he says, holding us both close.

"Group hug!" I declare and turn my body so I can hold both of them, their bodies pushed as close to me as we can get them.

My stomach has decided we've waited too long and lets out an embarrassingly loud grumble. I can feel the blush on my face, and I apologize for the noise. I get rewarded with laughter, and we move on to the food portion of the evening. Once full, we all collapse onto their sofa, resting and trying to decide what we should watch.

"Can we talk more about all this?" I ask tentatively as Simon flips through the movie options.

"Sure," Vic says easily, "Where do you want to start?"

"Well, I have three Matches now, and I know Jesse is a bit anti-social, Simon, you're not sure you want a Pack, and Vic, you're always so easy going that sometimes I'm not sure what you're thinking. What do we do?"

"What do *you* want, Josie Girl? I think that's the most important."

I think about his question a moment before answering. "I want a Pack that loves me for who I am, not necessarily for a Match. I want to experience life as a unit, always there for each other, and sharing joy. Maybe even kids someday, I don't know."

Vic and Simon are both quiet for a moment, thinking through my words. I'm more worried about Simon's response than Vic's. Predictably, Vic answers first.

"Honestly? I want the same. If it never happens, I'm also okay with that. I don't want to force anyone into choosing Pack life, but I can see the life you've described, Josie Girl, and I like it," Vic says.

Simon hums before answering, "I don't know if I want Pack, honestly. I know I want both of you—"

"Excuse me, are you guys *together* together?" I interrupt Simon.

"Is that a problem?" Vic almost sounds angry with his question.

"No, no, just expanding my imagination is all. Maybe plans for later, too." I hurry to soothe any insult he may feel.

Chuffing a laugh, Simon continues, "I want you two, but that's as far as I can go right now. I'm open to talking about Pack, but I just don't know if it's something I can really commit to."

I'm disappointed with Simon's answer, but I also recognize that I don't necessarily know him as well as I want to. If he's willing to talk, I'll take that for now.

"Okay, maybe the three of us and Jesse can talk about it?" I suggest.

"You're forgetting someone," Vic chides me.

Henry's face pops into my mind. I haven't forgotten him, not by a long shot. But, I don't know if we're a Match, and I absolutely am with Simon and Jesse. It doesn't seem fair to include him without a Match.

"What if he's not a Match?" I ask quietly.

"Does it matter?" Simon challenges.

I give him a small smile, "I suppose not, in the end. What matters is how we treat and love each other."

"Damn straight," Vic agrees.

He pulls me into a snuggle as Simon finally picks a movie, and Simon snuggles in on my other side. This moment feels pretty damn perfect.

HENRY

I've been dragging my feet on texting Josie about a date. At first it was nerves, but then I realized I'm being a chickenshit. Sure, we've texted back and forth, and she came over for the friend dinner, but that's not a date. Plus, knowing that Vic and Jesse both have a Match with Josie makes me nervous. What if she doesn't have one with me? What if she doesn't want one? I'll never know until we talk about it, which means I need to put on my big boy pants and just text her.

ME

Hey Josie! Are you free today, by chance? I know it's last minute.

JOSIE

Hello, handsome! I have a session today in an hour, but after that I'm free. What's going on?

ME

I'd like to take you on that confidence seminar we've discussed. I think a good place to start would be Nature Art if you're interested.

JOSIE

Oh, I haven't been there in AGES. Sure, that
sounds great!

ME

Awesome, text me when you're home, and I
can come get you?

JOSIE

Perfect. I'll talk to you soon <3

MY FIST PUMPS into the air, victory sweet in my brain. I can't wait to
take her out to look at art in the woods. It sounds cheesy, but some of
the permanent installations are breathtaking, no matter how many
times you see them. The seasonal displays are always intriguing, too,
and I can just imagine wandering around with Josie, hand in hand, as
we talk about the art. Or life. Or whatever makes her smile. If she
wanted to spend two hours talking about snails and slugs, I'd happily
listen.

I make sure to put on casual clothes, but then realize I don't have
anything to do until she texts. Maybe I'll check in on Ray. She seems
to be improving with Josie's sessions, and I should probably let her
know I want to date Josie. The last thing I want is awkward tension
between them. Ray is actually out of her room today, sitting in the den
with some blankets and textbooks in front of her.

"Hey you," I say gently, knocking on the doorframe.

Ray looks up at me with a small smile before going back to her
books. "What's up?"

"I wanted to ask you about something. Do you have a minute?"
I ask.

"Yes, just let me finish this page," she says distractedly, grabbing a
highlighter.

She finishes whatever passage she's reading and sits back, resting
against the back of the couch as she looks at me. I clear my throat.

"Do you like working with Josie?" I ask first.

111

Ray's face lights up, "Yeah, she's great! Our scents aren't great together, but we're totally used to it now, and I don't mind it. I'm glad you found her."

"I, um, how would you feel about me dating her?" I ask, stumbling a bit over the words.

Ray grins, "I think that would be an excellent idea. Especially since you're Matches."

"Uh, we don't know that. Why are you saying that?"

"Puh-lease, the way you reacted to each other's scents? You have to be Matches," she informs me with all the teenage attitude she can muster.

"You're such a brat," I grin at her.

Ray just grins back and turns back to her studies. I hope I've encouraged her enough, but I decide to give her one more thought before I go.

"Ray?" I get her attention.

As usual, she just looks at me, waiting for me to talk.

"I'm glad you're here, and I'm glad Josie is helping. I can see the change."

Her eyes tear up, but she holds them in as she gives me a wobbly smile before nodding and going back to her books. Emotions are not her strong suit. Noting that there's still time to kill, I head to the living room with a smile, watching a show about finding cake. When Josie texts to say she's ready for me, I jump up like I've been burned and speedwalk to my wallet and keys.

"Have fun!" I hear Ray yell from the den.

"Don't get into too much trouble!" I yell back, then leave the house.

By the time I pull up to Josie's condo, my stomach is in knots. We haven't really spent any time with just us two, and I hope I don't push her away. Sometimes my foot gets in my mouth, and it's hard to pull it out again. I glance around as I walk to her door and notice Jesse in his condo. He glances out his window and gives me a small hand wave before walking to a different room.

Josie's opened the door before I can knock, and the air gets knocked out of my lungs. Even dressed for a casual date of walking around in some woods, she's breathtaking. Her hair is bound up in a messy bun, some tendrils falling around her face, her jeans fit like someone molded them to her body, and her oversized t-shirt makes me smile. It's black and a bit worn, featuring a side knot and a graphic of Rick Astley.

"You look amazing," I tell her with a smile.

"Flattery will get you everywhere," she winks, "You don't look too bad yourself!"

I'm wearing a long-sleeved flannel with the sleeves rolled up, so I hold out my arm for her to take. There's enough fabric left on my forearm that she can avoid my skin if she wants to. Josie grabs my bicep instead and nods at me. Grinning, I walk her to the car and we get settled in.

"When was the last time you went to Nature Art?" I ask.

"Gosh, I want to say four or five years? It was right before or after I started Touch Helpers. I just remember being so overwhelmed with everything to do with a start-up that I needed some Zen. Nature Art was exactly what I needed at the time."

"That's amazing; I can't remember if I've told you, but I think it's badass that you saw a problem and created a company to help fix it."

She blushes a little, "Thanks, it's been a lot of work and I couldn't have done it without Georgie and James. They've been a rock for me since I hired them, and we're almost at the point where I'll need to hire a third Beta for Touch Helpers!"

We talk a bit more about her business, the challenges she's faced, and what her strategy has been. It brings so much joy to her face that mine is smiling consistently. I share some of my business experience with her, and we throw ideas back and forth. Most of my family are investors or silent partners, but I've always enjoyed the idea of being more hands-on in business. So, I worked my way into a CEO position.

We arrive, and I grab two water bottles from the backseat to bring along. I want to make sure Josie stays hydrated while we wander around. Grabbing my wallet, I pay our fee and we walk into the park, side by side. I hold out her water bottle, and she grabs it well away from my hand before smiling at me.

"Glad you thought to bring these!" she says.

I shrug, "I like providing for you."

Josie's face flushes red, and she gives me a shy smile. I wish she was used to people providing for her, and I promise myself now that if she accepts me, I'll spoil her rotten. I point out some ridiculous sculptures and we joke about what we see in them, but we also have thoughtful conversation about some of the pieces that do move us. She has an interesting view of the world that I probably never would have considered as an Alpha. Being around her and listening to her makes me feel like I'm a better person just for knowing her.

"So, how are Jesse and Vic?" I ask her, knowing she has a Match with both of them.

"Uh, good, Jesse pops by every now and again, and I actually got to go see Vic's rental. It's a cute house, a little small for a Pack bigger than three, but it's perfect for him and Simon right now," she responds.

"Oh, I'm glad you got to go check out their place! Did you get a chance to see Simon too? Us guys actually went out and did an escape room, and it was pretty fun."

Josie smiles, "Oh yeah, I heard all about it from Vic. He enjoyed it too."

Her neglect to mention Simon doesn't escape my notice.

"Simon's goofy side took me by surprise," I confess, "I hope I get to see more of it. He's really fun."

"Yeah, he is," Josie says softly.

I sense she's still avoiding the topic of Simon. When we stop moving next, I take the chance to turn and face Josie directly.

"Are you okay with Simon? Did something happen? You don't seem to want to talk about him, but I want to make sure he didn't hurt you somehow," I tell her.

Josie turns to me, surprised, but it evens out into a smile. "No, nothing like that. You're sweet for caring. I... Well, we were... Um... I accidentally touched his face."

Her speech slows by the end of her sentence, and she looks unsure of herself. Not on my watch.

"Did he accidentally electrocute you with his face? You know, like static electricity?"

Josie lets out a full laugh, "No, no, not that. We're... well, we're a Match."

Another piece fits into place as I imagine our future together. I knew about Vic and Jesse, obviously, but I suspected Simon was part of it too. Assuming Ray is right, I'll Match with Josie as well.

"Is that bad?" I ask.

She wanders to a bench and sits. I take the seat next to her and twist my body so I can see her better.

"No," she sighs, "It's not bad, but I had a panic attack over touching him without consent. It's my number one rule, and I broke it while we were all goofing around. I'm glad he's a Match because hopefully it won't cause a rift between him and Vic, but he also said he's not sure he wants a Pack. I know I want one eventually, so I just feel unsettled. Like I don't know where I stand."

"That would be hard, I agree," I tell her, "Sometimes the best thing to do is focus on the moment instead of worrying about the future. I get caught up in the future too much at work, so I make a point to appreciate those smaller wins, the things that are happening in the moment."

"I can see that. It's knowing where you want to go, but stopping to smell the flowers on your way," she says.

"Pretty much," I agree with her.

Josie looks over at me, "Look at you, Mr. Wiseman."

"Sometimes. Sometimes I say things that make no sense and make everything more awkward," I confess with a grin.

Shoring up my nerve, I ask the question that's been burning on my mind for weeks. I want that confirmation of a Match, but I know Josie is huge on consent, and I won't touch her without it. It's hard not to imagine how soft her skin will be when I finally do touch it, and my dick stirs with the thought.

"Josie, may I touch you? I want to know if we're a Match," I spit out quickly.

One eyebrow raises on her pretty face, "You say that like you're worried about the outcome. You don't have to touch me, we can just date. If you're worried about a Match, we don't have to go on another date."

"Fuck, no, shit! I want to be a Match. You're amazing, and I want that connection with you."

"So, you want me because you think we're a Match?" she asks, face full of confusion.

"Goddammit, I'm fucking this up. Hang on a second." I take a deep breath and rephrase my awkwardness, "Josie, you are wonderful, and I would be overjoyed to just spend time with you. You're funny, smart, and so, so kind. I also want to be your Match. I want to know that we're meant to be together, like I hope we are. Knowing we're a Match would be the most amazing connection ever. If we're not, though, I have no intention of letting you go."

Josie searches my face for a moment, taking in my words, before she gives me a slow smile.

"Okay, if you really mean that, then I guess let's find out. If you run away, I'll just have Vic, Simon, and Jesse chase you down." She winks at me.

Chuckling, I raise my hand slowly, wanting to cup her face with it. She leans toward my hand, and the moment we connect, she closes her eyes with peace. My body lights up like a firecracker, the Match firing through my synapses, changing my world in the blink of an eye. My nerve endings feel electric, and I swear I almost come in my pants. Finally re-focusing enough to look at her again, Josie is happily leaning into my touch, and I feel contentment like I've never known.

I meant what I said, I would have been sad without the Match, but I would have courted her anyway. Now, though? She's mine just like I'm hers. She can't feel the Match, but she trusts me to feel it for both of us. It's a heady feeling on top of my world shifting to center around her. I can't find words yet, so I lean in and lightly kiss her. She responds beautifully, and it's everything.

nineteen

JOSIE

Suspecting that Henry might be a Match, and finding out he *is* a Match are two vastly different experiences. My mind is still reeling from his kiss, but I could almost feel the moment when he experienced the Match. His hand on my face is the best feeling. A sense of peace has washed over me, still lingering while he touches me. His nervous energy faded away the second he touched me, and I knew. While neither of us is ready to be done with this kiss, Henry pulls back and places our foreheads together. We're both breathing a bit heavily, but there's a sense of peace between us.

"Wow," I comment, unable to find any other words.

"Absolutely," Henry chuckles.

He pulls back again to look me in the eye, and I find I'm irrationally irritated that he keeps pulling back. I want all of us to be touching, dammit! Henry smiles at me, and it's like the sun emerging from the clouds.

"I never expected to find a Match. I'm eternally grateful that it's *you*, Josie. You amaze me and bring so much good with you that I'm better just for having you in my life."

My cheeks almost hurt from how big my smile is. Tentatively, I lay my hands on his chest, wanting to touch as much of him as I can.

Biting my lip, I meet his eyes, blown away by his words and how my body buzzes with his touch. His light blue eyes are almost white with how the sun shines on us, and I'm drawn in by the bright intensity.

"I'm glad you're a Match, too. You made me feel special from the first moment we met, even if I didn't recognize it at the time," I confess.

Henry pulls me closer and captures my lips again. A soft moan escapes me as his lips explore mine, exchanging light nips and sucking on each other. My hands slide from Henry's chest to wrap around his neck, grasping him as if my life depends on it. Our kiss depends, and Henry's tongue teases my lips, so I happily open to allow him more access. My tongue darts out and tangles with his, and I lose all trace of my surroundings. Everything is Henry, and I feel slick begin to build up, my body primed to go further.

"Fuck, can I take you home? The things I want to do to you are not for public eyes," Henry says against my lips.

I let out an unintelligible affirmative sound, and Henry sweeps me up into his arms, walking quickly out of Nature Art. A giggle comes loose, and as ridiculous as it feels to be carried out, a part of me is basking in it. When he asks my house or his, I insist on mine. I want my nest. We pull into the driveway in record time, and I bring him into my home.

"Tour later," I say, grabbing his hand to pull him toward my nest.

I hesitate by the door, suddenly understanding that this is a big step. My final Match being invited into my nest. At least, I hope he's my final Match, I don't know what I'd do with more than four men.

"Just one moment," I tell him, holding up a finger.

I open the door, but leave it open so he can see what I'm doing. My Omega wants me to show our Alpha how good of a nest I can build so he knows I can create a special space just for us. When I get everything in the right place, I give the nest one more look and then turn to Henry. He's standing in the doorframe, watching me with awe, as if I've solved all the world's problems. My Omega preens at his expression, and he waits for me to speak first.

"You can enter," I tell him, giddy with delight that he waited for permission.

Good Alphas wait for permission. It's not taboo to come in without, but it signals to Omegas a lack of respect and causes strain between the designations. Henry removes his shoes and steps into the room. Button by button, he takes his flannel shirt off, revealing a short-sleeved white shirt underneath. My hands twitch, wanting to take one of his shirts for myself, and he reads my mind.

"Which one?"

I point to the white t-shirt, it's been closer to his body. Henry grins and whips it off, handing it to me gently. I snatch it out of his hands and bring it to my nose, inhaling deeply. The scent of cedar and light eucalyptus captivates my senses, and I know just where to add this treasure. Once it's in place, I kneel on the bed and face him. He grins at me and slowly, reverently steps into the nest itself.

He moves as if we're on hallowed ground, not rushing anything, but clearly savoring the mixed scent of him, Jesse, Vic, and me. I haven't gotten Simon in here yet, but I hope to. Henry cups my face with both hands and worships my lips. Moving steadily, he controls the speed and depth of the kiss, leaving me to cling to his biceps and enjoy the ride. Touching his bare skin is a thrill that I don't think I'll ever tire of. It's been so long since I've had skin-to-skin contact, and feeling his smooth skin covering strong muscles is heady.

I move my hands down to pull my shirt over my body, and Henry obliges by helping, then unclasping my bra. I'm bared before him, but before I can bring our chests together, one of his hands cups a breast, holding it so that his lips can wrap around my pointed nipples. He oscillates between sucking and nipping on both nipples now, driving me higher and higher. My panties and jeans are soaked through, and Henry starts to kiss down my body, groaning as he does. Gently urging me onto my back, he unclasps my jeans and pulls them down, bringing my underwear with him.

Part of me feels self-conscious as he looks at my naked body, and my first instinct is to cover. My hands start to move, and then I take in the look on his face. He's staring at the apex of my thighs as if I'm his next meal. With gentle pressure, I let him part my legs so he can lean down and take a deep inhale of my scent where it's strongest. My body is so tuned to his that I whimper in desire as he savors my scent. Then, slowly and steadily, he lowers down and swipes his tongue through my slit, bottom to top. His tongue takes an extra second to flick my clit as he goes. My hips buck in response, and I moan in ecstasy.

Henry chuckles, "Did you like that? Does my Omega enjoy my tongue on her needy clit?"

"Fuck, yes please, Alpha, more!" I say, my words almost slurred together.

"Oh my Omega, there's nothing you can ask for that I won't give," he growls before diving in deeper.

He thoroughly explores me, using his thumbs to hold me open, his tongue slipping around my hole before teasing in and out, pushing his face as far into me as he can. I can feel his tongue testing out my body, how far it can go, what spots make me squirm the most. My head is thrown back, my eyes closed in ecstasy, even as one of my hands grasps his hair. The sensations change as Henry slides one thick finger into me, now using his tongue to flick my clit. It's a steady, slow torture of his finger and tongue teasing me and pushing into my body. He adds another finger and speeds up, now alternating between sucking and flicking my clit. I cry out as he goes faster and harder, and he growls as he sucks *hard*. I shatter, my walls clenching down on his fingers, tingles erupting down my legs, and waves of pleasure overtaking my body.

When I come down from it, my eyes lock on his, "More."

Henry scrambles to get his pants off and my mouth waters at the sight of his cock. It's absolutely perfect, and now my Omega is imagining him and Jesse pleasuring me together. My time with Jesse was intense, but my time with Henry is almost soul-deep. His eyes meet mine as he crawls over me.

"Protection?" he rumbles.

"No, I'm clean, birth control," I pant.

His response is a growl, "Me too, thank God."

He pushes in after that growl, and my eyes widen at how beautifully he fills me. There's a slight stretch to it, but nothing painful. It's like we were made for each other, and I remember feeling this with Jesse, too. I hope it's the same for all my Matches. I feel our hips connect as Henry pushes in as far as he can, savoring the feeling of us coming together. My hips buck to try and get him to move, but he chuckles before he obliges.

"Needy Omega."

Pull out.

"Taking my cock."

Slam in.

"So damn good."

Pull out.

"Can't wait to knot you."

Slam in.

My mind is lost to his words, my body a slave to his. His tempo speeds up, steadily driving me to the brink by hitting that one spot that makes me see stars. I can feel his knot growing, and it's preventing him from thrusting in as far as he was when we started.

"Alpha, please," I whine, not even sure what I'm whining for. I just know I want *more*.

"You want my knot? You want me to lock into you and fill you with my cum? Gonna fill you up, baby, breed you until we can't move anymore."

His filthy words drive me higher, and I realize I'm chanting "yes" as he speaks and slams home.

"Tell me you want my knot!" he growls.

"I want your knot, Alpha! Please give it to me!" I all but scream.

He shouts wordlessly as he drives his knot into me, stretching me almost painfully until he locks into place. Henry's knot triggers my release, and I scream his name as I come, slick flooding me, but stuck inside with Henry's knot in the way. His own release comes a moment later as he's rutting into me, and he comes with a deep guttural groan. It's so masculine that I come again, not quite as hard but still feeling my walls pulse and pleasure spread through me.

Henry holds his body above mine, his head ducked down into my neck as he breathes heavily. I can feel his exhaustion and overwhelm, so I rub his back up and down while we both revel in the feeling of being locked together. Eventually, he turns us so that I'm on top, and pulls one of the loose blankets over us to keep us warm and cozy. We stay like this, enjoying the quiet and the feel of each other. Hands gently exploring, rubbing soothing circles into the other's body.

"Henry?" I ask quietly.

"Yeah?"

"Will… would you want… I mean, um, I'd like… I'd like your bite someday," I confess.

As I continue to relax after coming together, the rightness of it all hits me. There's nobody else, other than my Matches, that I want to do this with. It was easy, like breathing air. If we had the bond, too? I just can't imagine the level of explosiveness that would have been.

Henry kisses the top of my head before resting his chin on it. "I'd be honored if you wore my mark, and I would proudly display yours to the world."

"You're so cheesy," I giggle.

"Only for you, baby girl," he chuckles along.

Now I just need my other three Matches and everything will be perfect.

twenty

JOSIE

I can't stop thinking about my guys. It feels weird to call them that, but it's alright, right? They're all a Match, they've all expressed that they want me, so I'm claiming them. Verbally, at least. I hope they'll all want in during my next heat. I want to bond with them all, which means they have about two months to get their shit together. Me too, if I'm being honest with myself.

So, I declared a date night with my Matches. My Omega pushed for me to call it a Pack Date when the idea struck, but despite that instinct, I know that we're not *really* a Pack. Not yet. Simon expressed concern that he might never want a Pack. I hope that tonight changes their minds. I did some searching and found a business that takes cute ideas for first dates and creates them for you. There are tons to choose from, but I decided to do the classic "Dating Game". I pre-wrote some questions for the guys, but we also have a chance to write our own. The guys will answer the questions, and I have to pick which answers go to which guy. They have a voice modulator as well, so I can't go based on their voices.

After, I'm hoping we can go out for some dessert and just spend time together. Hopefully they're all up for it. Jesse offered to drive me since we're literally neighbors, and I took him up on the offer. Never hurts to save fuel and the environment. Since we're doing something a little more old-school, I decided to play up my love for the 80s tonight. I've got teased hair in a high side pony, jeans with a jean jacket, a neon pink tank top, and some Chucks to complete the outfit.

Once I'm dressed, I grab my purse and bounce over to Jesse's door. He offered to come get me, but I'm ready a few minutes early, so I decide to surprise him. I raise my hand to knock on his door just as he opens it to leave. Thankfully, my hand stops, but he's already seen my hand, so now we're standing awkwardly with my hand fisted and reaching out toward him. I unfurl my fingers into a flat palm.

"High five?" I ask.

He laughs and accepts the five, and my own laughter starts in response, and he gives me a hug before turning to lock his door.

"Didn't expect to see you here," he teases.

"I got done early, so I figured I'd save you the hassle of traveling to my door."

Jesse wipes at his forehead, pretending to be relieved. "Phew! I was worried about the long trek, you know."

I giggle as he opens my door for me before jogging around to his side and climbing into the driver's seat. He drives a well-kept mid-size car. Probably a CR-V or something, I'm terrible with car brands and models. I do appreciate a well-kept car, though, and Jesse's is really nice. It's not immaculate, but it's not a sty either. If it was immaculate, I'd be nervous to touch anything.

"So are you gonna tell us what we're doing tonight?" he asks as we ease into traffic.

"Nope! It's a surprise. I didn't want you guys to form opinions before we start."

Jesse looks over at me quickly, giving me a side eye, "You're a sneaky one, aren't you?"

"When I need to be," I say, flicking imaginary dirt off my shoulder.

He chuckles, and after a few more minutes of small talk and traffic, we arrive. The location wasn't a surprise to anyone. It's a fairly popular spot for dates, but they don't know which package I selected. I'm almost dancing on my toes, I'm so excited for this. All I can imagine is fun, and hopefully some silly answers. I hop out of the car, Jesse not far behind, and we wait by the doors for the rest of the guys. I don't see their cars here yet, but they quickly appear as we wait. Simon and Vic rode together, with Henry separate.

"You're here!" I squeal as the three of them converse on us.

"Whoa, Josie Girl, feeling the 80s today, I see," Vic teases, landing a kiss on my temple.

All I can do is grin at him. The combination of the four of them being here, plus all of them being Matches, has gotten me so excited that I think I'm beyond words.

"Looking forward to this?" Henry asks as we walk in the door.

"Uh, duh!" I say to him, putting as much sass as I can into it.

Henry growls playfully and snatches me from behind. I squeal in surprise, and when he bends down, I wait for his kiss to land on my neck. However, a raspberry is what I get instead. My skin tickles like crazy, and I can't stop the high-pitched giggles that escape me.

"Stop! Stop! Uncle!" I say, laughing and enjoying myself.

Henry stops and gives me a real kiss on the neck before pulling back. A Beta receptionist is smiling fondly at our antics and greets us when we get around to moving beyond the entryway.

"Welcome to Date and Busters! Where we serve up dating fun for everyone! Do you have a reservation?" she says chipperly.

"Do you hate having to say that every time?" Simon asks from behind me.

"Yeah, I really do," she says, a little less chipper now, sounding like a normal person.

"Reservation for Josie?" I say with a smile.

She types something into the computer and grins, "Oh, I love this one! Okay, let me take you to your space, and your date guide will get you going."

We walk behind her, Simon whispering things to Vic to make him laugh as we go. I bite my lip, enjoying the sounds of their camaraderie behind me. The receptionist stops in front of a door with large letters above it stating "The Dating Game". She opens the door to usher us in.

"Have a great time!" she says kindly before closing the door.

A Beta male is adjusting a few things as we walk in, and he turns to look at us.

"Welcome! I'm Jim, I'll be your host tonight!" he says with a warm smile.

My mouth opens before my brain registers words: "Is that actually your name?"

I'm horrified for a moment before he laughs.

"No, it's not, but it's kind of fun to use the original host's name so we go with it," he says.

"Alright, then, Jim, tell us what to do," Vic says.

"Jim" situates us so that the four guys are to my left, and there's a panel between us that I cannot see through. All our stools are high-backed and surprisingly comfortable. Once seated, he steps back so we can all see him. He explains the rules, that I've given them three questions and I have to guess which answer belongs to which guy. Their voices will be disguised, so I can't tell based on that. Then, if they want, they'll all have a chance to have me answer those same three questions.

"Alright, question number one: What animal, if you could pick any, would you be? The cheesier your answers, the more fun the game is. Let's start with bachelor number one!"

"Well, seeing as how I'm so full of *pride*, I would clearly be a lion. Ready to protect you at any cost." One says.

The voice modulator makes them sound like chipmunks, and I almost fall off the stool laughing. When the guys laugh, it just adds more chipmunk sounds to the situation, and I'm now laughing so hard there are tears streaking down my face. "Jim" comes over with some tissues, and I mop the tears and take some deep breaths to compose myself.

"Oh my god, I didn't know it would be chipmunk voices, sorry, phew," I say, taking one last big breath at the end.

"Bachelor number two?" Jim prompts.

"I'm always watching over you, baby, so I'd be an eagle, ready to keep an eye on you." Two responds.

I fan myself, pretending to be overcome by the answers. The guys have a small feed of me that they can watch, even though I can't see them.

Three doesn't wait, "Having you touch me is the best feeling in the world, so I'd be a chinchilla, ready for you to caress me all the time."

"What you really need, bachelorette, is someone to hold *you*, so I'd be a monkey, holding on to you all day long." Four wraps up.

I can't stop the giggles that burst from me, "You guys are so cheesy and I love it so much!"

Jim moves on to the next question. "Question two: Is a narwhal a unicorn? Why or why not?"

The chipmunk laughter comes through the speakers again, and I try so hard not to crack up at the sound. It doesn't work great, but at least I can pay attention through the laughter this time.

Bachelor one, "No way, Unicorns are considered to be non-existent, but we already know Josie is a true unicorn, so narwhals cannot be unicorns."

Bachelor two, "Narwhals are definitely unicorns, the unicorns saw Josie and knew they couldn't compete, so they submerged into the sea."

Bachelor three, "Narwhals can't be unicorns, there's no such thing. Now, an Alicorn, those are *definitely* real."

Bachelor four, "Narwhals are definitely unicorns, they bring joy and magic to the sea, there's no other explanation."

Jim watches me laughing, waiting for his cue to continue. He clears his throat and asks the final question.

"What is your favorite thing about Josie?"

Bachelor one, "Her laugh, it brings me joy any time I hear it."

Bachelor two, "Her mind, she's so smart and so caring, it blows me away."

Bachelor three, "How mischievous she is while looking so innocent."

Bachelor four, "How good of a snuggler she is. I don't know many people who can snuggle at a Josie level."

My cheeks turn red, "Aw, guys... thanks. I had expected silly answers, but that's so sweet."

Jim is smiling as he looks at the guys. "What question do you four want Josie to answer?"

There's high-pitched murmuring coming from the speakers, and more laughter spills out of me at the sound. I'm not sure I'll ever not find the noise funny. One of the bachelors answers Jim after a moment of whispers.

"We want to know what Josie's favorite thing about each of us is."

Jim turns his attention to me. "Josie?"

"Can I guess who they are while I answer?" I ask.

"Absolutely, I'll write down your guesses as you go, and we'll do the grand reveal after," Jim says.

I squirm a little in my chair to get comfortable before I start talking.

"Bachelor one, Henry, my favorite thing about you is your confidence in us. Even before we Matched, you liked me enough to buy me a gift. It made me so happy. Bachelor two, Jesse, my favorite thing about you is how clever you are. You like to hide it, but I can see it, and it's amazing. Bachelor three, Simon, your humor and zest for life bring out my own, and it's so much fun to be near you. I would definitely pet you if you ask. Bachelor four, my Vic, thanks for being my monkey for years and holding on to me. That's my favorite thing about you." I clear my throat, surprised by how deep that went. Didn't expect to get emotional.

"Are you ready for the reveal?" Jim asks.

"Yes!" I shout, both hands in the air.

"Bachelor one, was Josie right?"

A moment later, Henry walks around the partition, grinning like crazy. I squeal in delight and fling my arms open, allowing him to swoop in for a huge hug.

"Bachelor two, who are you?" Jim asks.

Jesse walks around the partition, a shy smile on his face, and he ducks his head when he gets close. I grab his arm and pull him to me, making him look into my eyes before giving him a soft kiss.

"Bachelor three, is Josie going to be correct on all counts?"

A moment later, Simon rounds the partition, and Vic isn't too far behind. My hands fly into the air again.

"Yes! I knew it!" I hop down and skip the few steps to the two of them, and throw my arms around them.

We spend a moment laughing with each other over answers and the chipmunk voices before turning to Jim. He's smiling wide, clearly enjoying the sight of happy customers.

"Thank you all so much for coming, you were a joy to work with," he says, reaching out to shake my hand first. Jesse steps in front of me, grabbing Jim's hand instead.

Internally, I roll my eyes as all the guys follow suit, nobody wanting me to touch this guy. I also internally melt at their protectiveness. My Omega instincts scream that these are good mates, and I intend to keep them. Jim has gotten the subtle message not to touch me, and he just nods in my direction. Pleasantries exchanged, he leads us to the main lobby and we see ourselves out.

"Did you guys have fun?" I ask nervously.

"I don't know about these guys, but I had a blast," Simon assures me.

The guys all agree, and I dance in place, filled with excitement and pleased that I did well on picking a date.

twenty-one

SIMON

I'm pleasantly surprised at how fun that date was. I was feeling unsure at first, worried she had picked some odd "Pack building" thing, but she kept it fun and light. I appreciated that and was extra happy that she could tell who we all were. She's glowing as we leave the building, and we agree on a restaurant to grab drinks and dessert. We get a table outside in front of the building. The sidewalk is wide enough to comfortably seat us.

"So do you think a narwhal is a unicorn?" Vic asks Josie.

She sets her drink down and spears him with her eyes, "No, I think *unicorns* are *narwhals* in disguise."

The table is silent as Josie looks each of us in the face, but by the time she gets to me, her serious facade cracks at my skeptical reaction. She's trying to hide a smile, so I lean in further, resting my arms on the table, my eyebrow raised. Josie leans in to match my posture, and we stare at each other.

"I hate to break it to you, but narwhals are not what unicorns disguise themselves as," I tell her as seriously as I can manage.

"Oh? Do enlighten me."

"They clearly disguise themselves as rhinos."

Josie throws her head back in laughter, her eyes bright as she looks back at me.

"I like that argument, we can go that route," she says.

We relax into bantering and snacking on food for a while, just enjoying everyone's company, and even Jesse adds some comments. As unsure as I am about Packs, I'm finding that we flow pretty well. This is only the second time we've all spent time together, and I can see how our pieces might fit. It's terrifying. I have no idea how that would look long-term. What if my piece doesn't fit like we'd expect? Will they kick me to the curb? The last thing I want is to be left behind again. I want Josie, but do I want a whole Pack?

The waitress comes by with our dessert, and once we have our plates, Josie looks at all of us before clearing her throat. All our eyes turn to her and wait for her to speak. I hope she's about to speak because otherwise it's real creepy that we're all just staring at her.

"I was hoping we could talk about some serious stuff," she says hesitantly.

Henry places his hand on top of hers. "What's up?"

"So, um, my heat is coming in a couple of months. I usually medicate through them, but since we're all a Match, I thought maybe we should talk about what this means. Do we want to bond? If so, we'll need to Pack Bond as well. We could wait a little bit after to Pack Bond, but I guess I want all of it. I don't want to pressure anyone, though, I just wanted to get my thoughts out there."

The words take me by surprise. I wasn't really expecting her to be so bold or blunt with her thoughts. Especially in regard to something so sensitive. She wants to bond, but she also wants a Pack Bond. That seems fast to me. She doesn't want to pressure me, but isn't that exactly what she's asking for? I try to shove down the simmering anxiety in my belly and focus on the table.

"Pack Bond, huh?" I ask, my voice pitched low.

She fidgets in her chair. "Only if you want to. I don't want to force anyone, that's not fair to do."

"I think we all *want* to help you with your heat, but the rest of it may feel rushed for some," Henry says gently.

I lean back into my chair and glance at Jesse. He looks like I feel, a little nauseous and incredibly insecure. Where is this conversation going? Is anyone going to actually ask Jesse or me what we want? Maybe they'll just refer to us as "some" of them. My eyes glance at Vic, sitting between me and Henry. I'm curious to hear what his response will be to all of this. I know he feels like he's in a precarious position right now, but as much as I don't want to give him up, I will if he just wants Josie. I'm not going to push him one way or the other.

"Josie Girl, what do you think about us just all saying how we feel and what we want? No judgment from anyone, but when we're done sharing our opinions, we can talk about it as a group." Vic suggests.

Josie bites her lip, but nods, "I think that makes sense. Open communication and all that, right?"

"Exactly, why don't you go first?" Vic replies.

"Well, if I'm being honest with myself, I want all of you. I'm nervous about bonding, because if we do, it's all going to be a Mate Match bond, and it's a lot. I do want you all to be my Pack, though, I truly do. The idea of opening myself up that deeply scares me, but I know none of you would intentionally hurt me."

She looks over at Jesse, encouraging him to take his turn. Jesse shifts in his seat, looking supremely uncomfortable, but I also know Josie is it for him, so he won't evade her questions.

"Well, Jojo, you're it for me. I don't want another Omega. I never expected to find a full Pack, though, and I don't know if I can do it. Share myself with that many people and be so open. I like my privacy; I *like* being alone, unless it's with you. So, I guess I don't have a good answer."

Josie nods, her eyes glossy with unshed tears, but she also reaches out to squeeze Jesse's hand. Why does she have to be so amazing? I don't know how to deal with any of this, and it's my turn.

"Well, if I'm being totally honest, I've been avoiding the entire situation. I don't know what I want. For the longest time, it's just been me and Vic, and now there are two other guys and my Match thrown into the mix. It's confusing and I don't know if I can bond when I'm this fucked up," I tell the table, my eyes downcast to my hands that are clenched together.

Vic reaches out and squeezes my shoulder, and the gesture makes me turn my head toward him. His eyes are filled with understanding, but also sorrow. He clears his throat before speaking.

"I hear what you're saying, Si, it's a lot. I… I'm all in if I'm being honest. Josie Girl, you've been it since we met back in high school. If you have other Matches, all that means to me is that you're going to be well loved, and I'm more than okay with that outcome." Vic's voice cracks at the end.

"What's wrong?" Josie asks.

"Uh, let's let Henry go first before we talk more. I want to make sure we all get heard."

"I'm simple, I want Josie and anything that goes with her. I'll bond whenever Josie wants to," Henry says.

"Just like that?" Josie asks.

"Just like that, babe."

Henry gets the brightest smile from Josie, and I can't deny that there's a little bit of jealousy. I want that smile to be directed at me, even though I know why it's not. My ridiculous Pack issues are going to break her heart, I just know it.

"Okay, Vic, spill it, what's up?" Josie says, turning to him again.

"I want Si to be a part of things, but," he turns to me, "I'm not sure you're ready. I don't want to lose you."

All I can do is nod. I'm not sure what else to say at this point.

Josie turns to Jesse, "Okay, I don't want to be in the middle of Simon and Vic, we don't need to all watch them work their shit out like it's a soap opera. Jesse, how… how do we get past this? I meant what I said, I'm not letting you go."

He smiles gently at her before taking her hand.

"I know, but I'm just not sure about being a Pack," he says.

We sit in silence for a few minutes, nobody quite sure what to say. It's awkward, Henry's trying to subtly comfort Josie while Vic does the same for me. Jesse sits mostly alone, but I can see Josie trying to give him some comfort when I'm not sure she has much comfort to give. This woman is too good for me. Jesse pulls away from Josie's comfort and stands.

"I'm sorry, I just don't think I can deal with this right now," he says softly before giving Josie a kiss on her temple.

Then he throws $20 on the table and walks out. Josie's trembling hand covers her mouth, and I can hear a soft whimper as she tries to keep any noise in. She doesn't want to cause a scene, but I think one has already been caused.

"Didn't you guys ride together?" I ask before my brain registers what my mouth is doing.

"Simon!" Vic hisses at me.

"Oh, shit, I'm sorry, I didn't think," I try to apologize to Josie.

"It's fine, uh, I'm sure I can call a ride share," she stumbles over her words.

Henry growls, "Absolutely not, I'll take you home."

The first tear escapes her eye as she nods. Henry helps her stand and looks at Vic, one eyebrow raised in question. Vic nods, and I sit there with him, somewhat dumbfounded at what just happened. We had a great time earlier this evening, but now I'm sitting here feeling unsettled and upset with Vic. Josie's run off crying, and Jesse just left everyone at the table.

"What the hell just happened?" I ask Vic.

"What just happened is that you and Jesse just about broke Josie's heart while Henry and I sat and watched." Vic's hand is now over his face, shoulders hunched.

"I'm sorry," I whisper.

Vic sighs before sitting upright and looking over to me. We look at each other for a moment, neither of us sure how to move forward.

"It's not your fault, man, she wanted honesty, and that's what you gave her. I think... I think you need to do some deep soul searching, though. This group would make a Pack that's incredibly different from the one that hurt you. Don't sell us short because of some other assholes," Vic pleads with me.

I nod and reach out to grab his hand.

"I'll do my best," I tell him, "I don't want to let you *or* Josie down."

Vic flags the waiter to grab our group's tab and pays what Jesse's money didn't cover. We walk to the car together and drive home with only the radio for noise, playing low in the background. When we're home and ready for bed, I move to sleep in the extra room we have before Vic stops me.

"Where the hell do you think you're going?" he asks.

I gesture over my shoulder with my thumb, "To sleep."

"Our bed isn't in there."

"Oh, you're not kicking me out?" I ask, a bit surprised.

Vic's eyes soften, "No, Si, we had a rough evening, that's all. We still belong to each other. It takes more than this to break us."

I walk across the hall and pull him into me, needing to feel him anchoring me to the present. My insecurities swim in my stomach, reminding me that I'm not good enough, not clever enough, just not enough.

"Thank you," I tell him.

Vic pulls back and places his hands on either side of my face, "I love you. Nothing will change that."

twenty-two

HENRY

I think it's safe to say that our Pack outing ended in disaster. It's been a few days, and while we still have a group chat with the guys, it's been quieter than usual. Vic and I are the only ones chatting, and at this point, I'm ready to start a thread with just the two of us. My heart is still feeling sad and sore from the group talk where I drove Josie home. She was so heartbroken that my own heart got sad. She told me that what they said wasn't a surprise, but it still made her sad to hear.

When we got to her condo, Jesse's car wasn't in his driveway, and I could see the disappointment in her body language. So, as the chivalrous Alpha I am, I offered her snuggles. She accepted, and I spent the evening snuggling with her until she fell asleep. It was one of my happiest moments, and I'll be treasuring it in my heart. Now, though, Vic and I are trying to wade through the aftermath. I grab my phone from where it's sitting next to me on the couch and pull up a new thread with Vic.

ME

You busy?

VIC

Nah, done with work, Si's still workin.
What's up?

ME

Been thinkin on Pack talk from the other night.

VIC

Oh, is that why we're not using the group
chat?

ME

Partly. Well, mostly.

Okay fine, yeah, it's the reason.

VIC

😅

Well, what's on your mind?

ME

Bonding. We should talk. Wanna meet?

VIC

Yeah, how does a beer sound?

ME

Delicious.

WE TEXT MORE before landing on one of the breweries in town. It doesn't take long to get there, and we've arrived in time for their Happy Hour. Cheap, delicious beer? I'm totally in. Vic's already here, and he catches my eye by waving his hand in the air. My own hand raises in acknowledgement before navigating his way. I sit on a stool across from him at a two-person high top and settle in.

"Whatcha got there?" I ask, looking at his golden drink.

Vic inspects the glass before shrugging. "Honestly, I told them to bring their best-selling beer, didn't ask what it is."

My head tips back in laughter, and when the waitress comes

around, I order the same, grabbing an appetizer as well. We make small talk until my beer is delivered, and I decide it's time to get down to it.

"So, I want to bond with you and Josie," I spit out.

Vic raises his eyebrows in surprise, "Well, lube me up before you just jam it in there."

I chuckle, "I figure just get it out in the open and figure shit out, you know? Simon and Jesse are clearly not ready or not willing to join as a Pack, so I didn't want to waste time if you're not interested."

"No, I'm interested, no problems there. I don't know Jesse very well, but Josie seems like she's excited about him. I think our last Pack talk hurt her more than she wants to admit."

"Yeah, after I took her home, we just cuddled. She wouldn't let me leave until she fell asleep, but she also wouldn't talk about it," I tell him.

"She's always had a bigger heart than she cares to admit. There's a desire in her to be independent and not need anyone else, and I know there are a few areas that stem from that. Deep down, though? She is more focused on other people's happiness than her own."

"So all we have to do is convince the other two to bond with us, and everything's fixed. Easy." My voice is laced thick with sarcasm.

Vic just chuckles and makes a noise of agreement. Our appetizers appear then, and we abandon our conversation for food and more small talk. Vic is a fun guy, and I can see why Josie likes him so much. He gives me glimpses into their lives as they met and then were separated. It sounds like they've been enamored with each other since they met, and fuck if my heart doesn't melt a little at that.

"What if we really do get both guys on board?" Vic asks, swinging back to our serious conversation with no warning.

"Now who isn't using lube?" I tease him, eyebrow raised.

Vic chuckles, acknowledging the switch in position.

"What do you want to do to get them on board?" I ask.

"Well, I'm not totally sure about Jesse, but I know Simon's biggest issue is insecurity and fear. He's scared that we'll change our minds and leave him behind." Vic explains.

I grunt, "Something like that takes time to prove. It's not a short-term solution."

"You're right," Vic sighs, "I think we can get him there sooner, but it's going to take more time than I want it to. So, what's your read on Jesse?"

"It almost feels like he doesn't know how to interact. He seems more comfortable just observing. When it comes to Pack, we need everyone engaged or it doesn't work."

Vic hums under his breath, thinking through our conversation so far. My observation of him so far is that he tends to be more thoughtful in his approach, whereas Simon is a little more impulsive. Not in a bad way, I don't think, but it definitely means his emotions drive him more than he'd like to admit. When the waitress passes by, I order us a second round of drinks.

"Does Simon typically go with how he feels in life? Or does he think things through?" I ask.

"He definitely goes with his feelings more frequently than most with decision making," Vic replies.

"So if we talk to him, maybe we can convince him to give us a try. Appeal to his feelings and point out that we're not the same as what he's gone through in the past?"

"That would be something you need to do. I've talked about this with him many times in the past, and I think the problem is trusting new people. He trusts me already. At least, I think he does." His brow furrows, as if he hadn't considered that Simon may not trust him.

"I'm sure he does, he looks at you like you're the greatest thing in his life. Josie is a close second based on how he looks at her, too."

Vic looks up at me from his glass, "Thanks, man, I think I needed to hear that."

"Happy to remind you anytime," I assure him with a smile.

"So, Jesse. I actually think that's something I can tackle. We'll do a double-sided approach. You handle Simon, and I can take Jesse."

It's my turn to frown now, "How are you planning to approach Jesse?"

"I think I'm going to approach it as getting to know him, honestly.

Yes, it sounds silly, but I'm hopeful that if he knows we value him just for being him, he'll open up more."

"Well, let's hope we can put our Pack together, eh?" I say.

Vic smiles and holds up his beer. I hold mine up in salute, and we both drink, my brain whirling with plans. Another idea comes to mind, and I can't let it pass by.

"Vic?"

"Henry."

"What do you think about agreeing to bond Josie, even if the other two aren't in? You're a Beta, so we'd be balanced. We wouldn't have to worry about rushing to find another member." My voice is almost rushing at the end, excitement flowing through me now.

The idea had filtered into my head, but I didn't expect the excitement to heighten as I spoke. As I think it through, though, I realize that there's no reason we should wait to bond Josie if she's ready. She already said she is, so now it's a matter of telling her. Vic's eyes light up as he listens to my idea, and I can tell he's in.

"Yes, I absolutely think we should. It makes sense, and you're right; we have one of each designation, so there's no rush to find someone to balance us out. We need to talk to Josie first, though," Vic agrees.

I pull out my phone in response.

ME

Hey there, sweetheart, are you busy?

JOSIE

No, I'm just finishing up getting a job posting put together. What's up?

ME

Are you up for visitors? Vic and I wanted to talk.

JOSIE

… is everything okay?

ME

Yeah, all good.

JOSIE

You sure? Cuz you just gave me the "we need
to talk" but nicer message.

MY EYES MOVE TO VIC, my cheeks red, and a smile of embarrassment
on my face.

"I think I messed up a bit," I confess, and pass my phone to him.

Vic grabs it and reads our messages before cracking up. He's
almost crying from how hard he's laughing, and I cross my arms
defensively. He waves me away, trying to dismiss the embarrassment.

"Sorry, it's not funny, but it's funny. Can I?" he says.

I shrug, "Sure."

He types a message back and hands my phone back, certain that
he's now fixed the situation.

ME

Josie Girl, I just grabbed Henry's phone. Our
poor awkward boy and I want to see you
because we miss you.

I'M TORN between amusement and indignation when Josie replies.

JOSIE

God, you two are adorable. Get over here.

I LOOK UP and grin at Vic, "Bingo, we're in."

Grabbing my wallet, I pay for our bill, and we both head to our cars and drive quickly to Josie. The two of us park on the side of the road and almost race to the door. Vic beats me with a "hah!" and raises his hands in victory. He's busy looking at me and gloating, so he misses when the door opens. Josie looks at him and smiles in confusion, with her head tilted.

"You good there, Vic?" she asks, mischief clear in her tone.

He turns, arms still in the air, and grins at her. "Yes, yes, I am."

She laughs and opens the door all the way, inviting us in. As the two of us file into her condo, we both take the opportunity to kiss her on her forehead and temple. She's blushing and smiling furiously as we settle in on the couch. Vic and I settle in on either side of her, and I can't stop myself from bringing my nose to her neck and inhaling deeply. Her head tilts with a smile of contentment, but I pull myself back before I can get lost in her.

"Well, we do have a question for you," I admit to her as I pull back.

She settles back into the couch so we're both slightly in front of her, where she can see us.

"Okay, shoot."

"Were you serious about wanting to bond us the other night?" I ask.

She frowns a little before looking between us. "Yes, I want to bond with all of you, but I'm not sure how we can with Jesse and Simon out. They really don't seem to want it, and I'm not about to force them."

"Would you bond with just us?" Vic asks softly.

Josie looks between us, surprise clear on her face. She bites her lip just a little as she thinks before twisting her fingers together.

"I would love to, but it doesn't seem fair to keep them out. I want all of you," she says softly.

"We aren't giving up on them," I reassure her, "They need time, but Vic and I are ready. So we're hoping that you're willing to bond during your next heat, and we can try to convince them before that to join us. If they don't, we can bring them in later. We have balance with the three of us."

She nods, thinking through my words.

"Josie Girl," Vic brings her attention to him, "We don't want to deny you anything. We want to give you everything. We want Jesse and Simon to join, but we also recognize it may take time."

A smile finally begins to spread across Josie's face. "Yeah, okay, I think I can do that. I'm still nervous. It's a big step. We just feel *right*, though, don't we? I can't feel it physically, but the more time we spend together, the more sure I am."

"I'm pretty sure I was gone for you the second you knocked on my door and put me in my place for staring," I admit with a chuckle.

Josie beams at me and grabs the front of my shirt, pulling me in gently. Our lips meet softly, and I hum happily into her lips, savoring the taste of her on my lips. She pushes against me gently, and I pull away. She uses her other hand to grab Vic's shirt and pull him in where I just was. Watching them kiss is more erotic than I thought it could be.

I'm aching for her heat, now, and I can't wait.

twenty-three

JOSIE

My coffee steams in my mug as I ponder on this morning. I woke up to Vic on one side of me and Henry on the other. All of us still mostly clothed, solidifying how happy I am with them. We had plenty of opportunity to get dirty last night, but I'm still reveling in how touching them isn't draining. So, they obliged me and just held me all night, kisses passed here and there, but not taken further.

Was it torture? Absolutely.

Was it my decision to stop? Yup. Just torturing myself over here.

Both of them are gone now, needing their own clothes and showers to proceed through their day. It's almost like they have their own jobs. Crazy, right? I smile to myself as my hands soak in the heat from my mug. The two of them were so sweet last night, I almost begged them to stay. Maybe soon we can figure out somewhere to live together. Sure, it's fast, but we're planning to bond and we're Matches. As far as my Omega and I are concerned, it's a done deal.

I can't imagine my Alphas protesting it, but I know that Vic doesn't want to abandon Simon, so that might play into things too. My lips meet my mug, and I sip some more of the liquid gold into me. Simon.

He's so complicated and so simple all at the same time. Spending time as a trio, just him, Vic, and me, felt as natural as breathing. He doesn't want to bond with me, though, so what does that mean? Did it not feel right to him? He kissed me like he couldn't stand to ever be apart, but when push comes to shove, is he really all that interested in staying?

My mind thinks back to some of the information I have about him, specifically, being burned in the past. Who hasn't been burned, though? The number of times I've had someone declare us to be a Match when they found out I couldn't tell is astronomical. I've been fooled more times than I care to admit, but I know this isn't false. It can't be, everything feels like it fits exactly where it should. So, how do I get Simon to recognize that this is the real deal? I could just tie him up and keep him captive until he gives in. That might not be entirely legal, though. Better not.

I drain most of my coffee, spending a few minutes pondering on Jesse since I'm thinking about difficult Alphas. The two of us together are perfect, the chemistry is amazing, and he feels comfortable with me. It's like the prospect of an entire Pack makes him panic. That makes sense, I suppose, he's said he's not very social. Maybe tying *him* up would work.

"Stop considering kidnapping your Alphas," I mutter out loud.

Glancing at the time, I sigh. It's time to make a work call. Maybe I can get some Georgie time too. My laptop is on the other side of the couch, so like the mature adult I am, I tip my head back and whine. Why's it gotta be so far away? I crawl over to it and then scurry back to the warm spot I left behind. I get myself set up and dial Georgie and James.

"Josie!" Georgie greets me.

"Hey Jo," James is decidedly less enthusiastic, but still pleased to see me.

"How are my favorite Betas?" I ask.

"Livin' the dream, girlfriend," James quips.

My eyes roll at his words. "Okay, let's get down to brass tacks."

"Brass tacks?" Georgie asks, a smirk on her face.

"It sounds professional!" I insist.

"Whatever you say, boss," she giggles.

"Well, I completed the job posting and sent it to you guys via email. What do you think? Does it encompass the role well? I want to be clear about what the job is without scaring people away," I say.

"Let me look again right quick," James says, pulling up a tablet and flipping through it.

As he skims, Georgie peers over his shoulder to read it with him.

"I think it's really good, just needs a few changes," Georgie says.

"Yeah, I'm looking at the part about why we're hiring, and I think that's something we could move out of the posting and just let them know about it during interviews. You stepping back a little doesn't need to be in there," James suggests.

I make some notes in my computer's note app.

"What else?" I ask.

"Do we need to keep in the bit about the role not being sexual in nature? I mean, we don't want it to be, obviously, but I'm not sure how forceful we need to be in the posting," George speaks up.

I pull it up on half my screen to review it with them. Apparently, I was feeling extra sassy the night that I wrote this job posting. The words I used are "This job is not for hook-ups, good times, or getting your kicks in. You will under no circumstances be hired if these apply. We don't want creepers." Yeah, we probably should tone that down or remove it.

"What about just using reasonable language?" I suggest.

James laughs, "You mean, 'no creepers' isn't reasonable?"

"Well, it's definitely not professional," I shoot back with a smile.

"What if we just said, 'this position is to comfort only when working with our clients.'? Would that work?" Georgie asks.

James nods, "Yeah, I think that sounds good. Josie? It's your business, what do you think?"

I'm already making notes in my app, "I think that I trust both of you and agree with your assessment."

"Oh, you," James teases, waving me off.

I giggle, enjoying James' teasing. He's so ridiculous, kind of like the brother I never had. We go through the rest of the job posting, ensuring that the language makes sense and represents the position well. I finally decided to hire another Touch Helper, so I'm terrified and excited. At first, it was just me on my own, then when I met Georgie and James, it was like destiny. Not romantically, but sometimes you just *know* that someone is meant to help you.

Hiring this person means I can scale back to one client at a time. It will relieve my stress a ton and will allow me to soak in my Alpha and Beta snuggles. I'm still in the honeymoon phase about how I can touch them without my energy feeling drained. Honestly, I hope it's always like this. Cuddling without feeling exhausted afterwards. Maybe I'll write an opinion article and submit it to someone so other people with Touch Loss know they're not alone.

I look into my camera after making the final notes on the changes we've discussed. Updating some phrasing and a format change, and it's complete. I'll post it on some job boards, and if that doesn't get us anywhere, I can look into print media as well.

"Hey Georgie?" I ask.

"What's up?" she responds.

"Are you busy? I, uh, I was hoping you would be willing to talk something out with me," I tell her.

"Yeah, absolutely! You wanna do it over video here or meet up or something?"

"We can just chat over video here, no need to make an effort to be seen in public," I assure her.

"Are we more worried about you looking presentable in public or me?" she laughs.

James stands then bends back into view, "This is my cue, catch ya later bossman."

"Bye, James!" I say, probably louder than necessary.

The view jostles some as Georgie moves around, and when she settles, I can see she's surrounded by pillows. Looks super comfy.

"Okay, brought you to my bedroom. I have a pillow obsession, so, uh, forgive the plethora behind me," she says.

"Omega over here, remember?" I tease her.

"Oh yes, how could I forget!" she quips back.

I chuckle and get myself settled back into a cozy position.

"So what's up? How can I help?" Georgie asks.

I sigh and close my eyes for a moment before looking into the camera and unloading on my employee/friend because I have nobody else to talk about this with.

"I found my Matches," I tell her.

"Uh, WHAT? When did this happen? Give me *all* the details!" she exclaims.

Laughing, I go through the entire process with her, explaining how Jesse found me first, and how my best friend turned out to be a Match too. Georgie squeals in excitement and gasps at all the right places, including when I accidentally outed Simon as a Match. When I explain how Henry fits in, she swoons dramatically.

"Girl! You have been *in it*! Wow!" George says.

"I know, right? It's been a huge whirlwind, but it all feels right. It's so weird," I confess.

"God, I hope someday I find a Match. It sounds like it's the best thing ever."

I smirk, "Well, I can't speak for the first touch, but everything else lives up to the hype."

At this point, she demands all the details of intimacy, including just snuggles. I didn't expect to really get into detail with her, but the longer we talk, the lighter I feel. The goal of this talk wasn't to be a therapy session, but that's kind of how it's turning out. She has great questions and is a fantastic listener. I think this entire situation is going to push us into a friendship in addition to being co-workers.

"So, what's the issue? It sounds like everything is great!" she comments.

"Well, this is where it gets more complicated. I took the guys on a group date at Date and Busters, and it was so much fun! The talk afterward was not so much fun. Basically, two of them borderline rejected me," I tell her.

"Excuse the fuck out of me, what?"

"Maybe I'm being dramatic, but Jesse and Simon both said they don't want to bond. Well, more specifically, they don't want to be Pack. But they can't bond with me and *not* be Pack. That's not how it works."

"Sounds like a bit of a cluster, eh?" Georgie comments.

"Seriously. How am I supposed to take that from them? Do I force the issue? Do I leave it alone? What do you think? You're mostly unbiased, so I wanted your thoughts," I tell her.

"Mostly unbiased?"

"Well, clearly you're on my side in the end," I tell her breezily.

We both laugh and then go quiet in contemplation. I bite my thumb while I wait for Georgie to figure out what she wants to say.

"Well, considering I've never been and never will be in your shoes, take what I say with a grain of salt. I think Simon and Jesse need a proverbial kick in the ass. I say you bond Vic and Henry and make sure Simon and Jesse know it's happening. Let them know they can be in if they want, but you're not going to beg for them."

"Like an ultimatum?" I ask, feeling a bit uncertain about that idea.

"Not so much an ultimatum, but a reality check like you're not going to wait on them to get your happiness, but you also want them to be part of it. Does that make sense?"

I hum as I think over the idea. It has merit.

"I think I like that. I've told Jesse that I'm not giving up on him, that he's mine, but I think you're right. I shouldn't have to wait for him to be ready to get my own happiness. Simon's just so scared to be in a Pack, but maybe I can get him to come around. He already knows Vic, and I'm a Match, so it's not like we're going to kick him out. That seems to be his concern." I reply.

"Absolutely! I think you're on to something," Georgie encourages me.

We smile at each other and lapse into silence for a few minutes. I'm about to tell her we can hang up now, but she clears her throat and starts speaking.

"I know you're my boss, but I really like chatting with you. Maybe we could be friends too?" she asks.

My heart warms, and a smile spreads wide across my face. "I'd really love that."

We say our goodbyes, and I promise myself that I'm going to be a good friend to Georgie. She's amazing. For now, though, I need to come up with a game plan to get my hesitant Alphas in gear.

twenty-four

VIC

Henry and I have been trying to figure out when we want to break the news to Josie about bonding. We're both in and want to make the formal ask to bond her during her next heat. I'm not even sure when it's going to happen, but it's gotta be soon, right? I sure hope so, at least. I can't wait to spend it with her and Henry. I hope he's up to the task when it comes to the knotting portion of things. Maybe I should look up more information on how to keep Omegas satisfied while in heat. Yeah, I'm gonna do that.

I pull up a browser window on my work computer and type a search to learn more about Omega heats. Frowning, I realize that's a bit redundant, but what's typed is typed. A variety of results come, anything from shopping for supplies to links that look a little untrustworthy. After skimming the first page of results, I chose to go medical first. Understanding how the biology works is the first step, I think.

Helping an Omega through her heat sounds like a sexy idea, but somehow, medicine has a way of making it sound horrible. It talks about potential starvation from getting lost in sex, how the Omega will be essentially mindless, the way skin will swell, and potentially turn red from all the blood rushing to the genitals. I exit out of the browser and remind myself that the Internet isn't the best place to get information.

When my workday is finished, I swing through the library to see if they have any books on how to help an Omega in heat. I wander through the self-help section, but so far, all I can see are books on general life improvement.

"Improve your life in seven steps," I read under my breath, "Yeah, right."

I place the book back and wander some more. Just as I resign myself to asking for help, a librarian saves me from myself.

"You look a little lost. Can I help?" she asks.

She's an Omega, her scent muted. It doesn't seem like a chemical suppressant, thankfully, but I do see she has several bitemarks around her neck, showing she's taken by a Pack. That would explain it. It makes me hope that someday Josie will bear the same marks.

"Uh, yes, actually. I'm looking for a basic overview of heats. Basically, Heats for Alpha Dummies 101."

Her laugh is light and airy, and she gestures for me to follow her. We walk past quite a few stacks before finally turning down one of them. I was way off in terms of location.

"This is where we keep all the information on Omegas and Packs. Unfortunately, there aren't many books on Betas and Alphas, but hopefully someone will write those someday. We have a few different books on heats right... here!"

She gestures to the selection of books, and I let out a sigh of relief.

"Thank you so much! This is exactly the kind of thing I was looking for," I tell her.

"Not a problem, that's why we're here to help. If you need anything else, just flag one of us down. We're all wearing these lanyards, so it should be easy to find us."

With that, she walks back the way we came, her stride steady but soft so she doesn't make much noise. I'm pretty sure I would go crazy if I had to work in an environment that required quiet. I examine the title of each book before landing on a couple. One was made for Omegas to help them through a first heat, and the other is a Pack's guide to heat. I need to make sure Henry gets copies of these for himself, too.

I check out my books and head home, intent on sitting down and reading through them. Hopefully, it will give me some information on how Betas can help during the heat. We can't knot the Omega, but there's other stuff I'm sure I can do to help. I just need to learn. According to my library slip, I have three weeks in which to do that. Shouldn't be a problem.

I start with the Pack book, figuring that's going to have the information I need most. Pen and notebook in hand, I scribble down anything listed about the role Betas play in a heat. We are definitely not left in the dust during a heat. Josie is going to need to be knotted several times, and the book recommends making her swallow Beta cum and rubbing any excess cum into her skin. The words on the page aren't written in a way to be enticing, but now I have the image of Josie spread out for us, dripping with our releases and overwhelmed with pressure.

My pants feel tight, and if I were an Alpha, I'm sure my knot would be swelling. I tilt my head back against the couch I'm sitting on, my eyes on the ceiling.

"Dammit," I groan, wanting to touch myself but also wanting to learn.

Who knew learning could be torture?

Maybe doing it with Henry will be less of a turn-on. I refuse to think about how gorgeous he is and focus on the fact that there's no way he's interested in men, and that definitely helps some of the pressure in my pants. Grabbing my phone, I pull up his information and send a text.

ME

Hey, I found a couple books at the library on heats. Not sure if you want to take a look at them.

HENRY

Oh, sweet, that would be awesome. I could
ask Ray... but she's like a little sister to me.

ME

Yeah, no, hard pass on that one.

HENRY

Exactly! 😅

Are you free now? I could swing by if you want.

Do I want Henry in my and Simon's house? I'm a little self-conscious since it's not a mansion like his house is. I mean it, too. He literally has a small mansion for a house. Simon and I have a rental, but it's not fancy by any means. Although maybe Simon seeing Henry here will be helpful. Maybe he'll notice that Henry isn't uptight.

I need to get past my own insecurities. Henry won't care about the house.

ME

Yeah, swing on by. Si will be home in a few
hours, but if you're still here, he won't care.

HENRY

Cool, see you soon.

So I KNOW I said I need to get past my own insecurities, but I decide to run around our house anyway trying to clean up. It's not like the house needs to be scrubbed down, but it does need to be picked up. There's mail spread across the counter, old glasses sitting on the coffee table in the living room, basic stuff that you find in a house. About twenty minutes later, I've just finished cleaning the toilet (because men are gross in the bathroom, don't let us fool you), when the doorbell rings.

"Perfect timing," I tell myself.

Hurriedly, I put all the cleaning supplies away and get to the front door. I swing it open just as Henry is about to knock, and we stare at each other in surprise, Henry's fist hanging in the air. Instead of putting it down, he reaches out and lightly knocks against my forehead.

"I'm here," he announces.

"No, shit, huh?" I say in wonder.

I let him in with a chuckle that he returns as he takes his shoes off inside the door. A few steps in, and he has a decent view of the house set up. It's a pretty open concept on the main floor, but there are a few walls separating the kitchen and dining area from the living room. Henry takes a few steps in and looks around with a smile on his face.

"This is great, feels nice in here. Welcoming, you know?" he says.

I blush a little, "Thanks."

"Where should we sit?" he asks.

"Right this way, sir," I say, mimicking a butler, and lead him to the living room couch.

We settle in, ready to dig into these books. I grab both of them, holding them up for him to see.

"So we have one from an Omega's perspective, and one from the Pack perspective. Where do you want to start?"

Henry hums for a moment, grabbing both books and looking them over. He chooses the Omega one first.

"I know you and I will need the Pack information more, but I want to understand more about what Josie will go through, I think. Did you look at this one yet?" he asks.

"No, I've been worried how Betas contribute during heats, so I started with the Pack one. I know there's a place for Betas, but I also know we can't knot like an Alpha."

Henry's face relaxes as I talk. When I said I was worried about how to contribute, I could see the panic rising in his eyes. I'm glad he didn't interrupt me, that shit annoys me. In the back of my mind, I'm starting to wonder if I had a bias against Alphas that my brain never caught up with. The fact that Henry has pleasantly surprised me more than once indicates that maybe I do have one. I'm happy with Si, so it never occurred to me that on a bigger scale, things might be different for me.

There's a small smirk on his face now, as if he knows my moment of silence was an internal battle about being biased. When did I grow up and become so introspective?

"Sometimes it feels like all the focus is on the Alpha when you hear about heats, but that's a certain kind of pressure on its own. The push to be perfect, make sure you have stamina, hoping that you're enough to soothe the Omega. I'm glad you found more information on the Beta role. I need to make sure we're all balanced," Henry replies to me.

"Why does it have to be you?" I ask, not aggressively. I'm actually curious why he's burdening himself with this.

"I think I'm going to be Lead Alpha. It makes sense based on the other two, and I don't mind doing it."

I nod my head in agreement, "I can see that. I don't have an opinion one way or the other; I'll let you Alphas sort it out."

Henry grins good-naturedly before we both pick up a book and start reading. At first, I worry that things are going to be awkward, just reading in silence together. However, I'm surprised at how much time passed while reading. Henry snaps me out of it with a comment.

"So apparently, if you have Matches, meeting all of them can induce an early heat," he says.

"Oh shit, do you think that's happening with Josie?"

He hums, "I haven't seen many symptoms yet. The book says they'll be needier, moodier, and frantic about where things are in their nest. It mentions a greater need to cuddle or have physical touch, but I'm not sure how that's going to manifest with our girl."

"Our girl," I grin at him, "I like the sound of that."

He grins in return.

"We should probably discuss group intimacy at some point," Henry says.

"You mean sex?" I say bluntly, just to see if I get a rise out of him.

"Yes. That."

"What?"

"Um," he hesitates for a second before lowering his voice, "sex."

I lean in close, pitching my voice low, "Why are we almost whispering?"

Henry chuckles softly and leans in toward me, "I have no idea. It just felt weird to say sex when we're talking about her heat."

"You're gonna have to get past it," I reply.

Henry sits back with a laugh, "Okay, okay, sorry, old habits of being raised by uptight parents. Loving, mostly, but uptight."

"All good, man. I think we just go with the flow if that's okay with you? I don't mind touching or engaging as long as everyone's comfortable with it."

Henry nods, "I'm cool with that at least until we bond, then we can reassess if needed."

"Will you be drawing up the contract?"

"Shut up," Henry snorts.

Then, we make a plan to officially ask Josie to bond with us.

twenty-five

SIMON

I've been off kilter since the awkward ending of our group date. Something isn't sitting right, and I can't figure out what it is. It's chafing at me, trying to get my full attention, but there are too many other things going on. My business needs the majority of my attention right now, so there's no time to go on a soul search or something.

My mind keeps lingering on old, hurt feelings. The lingering pain in my heart, where I assumed my Pack bonds would exist. It feels empty, uncomfortable. Too light, as if that part of me will float away. When I was in college, I never thought I would actually find a Pack Pull, so I was happy to be part of that group for a time.

Looking back on it, there are obvious signs that it wasn't going to work out. They applied to the Bonding Catalogue and never told me about it. I wonder if they actually registered a Pack bond at the same time as applying for Omega consideration. When they started dating Omegas, I thought they just forgot. When they went out with Omegas, I believed them that they thought I was busy or it just slipped their mind.

I was so desperate to belong to a Pack that I let myself be fooled by them. Part of me wilts at the thought of them laughing at me, but there's another part that gets angry and resentful. Before I was so damn desperate, and now I'm resentful enough that I don't want to have one. I do have one, though, don't I? Just not bonded in.

Another order pops up on our digital screen, and I find the matching cup with the written order. Part of me felt that this system would be overkill when I first started using it, but having the order and cup match has been a lifesaver, honestly. We do online orders, so being able to match things together this way saves a lot of confusion. I select the new order and claim it under my name so nobody else makes it.

Crafting the latte is almost therapeutic. I can lose myself in the rhythm of grinding, pouring, and stirring. Today, though, it's not bringing me to a place of calm. Today, I can still feel that itching need for *something*, but I can't figure out what it is. I place the finished order on the pickup counter, then, as I glance over the room, I see Josie in line to get coffee.

I'm pretty sure my instincts take over my body as my mouth stretches in a wide grin. My legs move me from behind the counter to where she's standing, and when my arms wrap around her and I pick her feet up off the ground, she giggles and holds me back. Just like that, the need for what I couldn't name mostly disappears. I have to focus to feel it, so I let it go and focus on the girl in my arms.

"Hi," she whispers against my neck, unabashedly taking in my scent.

"Hey," I whisper back, my own nose buried in her neck.

Without thought, I rub my cheek against hers, leaving my scent on her for anyone to smell. When I realize what I'm doing, I freeze and slowly straighten. This is something I should be asking for permission to do since we're not bonded.

"I'm sorry, I should have asked," I tell her as I set her back down.

Josie reaches up and grabs the back of my head, dragging me the few inches down to her face, and immediately rubs her cheek against mine.

"I don't mind," she says softly.

We pull apart, and I grab her hand, bringing her to the front of the line.

"What do you want?" I ask her.

She looks at me, horrified, "I can't just skip the line!"

"You can when you're my Match."

"Oh my God, your Match is letting you go first? That's so sweet! Here, go ahead," the next person at the counter says.

I raise my eyebrow in challenge, and she just sighs, relenting her argument. When she gives her order, I tell the employee that Josie never pays for her drinks here.

She clicks her tongue at me, "Simon!"

"I'm providing for my Omega! Would you really deny your Alpha when being provided for?" I hold my hand to my chest.

She blushes furiously, obviously not wanting everyone looking at her.

"Fine," she hisses under her breath.

I grin unrepentant and make her drink, handing it off to her as I round the counter.

"Do you have time to sit for a few minutes?" I ask.

"Sure!"

I grab her hand and we settle in at one of the outdoor tables, the slight breeze ruffling our hair and bringing fresh scents of bakeries and food trucks to our noses. It's at exactly that moment when I realize what I've done. I gave in to my instincts and basically claimed her in front of everyone without asking. There was no rational thinking in my actions.

"Josie, I am so sorry," I tell her, looking at her.

She cocks her head, confused, "What for?"

"I just kind of mauled you in there. You know, grabbed you, made a scene, I don't know what came over me." My hand rubs the back of my neck.

Josie's eyes soften, "Hey, it's fine. Sometimes instincts get the best of us, so we just need to go with the flow. Besides, we're a Match, it's nice to see some display of possessiveness."

My face flushes, and I almost hide in embarrassment. Alphas don't blush. I don't blush. What the hell is happening?

"Did you mean what you said in there, though?" she asks timidly.

"What did I say? Well, which part?"

"About me being your Match."

I frown, "We already covered this. We know we're a Match."

"It's one thing to know, and another thing to say it in public," she says, fiddling with her coffee cup, avoiding my eyes.

"Hey," I grab one of her hands and hold it in mine, "I meant it. I'm more than happy to tell everyone that you're my Match."

"Really?" She's beaming now

"Yes, really," I say with a laugh.

She jumps up and plops back down on my lap, throwing her arms around me. I let her hug me for a moment before pulling back and bringing her lips to mine. She's so soft and sweet, it's like coming home every time I kiss her. Admittedly, it hasn't been frequently, but it is the best experience I can think of.

Our kiss intensifies, my tongue sneaking into her mouth, caressing her there, and enjoying the feeling of our tongues sliding together. It's slick, erotic, and I'm reveling in every second of the exchange. My dick is hard already, driven by the scent and the *need* of this Omega in my arms. When she shifts to straddle me and rub her core on me, I pull back.

"Angel, I'd love to do this, but maybe not outside on the street."

Her eyes pop open wide, as if she'd forgotten where we are. I can see the blush rising on her cheeks, and I capture her chin with my finger and thumb.

"Make no mistake, though, I *want* you," I tell her, grinding up to tease her.

Josie gasps in pleasure before swatting my chest. "Heathen."

All I can do is grin in response. She giggles and slides off my lap, sitting back on the chair and grabbing her drink. We sit in peace, giving each other "fuck me" eyes as often as we can, and right when I'm about to snap and bring her home, the door to the cafe opens and my employee sticks their head out.

"Um, boss, sorry to interrupt, but the milk steamer stopped working."

I tip my head back, "Shit. Okay, be right there."

She looks at me, sympathetic to my plight.

"Thanks for the drink and the public claiming," she says as we stand.

"You are most welcome, Angel," I reply.

"Angel?"

"Yeah, there's no way you're anything less than an angel for putting up with three Alphas and a Beta." I grin.

She giggles and takes a step back. "Well, good luck at work, and don't worry about the claiming thing. Vic and Henry already offered the bond, so soon you'll be able to feel how much I enjoy it."

With that, she turns and leaves, but my heart has stopped working. Bond offer? What the hell is she talking about? Vic never told me... oh. Vic didn't tell me. I didn't really expect this experience twice, but I guess here we are.

My legs carry me back into the cafe, but my brain is in a fog. The milk heater is broken, so I fiddle with it a bit and realize it came loose. I pop it back into place, and it works like a charm again. Once that's fixed, I find myself in my office, sitting in my chair and staring at nothing.

Well, fuck, I think my heart broke.

WHEN I PULL into the driveway, I see the lights on in the house. Good, he's home. We need to have a chat, but I honestly don't know how calm I can be about this. I sit and think for a moment, not wanting to leave my car quite yet. Rational and calm. I need to be rational and calm. There's no reason to get overly angry or start accusing him right away.

If I repeat that enough times, maybe it'll work.

I sigh and open my car door, shutting it a little harder than needed. When I walk into the house, I calmly shut the door behind me. Well, as calmly as I closed my car door. I wince a little when I hear the door rattle slightly, and toe my shoes off. Vic pops his head out from the kitchen, frowning.

"You okay?" he asks.

"Fine," I shrug.

"You slammed that door awfully hard."

"Could have done it harder."

Vic sighs, "That's not the point."

All I do is shrug again, and that seems to piss him right off. Good, I'm pissed too. Any consideration of calm is out the window now that I've seen him.

"What is your problem?" he asks sharply.

"I saw Josie today," I tell him, walking into the kitchen to rummage for food.

Vic has already started dinner, but I'm not sure I can eat with him. So, I dig until I find a protein bar.

"Okay? Did she say something?"

I huff a bitter laugh, "Yeah, you know, she did."

Vic frowns, "What the hell? I thought you two were doing well together! I'll call her and ask what's up. This is not cool."

A small piece of me warms at Vic's protectiveness, but then I remember that he's lying to me.

"You're not my parent, you don't need to go defend me to other people."

"We're Pack, of course, I'm going to defend you."

"Are we?" I ask.

"Are we what?"

"Pack? Are we Pack?"

There it is. Vic's face goes a little pale, and he looks extremely uncomfortable. I shake my head, unwilling to suppress the disgusted huff that comes out of me.

"I thought maybe it would be different this time, you know? I'm real fuckin' hesitant to do the Pack bond thing, but I figured if I have you, it won't be so bad. You'd have my back. You'd understand my fears and help me through them." I say.

"Si, can you wait long enough to hear my side?" he asks.

"I tried to be calm enough to do that, I really did, Vic," I tell him, my voice tight, "Then I realized you did the same thing as they did.

You made me think I was wanted, then went behind my back and excluded me."

"You said you weren't ready!" he exclaims.

"You said Pack looks out for each other! Is this looking out for me? Is this helping me 'see the light'?"

Vic throws his hands in the air, "God, Simon, I don't know how the hell to explain anything to you when you're so consistently closed off about this!"

"Don't bother trying, I hope you and your Pack are happy with your Omega," I tell him.

I can hear Vic make an attempt to stop me, but he doesn't try for long. When I make it to my room, I toss the protein bar on my dresser and flop back onto my mattress. My heart is shredded. I know I said I wasn't sure if I'm ready, but dammit we didn't even sit down and talk about it one on one. They didn't even try.

Clearly, they didn't inform my Angel about it either. She was so excited when she told me. There have only been a few times in my life as an adult that I've cried. I hate crying. It makes me feel too vulnerable. As I lay here, though, it feels inevitable.

So, I let the tears flow down my face and just let it come.

twenty-six

JOSIE

I've been restless all week, and subconsciously, I understand what's happening. I refuse to think about it. If I don't pay attention, it will go away, right? That's exactly how this works, I swear. My hair falls into my face, and I blow it out of my face, irritated at the distraction.

Finally, after determining the bathroom floor is clean, I pull myself up and stretch backward. Maybe scrubbing the floor wasn't the best course of action to dispel this restless feeling. My back aches, and my hands are red from scrubbing without wearing gloves. Probably not my smartest decision, but I admit to not thinking it through; I just acted on the need to *do* something.

My phone buzzes, and when I check it, I see several messages from the guys. A smile appears automatically when I see their names. These guys have completely wormed their way into my heart, and even though two of them aren't excited about the idea of Pack bonding, I can't help being head over heels for them. It feels like I'm finally coming out of a world of gray and seeing color everywhere.

Before I get a chance to sit down and dive into whatever shenanigans are happening virtually, there's a brief knock at the door.

Looking through the peephole, I see Jesse standing on my small porch. Grinning, I fling the door wide open.

"Hey you!" I greet him.

Jesse gives me his shy smile, "Hey Jojo."

I stop back to let him in, and Jesse takes full advantage of the situation and pushes me back against the open front door. I happily let him pin me down and ravage my mouth with his own. My body lights up as his lips press into mine, his tongue demanding entrance. He pulls back way too soon, and I chase him a bit with my lips.

"Let's get all the way inside," he chuckles, pulling me away from the door.

Jesse smells *amazing* today, and I can't help but stick right next to him. I'm giving him zero personal space, and he chuckles as he maneuvers the door shut and brings me to the couch to sit.

"Feeling a bit needy today?" he asks softly.

I nod, "A little, yeah."

"I'm here for you to use however you need, Jojo," he says.

I melt into his embrace, my body fully leaning into his as he rearranges us to be more comfortable. My nose is just about buried into his neck, drinking down his scent like it's the air I need to breathe. It might very well be based on how I'm feeling right now. Jesse chuckles and peppers my head and face with light kisses. My head is almost dizzy between the light kisses and the intense scent.

Unable to hold back, I turn my head so we're face to face and reach up to bring him to me. A purr of contentment starts up in my chest, and I let my body relax into the noise. An Alpha's purr is meant to soothe, to remind the other person that they're protected by the Alpha and they can trust them. An Omega's purr is also meant to soothe angry situations, but it can also be used to stake a claim. Right now, my Omega is purring and staking our claim on Jesse. I promised him I would keep him.

Our tongues dance together, exploring and teasing, the feel of our tongues sliding causes my body to produce more slick. I'm so glad I wore absorbent underwear today. I don't want to worry about soaking through my clothes right now. I want to embrace the moment and keep Jesse close to me. His hand inches up and cups my breast, thumb lightly teasing my nipples. I'm not sure if he can feel them, but the slight tease is causing them to pucker, like they're begging for him to suck and bite them.

We break apart and stare at each other in wonder, breathing hard and letting our hands explore. I trace his strong arms and the soft skin of his neck as I slide from his shoulder up to his face. Jesse's hands are winding around my back, wandering up and down, brushing my ass just enough to ramp me up even more.

"You're such a tease," I tell him, my voice light and breathy.

He grins, "No idea what you're talking about."

As he says that, his hand brushes against the side of my breast, causing my breath to hitch. Jesse's face is full of mischief, and my answering smile stretches wide across my face. My phone dings again, and I startle. Apparently, I forgot everything when this man kissed me silly. I tell him as much as I pull my phone closer. He just chuckles.

VIC

Josie Girl! How are you feeling?

HENRY

Did something happen to Josie?

VIC

What? No, why would you ask that?

HENRY

You just asked how she was feeling! That indicates at some point she wasn't feeling well.

VIC

Bro, you need to take a breath. Nothing bad happened.

I SHOW JESSE THE CHAT, but he just nods with a small smile. "It may or may not be why I popped over."

Throwing my head back, I laugh with abandon, absolutely loving this chaos.

"Should I wind them up more?" I ask.

"Well, obviously!"

Cackling, I type out my reply.

ME

Vic, why would you tell Henry that nothing happened? I am beginning to feel better, but things are rough right now.

HENRY

Shit! I'm coming over, Josie, be right there.

SIMON

Are you okay, angel? Seriously?

VIC

Huh, is this what it's gonna feel like? Being the only one not freaking out?

ME

You don't know, Vic, I could be terribly injured! Simon, I'm always okay when you're around.

VIC

Are you??

ME

… well, not, like, terribly injured. Just a little swelling.

NOBODY RESPONDS TO THAT, and I'm concerned that Henry wasn't joking when he said he was going to be right over. Why did Vic and Si stop talking? I look over at Jesse with a small smile, confused about what's happening. Jesse, however, is red-faced, trying not to distract me with laughter. His hand is in a fist over his mouth, and I can tell by the crinkles in his eyes that he's dying to let loose.

I sigh, "Let it out."

Jesse starts cracking up, tears running down his face from holding it all in. I giggle at him, enjoying the laughter that he's locked into. I'm not sure I've seen him laugh this much or enjoy interaction so much. Maybe the bond will be a good thing for him. He said he's not sure, but how can he say he's not sure when he's got me and plenty of time to get to know the guys?

His laughing dies down to low chuckles, and my head is on the back of the couch, my eyes glued to his expression. On a normal day, Jesse is gorgeous. When he's laughing? My breath is about taken away. He's got the slightest dimple on his cheekbone, just by his eye when he smiles this wide. He looks lighter, freer, like this. It's how he should always be.

I push my way off my cushiony seat and fill up a glass of water for him. He accepts it with a "thank you," and sipping it seems to help the final giggles stop. Just as he's about to speak, there's a heavy knock at the door. My eyes shoot to it, wide and surprised by the heavy impact on the door.

Jesse pushes off the couch and steps in front of me faster than I can track, and my little heart melts at the protective action. He gestures for me to stay behind and moves to look through the peephole. A huff of air escapes him, and I can only imagine what he's seeing on the other side.

"Looks like a bunch of stray guys. Should I call animal control?" he asks, projecting his voice to be heard on the other side of the door.

"Goddammit, Jesse, open the door!" I hear Henry yell back.

I'm cackling with laughter as Jesse opens the door for Henry, who marches into the house. He's a mix of concern and anger, and while I *know* I should stop giggling, I can't. He's just so adorable. Each time I try to stop, my mouth just keeps going. It doesn't help that I can hear Vic yelling outside with the door still open.

"Si! Wait up! I'm sure she's fine!"

Simon steps in, and I *really* should stop laughing now. He's not amused. My body doesn't seem to understand that, though, and the giggles and cackles continue to escape me. Henry crosses his arms and glares at me. Fuck, that's hot. I kind of want to climb him like a tree right now. My legs lock together as I feel more slick escaping me. I'm not sure how much these panties can hold up to what these men do to me.

"Guys, I think this little Omega took us for a ride," he says, tilting his head as he looks at me.

Simon follows suit with the arm crossing, and Jesse looks over with a gleam of excitement in his eyes. Vic looks up at the ceiling with his hands on his hips, his head shaking back and forth in an exasperated motion. That restless feeling that's been plaguing me the last few days comes back in full force, and my hands and feet fidget. Henry stalks slowly toward me, and I step back out of instinct.

"Oh, my pretty Omega, don't you know not to run from your Alphas?" Henry continues, his voice low and rumbling through me.

I shiver as his words wash over me and bite my lip, wondering if I can beat them to my nest. They need to work for it, and my Omega wants them to chase me. My eyes flick to the side, judging the distance for a millisecond before locking back onto the guys. All four of them are now looking at me like I'm dinner, and I think my panties are officially wrecked. I found the limit.

Turning, I take two running steps before I hear Henry growl and catch me on the fourth step. His arm wraps around my waist, pulling me back to him, my ass happily rubbing into his hard length. His second arm wraps around one shoulder before landing lightly on my neck, holding me in place. Henry dips his head down and takes a drag of my scent before raking his teeth over my skin. A whine explodes out of me, and I can feel a sort of haze descend on me. I'm fully aware of what's happening, and they'll stop if I tell them to, but that's the last thing I want.

"Seems like we should teach our Omega a lesson," Vic says, his eyes almost feral as they roam my body.

Henry hums and the low vibrations that makes runs through my body, pulling a delighted shiver out of me. He then bends down and sweeps me off my feet, carrying me bridal style to the couch before sitting on the edge and twisting me around so I'm suddenly face down over his knees. How the hell did he do that so fast?

One hand gently caresses my ass, and I realize I've been hyper focused on his touch when I hear my name called.

"What?" I ask, feeling out of breath and more turned on than I've been in my entire life.

"I *said* you need to consent before I give you your punishment. The guys will be counting along with you, and if you miss a single one, they get to give you an extra," Henry tells me.

"Consent to what?" I ask, knowing I'll agree to anything he says.

Henry's hand makes another circle on my ass cheek before lifting. I almost raise up in confusion, but not a second later, a sharp bite lands on me, over my clothing, but still sharp. After the sharp? A world of languid delight seeps in, and I groan in pleasure.

I hear one of the guys chuckle, "Looks like our Omega likes that."

My body feels Henry's chuckle as he soothes the sting with his hand.

"So? Omega? Think you can handle it?" Henry asks again.

He's laid down a challenge now and fuck if I'm going to back down.

"Yes," I moan, "I can. Please."

"Please, what?"

I almost cry with anticipation and frustration, "Spank me!"

"What do you say, guys? Ten total?" he says.

"Unless she misses a count. Then we add on more," I'm pretty sure that was Vic.

"Safe word is 'Red', sweetheart," is the last thing I register Henry saying as blows begin to rain down on my ass. Each one interrupted by a soothing hand.

When he finishes, my body is languid, and I'm pumping out pheromones like it's my only job. A whine builds up in me, but I'm not sure why. There's an itch under my skin, like I need something, but I can't figure out what. Is it hot in here? God, it feels hot. I whip off my shirt, complaining about the heat, when I feel a strong set of arms lift me into the air.

twenty-seven

HENRY

I spanked our Omega into heat.

My Alpha is preening with pride that we pushed her into heat, that we were the ones to get her there. Much to the guys' dismay, she didn't miss a count despite her slurred words, so I let them each have one at the end. She was enjoying herself too much not to. When she whips off her shirt, I know it's go-time. Josie, on a normal day, wouldn't be quite so bold.

My arms sweep her up, and I call to the guys to get moving as I bring Josie to the door of her nest. I set her down on her feet, concerned she's going to fall over, but she surprises me by turning and yanking at my shirt. Her other hand reaches out to grab the next closest shirt, which happens to be Vic's. He relinquishes it, then she turns her back on us, scurries into the room, and closes the door in our faces.

"Well, then," I hear Vic say.

Turning, I see Vic grinning like he's won the lottery, and we chuckle for a moment together. When I look, Jesse and Simon are hanging back a bit. Frowning, I look between them. I step closer so we're not immediately outside Josie's door.

"Why aren't you guys closer?" I ask.

Jesse scuffs his foot on the ground like a little kid would do, "I'm not sure I'm going to stay. I... I'm not ready to bond yet, and she was really clear about wanting to bond during her heat."

"Are you kidding me right now?" My voice is low.

"I didn't... I didn't expect all of this to happen tonight! I came over to spend time with her, not to bond her!"

"So you're just going to give up your chance? Maybe this is the universe telling you to get your ass inline."

"Doubtful," he scoffs quietly.

My eyes laser-focused on him, "Then leave now, it's going to be painful for her either way, but if she sees you leave, it will be worse."

Jesse ducks his head in shame and nods before he ambles to the door. He hesitates for a moment, but then lets himself out. I blink, watching the door, assuming he'll come right back in, rethink things.

Why... why would he *actually* leave? I know I told him to go if he wasn't in, but how can he just walk away from his Omega when she's going to be in so much pain and need?

Simon is looking at the floor when I turn his way, his arms are crossed, and he's shaking his head. Vic's heart looks like it's breaking, his body leaning toward Simon almost unconsciously.

"I shouldn't have driven over here. That was stupid," he mumbles.

"It was stupid to come make sure your Match is okay when you were concerned?" Vic asks.

"Yeah, I mean, no, I mean." Simon stops and pinches his nose between his fingers.

We wait for a second, letting him have a moment to gather himself. In the background, I hear a small noise, but I keep my focus on Simon. He takes a deep, shaking breath.

I scoff at him, "Are you going to man up and take care of our girl or bail?"

"Our girl? Really? From what I heard, you two are happy enough to handle her all on your own. I want Josie, she is everything to me, but not if you assholes are attached."

Simon storms out of the house, and I look wide-eyed at Vic.

"What the hell just happened?"

Vic shakes his head, "Old fears and my dumb ass mistakes."

I glance at Vic, feeling insanely guilty suddenly. We had every plan to try and pull them in, but then tonight happened. Maybe we should have stepped up sooner. Apparently, I need to rethink how I'm going to lead this Pack.

"We fucked up. *I* fucked up. I'm sorry, Vic."

He claps a hand on my shoulder and squeezes once, so I know we're good. Now we need to address the little Omega spy.

A deep waft of Josie's cinnamon-sweet scent escapes the room as she steps fully out. Turning, she's just in a bra and panties, her skin slick with sweat, and her eyes heavy and needy. She looks down the hallway with a mix of devastation and horniness.

"Alphas?" she asks, a whine laced through the word, "They left? Why?"

She wants her whole Pack, but I had naively hoped she would put them out of her mind if we stayed for her. Vic curses under his breath, so I turn and grab her in my arms, slamming my lips down to hers, distracting her as best I can. When I relent, I turn my head a little and address Vic.

"Go grab waters and snacks if she has anything easy to eat. We've got our work cut out for us."

I assume he goes to do that because I turn back to my Omega and land my lips on hers again. Kissing her is one of my favorite things to do now. She pours all of herself into the kisses, freely giving all of herself as we pour back into her. Breaking for only a second, I ask for permission to enter her nest. She nods rapidly, so I walk her backward into the room, my hands roaming as I do. Her soft skin leaves me in awe, and my fingers find her nipples, pinching them slightly through the fabric of her bra, bringing more of her perfume into the air.

I go to my knees in front of her, needing to get my mouth on her, her slick down my throat, and covering my face. My hands reach out and peel her panties down, watching as her slick drips out, trying to follow the absorbent fabric. Helping her step out, I toss them behind me, and hear a deep groan behind me.

"Fuck me, she smells amazing," Vic rumbles.

Taking a glance back, he caught her panties and held them to his face, inhaling deeply. He may be a Beta, but his instincts are just as possessive as an Alpha's. Just a bit less aggressive. Turning back to Josie, I run my hands up her legs, encouraging her stance to be a bit wider.

"There you go, baby, just a little wider. That's it, I'm gonna lick you now. I want to feast on you tonight, you smell so *fucking* perfect."

She whines lightly as she begs me, "Please, Alpha."

Quick as I can, my face is buried between her legs, my tongue lapping at the slick she's produced. Once I'm satisfied with her lower lips, I pull them a bit wider with my thumbs and I about come in my pants when I see how perfect her wet pussy is. My tongue dives in, spearing into her hole over and over again. I fuck her with my tongue as she grabs my hair and babbles nonsense in her pleasure.

There's a shift in gravity, and when I realize Vic is supporting her weight, I dive in harder. Her clit is swelling and ready, so I flick my tongue over it, tracing circles and alternating between small flicks and long licks. My tongue flattens and I dip in as far as it will go before I drag it up to her clit, wrapping my lips around it. I suck and swallow the slick that my tongue gathered and then increase my suction, pulsing it just a little bit. When I put two fingers in her tight heat, I can feel the first fluttering of her orgasm. When I scrape her clit with my teeth she screams out her pleasure, her walls milking my fingers and trying to suck them in farther.

Vic takes the moment to unhook her bra, and we lay her down gently as she comes down from her high. The two of us shed our clothing, and when she notices it, she grins at the sight. Josie licks her lips at us, but then her face falls a touch. Her eyes search the room, panic starting to set in.

"Alphas? Alphas?" she asks again, a full whine present in her voice.

"Your Alpha and Beta are here for you," Vic coos at her, caressing her body and tweaking her nipples as he reassures her.

We both know that's not what she's asking for, but we'll do our damndest to keep her distracted. She starts to wiggle and writhe again, and I can't wait to get my knot in her. Giving her hip a light pat, I demand what I want.

"Present for your Alpha, Omega."

She scrambles to flip over, her ass high in the air, her face and shoulders pressed flat into the bed, arms stretched out in front. Before I give in to instinct, I look over at Vic.

"You good?" I mouth.

He smiles and nods, gesturing to me to get moving. We grin at each other, and I slide home into our girl. We both moan in pleasure, and I pound into her with a steady rhythm at first, picking up the pace and moving faster and faster. My hands are clinging to her hips, and I'm a little concerned about leaving bruises, but her eager body pushes back into me, asking for more.

"Fuck, Josie, you feel so damn good. Do you want my knot? I bet you do. You want me to slam deep into you? Lock us together so I can make sure you take all of me? Not a fucking. Drop. Lost."

I grit my teeth and slam into her at the last three words. My knot is pushing at her entrance, and I could easily pop it in now, but I want to feel her milk me first.

"Come, Omega, let go and let me fill you," I coax her.

Her walls clamp down as she sobs out her pleasure, and I slide all of me in, my knot swelling further to lock us together. My eyes roll back with pleasure, and I swear I'm going to black out.

"Bite, bite, bite," she chants as her orgasm continues.

Yanking her up, I move her hair out of the way and clamp my teeth down right where her neck and shoulder meet. The iron tang of blood enters my mouth, and I release her, licking at the wound to seal it. Josie's small hand reaches up and grabs my head. She turns, and I arch my neck so she can reach it. Her teeth sink in, and a burst of awareness comes over me before I lie us down and we both pass out.

twenty-eight

VIC

Henry and I have been tending to Josie for a full two days now, and while I never want to leave this nest, I want to ease the hurt that I can see on her face in the calm moments. She knows she's missing two of her Alphas, even deep into her heat haze. When we rest, she emits a quiet whine, like she can't quite settle without them.

Looking at Simon's face on the first night, I realized she must have told Simon about the bonding request from Henry and me. Henry took responsibility for it. Still, it slipped my mind to include him even though we live together, and it makes me wonder if I should have taken more responsibility for it.

My Omega stirs, and I banish those thoughts, needing to focus solely on her. I haven't given her my bite yet, but I think it's time. I've been waiting until closer to the end of her heat so I don't get too lost in feeling her.

Josie's hand softly lands on my cock, stroking it gently to life. Honestly, it doesn't take much with the pheromones we're all pouring into the room. I may not have an Alpha's stamina or rebound period, but I can hold my own well enough. I hum in appreciation of her strokes. The feel of her body fitting between my legs is perfect, and I wonder briefly if we could live in this position.

"Do you need my cock, Josie Girl?" I ask her softly, brushing her hair off her neck.

She gently whines and nods her head. So, I put my hands behind my head and gesture with my head down to the hard shaft between my legs.

"Get to it, baby. Show me how good you swallow me down."

I was nervous to dirty talk her in this environment since it can be completely different for an Omega, but Josie still loves the dirty talk. She can't come without it, apparently. I'm happy to deliver for her.

Her hot mouth seals around me, and she slowly takes me down into her throat. The feeling of her soft, wet mouth will never get old.

"Omega, fuck, you're so fucking good at that. Look at you, swallowing your Beta's cock like such a good girl."

Josie moans with delight, bobbing faster up and down, driving my pleasure higher and higher. I know she loves when we spill our cum in her mouth, but this round it's time for us to bond. The idea of bonding brings me close to the edge, and I know if we don't stop, I'll miss my plan to mate her. My hand reaches out to stop her, and I gently pull her off me.

"I need you to ride me now, I want to see those pretty tits bouncing," I say through gritted teeth.

Her perfume explodes, and she scrambles on top, where she gently guides me to her, lining us up perfectly. She's poised to take her time, but I'm not having any of that. My hands whip out to her hips, and I hold on tight as I pull her down, and my hips surge up. Buried to the hilt on the first thrust causes me to go cross-eyed with pleasure.

"Fuck, Josie Girl, you're so fucking perfect. Show me how you take your pleasure. Give it to me."

She emits another needy whine and I move one hand to her clit, rubbing vigorous circles. Her walls start to tighten, and I hear the change in her breathing as she continues to rock and bounce on top of me. We're both so close to the edge that it's not going to be long. That's not the point this time, though, so I'm happy to go quickly. I want her presence in my chest, to feel her all the time.

Right as I feel her clamp down, I surge up, pulling her closer to me and bury my teeth on the side of her neck, right above Henry's mark.

A muffled groan of pleasure escapes me as I taste the tang of her blood, and I can hear her screaming out her pleasure. I pull back from her neck, giving the bite a few licks to help it seal. My girl pushes me down and hovers over top, her hair curtaining around us.

"My turn," she says with a smile.

Her teeth sink into my neck, right where I bit on hers. She did the same with Henry, like she wants to mirror our individual bites. Awareness of her explodes inside of me, and I can feel the waves of love we each have reverberating between us. Henry moves closer while we bond and holds out his hand.

"Pack?" he asks.

I grab his hand and bite down on his forearm, just past his wrist. Henry's awareness rolls in gently, a steady and protective presence that feels like he'll always hold us. Licking the bite once, I hold my own arm out for him to bite wherever he wants to. He smiles and picks the same spot, mirroring us like Josie did. His eyes close, and he gives the bite a single lick as well.

"Pack," I say as we all lie together in a pile of love and exhaustion.

twenty-nine

JOSIE

My heat went for three days this time, and I can feel Vic and Henry right beside my heart in my chest. Henry's steady presence bolsters me, makes me feel like I always have someone in my corner. Vic's presence is a little more subtle, a steady affection and desire to ensure the ones he loves are happy and taken care of.

I'm not sure what I feel like, but it's probably not all sunshine and rainbows. When I woke from my heat, I cried for an hour straight. I knew, I *knew* that Jesse and Simon weren't ready, but they didn't even try. I watched as they left without saying anything to me. Once I was lost to my heat, I could tell someone was missing, but Vic and Henry kept me so distracted, I could never figure out why things didn't feel quite right.

My Omega is sitting in her proverbial corner, sad and a bit despondent that two of her Matches don't want her. Honestly? Same. I thought, well, I guess it doesn't matter now. I've managed to move myself to the couch today, now that the heat is over, but it's only been a day since things ended. Vic and Henry helped me get cleaned up, fed me, washed the sheets for me, and helped care for me the entire first day after the heat ended.

They both offered to stay longer, but I waved them off. I thought for sure I was fine, but after they left, I curled back up in my nest, feeling like part of me was missing. Today, though, today I manage to get to the couch to wallow instead of my nest. Improvement. It's been two days since my heat ended, and I'm torn between feeling comforted by Henry and Vic in my chest and absolutely devastated that there are two distinct missing bonds I can feel.

My 80s music playlist is filling my house with sound, so I don't go completely crazy from the silence. I snuggle further into the blanket pile I have on my couch and take a sip from the water bottle I promised Henry and Vic I'd drink. I have zero desire to drink anything, but I promised them both I'd stay hydrated.

The moment I set my water bottle down next to me, the song switches to "Jessie's Girl", and I lose all semblance of the calm and cool I was pretending to have. My throat closes up, and my eyes burn with new tears as I listen to the lyrics. God, I wish I was Jesse's girl, but I don't know that it'll ever happen. The guys must feel my sorrow down the bond, because my phone begins to buzz with incoming calls.

I ignore it and choose to wallow. Fuck maturity, my heart feels like it's in shreds from missing Simon and Jesse. Then I feel guilty for not being happier that I have Vic and Henry, and the tears double. How can everything feel so wrong and so right at the same time?

The songs keep playing, and while I'm no longer sobbing, there's a steady stream of tears running down my face. How do people survive this? This pain of knowing someone is missing, but threaded through with joy from who you have? It's maddening. Vaguely, I hear the door open, and my bonds flood with concern and love, bringing my awareness back to the moment. Of course, the minute this happens, I start to giggle.

Turning in my blanket burrito, I see Henry standing there, hands on his hips and a teasing look on his face.

"Did you do this on purpose?" he asks.

"Do what? I have no idea what you're talking about," I reply innocently.

He hums, "I think you Rick Rolled me on purpose."

My giggles take over as "Never Gonna Give You Up" plays on the speakers throughout my house. Henry doubles down on my giggles by doing Rick Astley's dance from the music video. Now my tears are from laughter instead of sorrow. How does he know exactly what to do? Maybe it's a Match thing.

Henry walks over to me and forces himself into my blanket burrito. I've never been more thankful that I bought a deep couch than in this moment. It leaves plenty of room for us to snuggle up together. He curves around me, the big spoon to my little. So I obviously scoot back with my butt to try and tease him and get closer. Squeezing me once, he sighs in my ear.

"Better?" he asks.

I hum in happiness, "Everything's better when you're around."

"Good." With that, he rips the covers off, smacks my ass and gets out of bed.

"What the fuck?" I borderline yell at him.

"Where are your bags?" he asks, walking toward my room.

I scramble off the couch, following him like a newborn foal trying to walk. The blankets have my legs so tangled I start to swear at them before finally getting free. In the meantime, Henry has found two of my suitcases and is raiding my closets, throwing in sweatpants, soft shirts, hoodies, all soft, lounge clothing. I dart in front of him to snag my favorite comfy pair of jeans. Just in case.

Henry starts to eye my bedding, and I step in between him and my bed. Nobody gets to touch my blankets right now. He'll mess them all up, and I'm not allowing that. A growl surprises me as it escapes from my throat.

"Don't touch my blankets," I tell him.

Henry holds up his hands in surrender.

"Okay, pack them up for me, I'm taking you home and I want you to have all the things you need."

I bite my lip, trying to figure out what to do next. Do I bring all my blankets? Do I bring things from my nest instead of my bed?

"Hurry up, Omega, or I'll do it for you," Henry threatens, despite telling me to pack things up on my own.

When I try to glare at him, he raises an eyebrow in challenge. My

Omega wants to roll over and submit, and judging by the slow heat building in his eyes, Henry can tell. Deciding I want my nest blankets, I turn to stomp out of the room.

"Pushy Alphas," I mutter.

A loud crack sounds in the air and my ass stings from the slap that Henry just delivered.

"Sassy Omegas," he mutters back.

I grin at the interaction, my sorrow lifting for a few moments as we finish packing things up. The second we step outside, though, I'm reminded that Jesse left. My feet stop moving as I stare at his condo, remembering how connected I thought we were. Apparently, it wasn't enough for him to stand by me through my heat. My eyes close against the pain as the memory of our time together plays in my head, and I feel a tear slip out.

Henry reaches around me to close the door before gathering me in his arms. I let myself lean into him, finding comfort in his strong arms. My eyes squeeze harder, as if I can block it all out by trying hard enough. Jesse was happy to help spank me, but he wouldn't stay with me when it pushed me into my heat. I wasn't far off, if I'm honest with myself, but I *needed* him, doesn't he know that?

Heaving a large sigh, I pull my head back from Henry's chest and look up into his light blue eyes. When the sun hits them just right, they're almost luminous, and it's easy to get lost looking at their color. He leans in and gently kisses my forehead. My silly little heart jumps at the sweet gesture, and I can't wait for him to do it again.

"Thank you," I tell him.

"For the kiss?"

"For being my Alpha."

His eyes soften as he gazes at me, "Thank *you* for being my Omega."

We part, and once the luggage is in the car, I climb into the passenger seat of Henry's car, which is a crossover SUV, so it's plenty spacious with just the two of us. I glance up once my seatbelt is fastened, and my eyes meet Jesse's blue ones. His blue is darker than Henry's, but they still pull me in easily. If I hadn't met him before, I'd assume he was casually standing there. Knowing him like I do, I can see the tension on his face and body, as if he's holding himself together by sheer will.

Another pesky tear leaks from my eyes, and I look away. Seeing him on the edge is too much, I can't watch him be on the edge when he's the one who walked away. I hear the door shut and a seatbelt click before a soft rumble comes from the seat next to me. I take a deep breath of Henry's cedar and eucalyptus scent and make an effort to relax. My eyes look up to his, where he's glaring at Jesse.

"Let's just go," I say gently, taking his hand in mine.

He looks down at our hands and smiles, "Okay."

When we arrive at his house, I feel even more tension bleed out of my shoulders. How can just being in his driveway make me feel better? I decide not to ask questions and heft my purse and tote bag over my shoulder. Henry grabs both of my suitcases and we head inside. It's a bit different walking in as Henry's Omega instead of a Touch Helper for Ray, but the familiarity is welcome.

"Did you finally get her?" I hear Ray call out from somewhere in the house.

Henry chuckles, "Yeah, she's here."

"Good! Maybe you'll stop being so pissy," she sasses before cackling and poking her head out from the living area to grin.

"Hey there," I say, waving at Ray.

Still grinning, she replies, "Glad you're here."

I return her smile with my own before Henry grabs my hand and leads me up the stairs. Pretty sure he's grumbling about sassy Omegas again, and it makes me snicker to myself. At the top of the stairs, instead of following the hallway in the direction of Ray's room, we turn right where double doors greet us. He turns the handles and pushes them open dramatically. I give him the appropriate gasp in response.

The Pack Suite is *perfect*. There are two feet of hallway before we walk into the sleeping area, which houses a large Pack bed. We would easily fit with some room to spare. I walk through the room and find the door to the bathroom, which holds a massive whirlpool tub, a few sinks, and a luxury shower. Seeing two more doors, one leads me to a walk-in closet and the other leads to a nest.

I open the door to the nest, and my eyes go wide, my mouth dropping in shock. It has a massive in-set circular mattress, so you have to step down to get in, and I immediately begin planning out how I can use the low wall around the mattress as sides of my nest. The ceiling of the room has twinkle lights around the perimeter, but nothing else has been done yet.

Henry's arms wrap around me from behind, "I wanted you to be able to change it as you see fit. Nobody else has used this room. Ever."

Turning, I all but attack Henry with my body, my lips slamming against his, begging for a taste of him. I hear the low, possessive growl that builds up in his chest, and he scoops me up, my legs reflexively wrapping around him. I'm pretty sure this is the first man who has held me this way, and I will absolutely be begging for him to do it more. His legs take us to the bedroom area, where he sets me down gently on the bed.

Breaking away from my lips, he apologetically says, "Unless we want Ray to hear everything, we should close the doors."

"Yes, let's not scar my former client and your chosen sister on my first time here as your Omega."

The door closes, and Henry races back to the bed, grabbing me and caging my body with his. Just a few hours ago, I was spinning in my solitude and sorrow, feeling like I wasn't good enough because of the two Alphas who walked out on me. Being here with Henry, though? I feel soothed, cared for, and content. There are still two holes in me that can only be filled by Jesse and Simon, but they get shoved to the background as Henry and I relearn each other's bodies.

As we snuggle later, I can't help but feel Henry's frustration and annoyance at himself through our bond. Wild.

"Hey, what's going on? I can feel you're a bit off," I ask gently.

Henry huffs a laugh, "Completely forgot about that part of the bond, which is funny because it's why I came to you today. I'm kicking myself for not staying with you, or asking you to come with me after your heat. Omega's need extra cuddles and pampering after a heat to feel secure, but you insisted you were fine, so I didn't push. Next time I'm going to listen to my instincts and not the words you say."

"I wondered how you knew. I didn't realize I was broadcasting it at all. Vic never called, though. He's at home with Simon now, but I didn't hear from him." I reply.

"I called and told him I was going to you, so he didn't have to worry. Fun fact for you that I learned last week, as Mated Matches, we can feel where the other person is. If it's somewhere you know, I think it's more specific, but you'll always know what direction they're in."

"That's so cool! It'll make finding you guys easier if we're all separated..." I realize at the end of that statement that we are, in fact, separated, but we don't all have bonds.

"They'll come around, I promise," Henry whispers in my hair.

I hold him tighter, "I hope so."

thirty

SIMON

I spent three days in agony, imagining all the ways that Vic and Henry were pleasuring Josie. Imagining how Vic and I could have pleasured each other while adding Josie to the mix. There's no part of me that doesn't want that experience. My imagination runs wild as I go through the motions for the three days that Vic is gone.

They both should hate me. I think *I* hate me right now. Vic has been home for a day now, and while I didn't see him at all yesterday, his presence was everywhere—shoes scattered in new spots, extra dishes in the sink. At first, my sorrow got more intense, but now that he's been home for a day, I'm starting to get angry. So he's just going to avoid me? Is that it? We almost never miss each other during the day, so it's got to be intentional.

Anger at him and myself grows throughout my workday, and by the time I get home, I'm ready to explode with anger and frustration. There's not even a true focus for all the emotions swirling in me. It's almost as if they've taken a life of their own, and I can feel them scratching at me under my skin. Everything's more intense and I can't focus for shit. My employees avoided me all day, and on the one hand, I'm glad nobody bothered me, but I'm upset that nobody even checked on me. How stupid is that?

When I walk in the door, I see Vic's shoes and his keys in the key tray. His scent is stronger today, and that tells me he's working from home. My instincts are torn between seeking him out jumping his bones or beating the shit out of him. I can feel the restlessness I've been struggling with rising, but I do my damndest to lock that shit down.

Instead of acting on my instincts, I kick my shoes off, dump my keys, and go to the kitchen for water. Maybe a cool drink will help. I can dream. I chug down a massive glass of water, noting that it's almost gone when I finish.

"Damn, I was thirsty," I mutter to myself.

My ass lands in a chair as I hold myself back from going after Vic. Deep down, I know I'm not really mad at *him*, he's just a convenient outlet. I'm mad at myself mostly, for my own damn cowardice. I just can't get past that feeling of rejection that resurfaced when I heard about Henry and Vic deciding to bond Josie. Now I might have missed out on something perfect, something special. I'm such an idiot.

Vic's footsteps sound in the house and get closer, telling me that I'm about to be put to the test. The knowledge that he's coming spikes the restless feeling crawling under my skin. Determined to control myself, I take a deep breath and try to ground myself. His footsteps stop when he reaches the kitchen.

"Hey." Vic sounds a bit surprised that I'm here.

"Hey."

The air feels thick with tension, but I'm not sure what else to say. Vic grabs himself a soda out of the refrigerator and opens it before sitting down next to me. He starts talking to me about something, but I can't hear him over the roaring in my head.

I can smell her on him. It's faint, but it's there, and I want to drown in the scent. It feels as if I can't breathe air that contains her scent, I'm going to die. The only thing that will keep me afloat is her scent. My hands start to shake a little, so I grab onto my glass like it will ground me. Instincts are screaming in my head to fight or fuck, and I'm a hairsbreadth away from exploding.

"You okay?" Vic asks.

I clear my throat a few times before I can speak. "No, not particularly."

I stand and move away from him, needing the space. Something is wrong with me, and I can't figure it out. My feet carry me back and forth, needing to walk but unable to leave the room just yet. Vic's eyes follow me, and I pace back and forth in the kitchen.

"Anything I can help with?" he asks. I can hear the genuine concern, but I can't accept it.

I laugh bitterly, "Like you helped with Josie and the Pack proposal?"

"That's not fair…" Vic starts, but I'm too keyed up to listen.

"Are you fucking kidding me? You're the one who pushed me out! Fuck you!" I yell, interrupting him.

Vic gets *pissed* and there's a small, vindictive part of me that is incredibly pleased. I want someone else to feel what I'm feeling. I need an outlet, and it looks like Vic is going to be the lucky winner to receive it. He pushes back from the table and storms over to me.

Now, here's the thing. I know that I'm being unreasonable. Vic should have been more open with me, sure, but me picking a fight like this isn't the best way to handle things. However, I can't seem to stop. It's like my body is begging for it, and I'm tired of resisting it. When he steps up to me, Josie's scent hits *hard*, it smells like her but amplified to the max. My Alpha is triggered. *Mine. Heat. Protect. Rut.*

A growl bubbles up from deep within my chest, and all I can see is a challenger to my Omega. Baring my teeth at Vic, I shove him out of the way with all my strength. He stumbles back a few steps before catching himself and looking at me in disbelief.

"What the fuck, Simon?" he yells.

"*Mine,*" I growl at him before advancing forward.

Vic's eyes widen in realization. He must know I'm going to beat the shit out of him for daring to touch what's mine.

"Aw shit, this is the last thing we need," he mutters to himself.

I take a swing at him, putting as much power into it as I can, but Vic ducks at the last second and rams his shoulder into my stomach, trying to knock me off my feet. The air rushes out of my lungs, and I fumble back, lying stunned as I try to breathe again. When I realize he's shouting at me and sitting on me, I buck my hips and throw him off me, scrambling to stand up.

We're circling each other now, Vic's hands up, pleading as more words come out of his mouth that don't register in my brain. My aggression won't let me idle, so I take a step forward and clock him on the jaw. Vic's head whips to the side before he looks back at me with determination in his gaze.

Then he gets serious and snaps out a punch so quickly that I miss it. I feel his knuckles make contact with my cheekbone, and while I register that there's pain, it doesn't faze me at all. My arm swings, and my fist lands on his side, a satisfying grunt of pain releasing from him. A savage grin takes over as I get lost in the red haze.

We trade blows back and forth, and I glimpse some blood here and there, but I don't know if it's mine or his. All I know is this challenger needs to be stopped. Fists fly as we battle for dominance, but I can see my competitor flagging, and the red haze that's taken over intensifies. Yes, I'm winning, I can feel it. My opponent surprises me with a tackle, though, and we both fall to the floor, grappling for the top position, fists landing on any body part that they can get to.

My arm wraps around his neck at one point, and I squeeze, trying to cut off his air supply. In a desperate move, he slams his elbow back and manages to land a blow to my solar plexus. The blow loosens my arms, and he wriggles out of my hold, both of us breathing heavily. Then he surges forward and lands on top of me, straddling my chest. My face takes another blow before a sharp hit lands on my temple, and everything goes dark.

MY EYES BLINK OPEN, and the first thing that registers is pain. My face feels like it's been put through a meat grinder, and my torso aches like I was a punching bag for a while. It's evening now, but I swear I came home early from work. I remember leaving the shop, but that's the last thing until now.

The restlessness and crawling feeling under my skin has abated, which is weird. Perhaps I passed out for a nap, and that's what fixed whatever was going on. My arms move to try and stretch over my head, but they're sore enough that I stop halfway.

"Ow," I complain, letting my eyes fully open.

I'm on the couch, which isn't unusual, but when I glance around the room, I see Vic on a nearby chair, looking beat to hell and pissed as all get out. My body freezes, and my eyes track the damage with concern.

"Holy shit, are you okay man? What happened?" I ask, hoping he didn't get mugged or some shit.

Vic just sighs and closes his eyes for a moment before speaking.

"You had to be a fighter instead of a fucker when you rut, didn't you?"

Rut? What does he mean... oh, oh shit. I can't believe I missed the signs. I've never gone into a real rut before, but I know the signs for one.

"Shit, am I the one that?" I gesture to his... well, everything.

Vic just nods.

"Fuck." I close my eyes for a moment before sitting up with a groan and looking at him, "I'm so sorry, man. Shit, I can't believe that happened."

Vic shakes his head and runs his tongue between his teeth and cheeks. I wince as I adjust how I'm sitting.

"You got me good, if that helps," I offer.

Our eyes meet, and I can tell Vic is still upset, but he laughs a little and tips his head back for a moment.

"I tried to talk you down several times, but you must have been deep in it. I'm not pissed that you went into rut, just for the record. I'm pissed at how much of a dick you are when you go into it."

I grimace, "Sorry, man."

He waves me off, "I owe you an apology. I should have talked to you about the Bond stuff before you heard it from Josie, and I should have showered. I just didn't want to lose her scent, but I know now that's what triggered you fully. It must have started when you were at her place."

"Yeah, I've been feeling restless for the last few days, like I'm about to crawl out of my skin. Haven't been able to figure it out, but it makes sense now. Restless, mood swings, and high aggression. Started right after I smelled her going into heat. God I'm a dumbass."

"True, but that's not new information," Vic smirks at me.

I flip him the bird with a smile, and it feels like normal banter again, not the stressful existence we've had lately. We lapse into silence, and now that the rut haze is gone, I'm thinking clearly again. Vic has never acted in a way to hurt me before. It's just not who he is. Obviously, I don't know Henry as well, but if Vic trusts him, I should take that into consideration.

Maybe I'm too hard-headed for my own good when it comes to Packs. The realization that I'm going to have to talk about this with Vic settles uncomfortably with me.

"So, not every Pack is like the one I met in college," I start with.

Vic looks at me, a bit shocked, "No, they're not."

Nodding, I add, "Some Packs are supportive and honest."

"I think *most* Packs are supportive and honest."

"You've never given me reason not to trust you. Josie is my Match. What the hell am I waiting for?" I ask.

Vic smiles, "I don't know. What the hell are you waiting for?"

My returning smile falls a little as I look at Vic, "Is it okay if I wait to bond in? Can I be Pack without bonding?"

I'm terrified about his answer, but I need to hear it from him. Vic's opinion means everything to me.

"Of course you can. You and I are already our own small Pack. We're just bringing more love into the fold."

Standing, I walk over to his chair, albeit stiffly and slowly, and gingerly pull him up with me. My arms wrap around him, holding him tightly. He returns the hold, and while it makes me wince, I don't tell him to ease up.

"I love you, Vic," I choke out.

"I love you, too, Simon. Always have. Always will."

thirty-one

JOSIE

It's been a day since I moved in, and although I've tried, I have checked my bond with Vic more times than I should have. He's been home, mostly, with some time at his office as well. Each time I check, I swear there's a small wave of reassurance that passes over me. I'm not sure if it's my own feelings or his, but either way, it's nice. I haven't had much time to explore the bond with him, but with Henry closer, we've played a bit with sending feelings back and forth.

The experience of having a Matched Mate Bond is otherworldly, and I can only hope that my other two guys come around. Do I want them to, though? I'm so torn on it. My Omega wants them no matter what, but she's a hussy who thinks of her pussy more than anything. My brain is more logical, realizing that what they did was incredibly shitty, and perilously close to rejection. At least, by my definition.

I messaged Georgie to let her know about my situation, and she reassured me that she and James would cover everything. It was reassuring but daunting to know that I'm dropping all my work responsibilities onto my employees. Thinking on that, I'm extra grateful that we hired someone new to take on a single client and paperwork for the time being. Eventually, they'll take more clients than paperwork.

My feet carry me to the kitchen mid-morning, after letting myself laze in the bedroom since waking, I can no longer ignore my hunger. There's a pot of hot coffee, some pastries, and some fruit on the counter. Happily, I make myself a plate, then find the creamer and pour a cup of life into a mug. Looking for a soft place to sit, I wander into the living room, full of a large plush couch and a few loungers.

I slowly get myself settled in and cozy in the multiple blankets lying around, then fully relax as I drink my lifeblood and nibble on goodies. My mood slowly sours as I sit on the couch with my treats. Henry will be home by lunch, and he held me all night long, so I'm not feeling alone and adrift. I'm feeling that hole in my heart where two other Alphas should be. It's easier to ignore those holes if I'm doing something, but when I slow down, the feels take over and it's hard to get going again.

"You gonna cry?" a voice from across the couch asks.

When I sat, I didn't see anyone, so I jumped a bit at the voice. Thankfully, I didn't spill anything. Looking over, I see Ray emerging from a pile of blankets I had thought were just thrown carelessly.

"Oh, hey, Ray," I reply.

"It's okay if you do, you know." She pushes.

I smile, "Yeah, I know, I feel cried out, but I still kind of want to. It's weird."

Ray hums, concern threaded through her voice.

"Did Henry tell you?" I ask.

"Just that you guys bonded, but only him and Vic," she tells me.

"Want to hear some drama, then?"

She holds her hands up, a signal to stop, "Yes! But this calls for chocolate."

Ray hops off the couch and scurries out of the room. When she returns, I've finished my food, but I'm taking my time with my coffee, savoring it as I go. Ray lays her stash of chocolate next to me on the couch, grabs her pile of blankets, and settles in on the other side of her stash.

"This is impressive," I comment, running my fingers through the options.

"Right? When Henry first told me to get what I needed, I went a little wild. Once I figured out what I like, I purchased a shit ton of it. Thus, our stash for today."

Grabbing a piece of chocolate from her stash, I smile at her as I pop it in my mouth. She reaches forward for her own piece, and her scent wafts towards me. I've gotten used to her scent, even though it's not my favorite, but now it almost smells different. Attempting a subtle sniff, I try to figure out what's different about it. It's still extremely floral, but I don't really hate it anymore. I wonder why that is. Ray takes a few moments to select her piece, so I lean forward and grab a second so I'm prepared once I finish chewing this one.

Ray glances up at me for a moment before going back to hunting, "Your scent is different. I'd heard that happens, but haven't really experienced it with someone I know."

"What do you mean?" I ask after swallowing my first piece.

"You're still all cinnamon-y, but now you've got some cedar hints and tiny hints of something else. I can't quite put my finger on it."

I must be emitting some of my Mates' scents now in addition to my own. When I explain that to Ray and clarify she's smelling sandal-wood, her response is a smile and a nod.

"That makes sense! Most people I've met haven't mated yet or have already mated. It's kind of neat smelling the change."

"It's weird being on this end," I tell her, "Your scent is the same, but it's not something I mind anymore."

Ray quirks an eyebrow and talks through her chocolate, "You sayin' I stink?"

"No!" I reply, laughing, "But it was too floral for my own tastes. I wonder if mating with someone means you don't mind other scents as much."

"Now *that* would be cool! Okay, stop stalling, tell me the story," Ray commands.

So, I do. I catch her up on some of the dates, some of my own history with trust issues, and how I got them. I tell her about how I tried my best not to touch anyone with my skin because my Touch Loss means I can't feel a Match through touch, and I didn't want to be lied to again. Then I talked about how each of the guys managed to touch me, and how easy it was to believe them, despite myself. Their smells were too perfect to be anything other than a Match.

I explain the dynamics of the three guys she doesn't know and detail our date to Date 'n' Busters, which gets me a lot of heart eyes and giggles from her. She probably got more detail than she bargained for on my feelings for each of them and how they've grown, but I keep anything beyond kissing out of the story. She gives me knowing looks, telling me that she's well aware of what happens between Matches.

Then, I explain the disastrous teasing of the guys that ended in my heat starting. Her eyes widen in surprise, and her face contorts into anger as I explain how Jesse and Simon didn't stay. How I watched Simon walk out the door after arguing with Henry and Vic. I described the deep loss I felt during my heat and the despondency I'd given in to once Vic and Henry left.

"Then Henry came and swept me away here. He apologized profusely, but I'm the one who pushed him out of the house, thinking I needed to be alone. So I don't think he needs to apologize, and I told him that, but I'm letting him do what he needs to do to feel like he's made amends. I do agree with him on the living together side, though. It feels fast, but it feels right," I finish.

Ray sighs, looking as exhausted as I feel after that story. Her first response is to lean over, toss some of the chocolate my way, then grab her own handful. We eat in companionable silence, letting the weight of my words sink over us.

"Well, shit." Ray finally comments.

For whatever reason, her response hits me and I can't help but giggle. She looks at me, a little confused as to why I'm giggling, but I can't stop now.

"That was so perfect," I explain through the laughter.

We both give in to the moment and just laugh. There's nothing particularly funny about what she said, but the simplicity and the accuracy of her response was so anti-climactic, and that just struck me as funny. A complete laughing fit hits us, and anytime we calm, our eyes meet, and we just start all over again. It's cathartic in a way I didn't know I needed.

When we finally calm down, Ray looks at me and asks, "So, are you, like, super angry?"

"No, I'm just sad," I sigh.

"Well, that's dumb," she says with the tact of all her teenage years.

"Oh?"

"Yeah, I mean, be sad, I guess, but you should be angry. You should be pissed!"

I can see where she's coming from, but I'm not sure if I really have the ability to get angry about it.

"I guess so, I just feel sad and abandoned, you know? It was their choice not to stay. How can I be mad at them for doing what they felt they needed to?"

Ray throws her hands into the air, "How can you *not* be? Yeah, they said they weren't ready for a bond, so why not just ask if they can join but not bond? You weren't exactly in a rational place to think about proposing that, and if they really wanted you so badly, why didn't they fight for you? I'm aware that I'm technically still in high school, but that doesn't mean I'm dumb."

"I never said you were!" I protest.

"I know, I know, I'm just saying I get it more than people would assume for someone my age." She waves me off.

"You are technically an adult," I say, nodding my head in mock seriousness at her.

"Ugh, don't remind me. Henry's going to make me go to college even though I am a legal adult," she whines.

"Don't you want to go? You could tell him you want something else, I think he'd listen," I tell her.

"No, I want to go, I just want to whine about it."

Her response makes me smile, reminding me of myself a little at that age. Knowing you need someone to push you, but not wanting them to do that at the same time.

"Back to you," she pivots the conversation seamlessly.

I sigh in response, "Back to me."

"I know you don't want to, but I think you need to get angry. Tell them how it is and make them Alpha up for you. They don't get something as precious as your sorrow. They deserve your wrath. They deserve to hear *exactly* how they fucked up. There should be romance novel level groveling happening here!" she exclaims.

"Romance novel level? That's pretty intense. How do you know what that looks like?" I ask.

"Never mind that, I just do." She waves me off again.

"Ray…" I taunt her, trying to get her to admit what romance she's reading.

Her phone alarm starts at that very moment, conveniently.

"Oh! Look at the time, I need to get ready and go to my afternoon classes. I tested out of a couple classes, so I get quiet mornings a few days a week. Remember, get angry! You deserve justice for yourself!" Ray cries out as she exits the room.

I watch her go with a small smile on my face. She is going to be a full force of nature when she fully comes into herself. I'm lucky I get to watch her grow and find out exactly who she is as she finishes high school and embarks on college.

The house is quiet once she leaves, and I put my coffee cup into the sink before giving myself a small pep talk.

"Right. Anger. I can do anger. I should do anger. Those two were dickheads and I deserve better! Who do they think they are, anyway?" I say out loud, looking at the tile behind the sink on the kitchen wall.

"Who does who think they are?" I hear Henry's deep voice say.

My head whips to the side, realizing I didn't hear him come into the house.

"Hey!" I exclaim before launching myself at him.

Henry catches me easily and we hum contentedly, neither of us hiding that we have our noses buried in each other's necks, savoring each other's scents. After a moment, Henry pulls back, and once I do as well, he greets me properly with his lips. He walks us further into the kitchen and sets me down on a counter. Unfortunately, that's all he does. I whine as he backs up a half step.

"Who are we getting upset about?" he asks, tucking a hair behind my ear.

"Jesse and Simon. Ray and I talked about things a bit this morning, and she said I should be angry, not sad."

Henry hums, "What do you think?"

"I think I'm both, if I'm being honest. Being angry isn't something I'm used to being, though, and I don't know what to do with it," I confess.

"You tell them *exactly* how you feel and how badly they fucked up."

I nod in agreement, "Okay, yeah, I can do that."

"That's my girl," Henry says with a grin.

"Um, can we have sex first? I would really love an orgasm right now," I ask shyly.

Henry groans, "Fuck yes we can."

He carries me upstairs, inciting giggles from me as we go. Having Henry on my side is everything, and I refuse to let the rest of my Matches back out of this.

This Omega is going to kick some ass. After she gets dicked down.

JESSE

I've done this to myself. I know. That doesn't make it hurt any less. At the moment that Josie was completely vulnerable, I panicked. They all wanted to be Pack and bond, and I chose not to trust them instead of asking for boundaries. Thinking back, I'm not even sure if I tried or not. If I had tried, I know the words would have gotten stuck in my throat.

New people take me a long time to work up to, and as quickly as Josie and I have clicked, it's not the same with the guys. Regret sits heavily in my stomach, but the anti-social part of me is relieved we made it out. We didn't have to have any awkward conversations, the guys didn't have time to give me odd looks, and I would look like a fool in front of Josie.

No, you just looked like a jackass instead.

My inner critic gets a mental middle finger from me. It's annoying when my inner critic is right, especially when I don't want to face my problems. So, I have been doing what I do best: burying myself in work. Today, I surface fully, realizing that I've been operating in a haze. I know I've gotten up and eaten, taken care of myself, but I haven't really registered my surroundings.

My coffee is cold, it probably has been for a while, so I head to the kitchen to pour in some that's hot. When I get there, I find that I've left the pot to sit, and the light is off. Fuck, now I gotta make more coffee. My problem with that is that Josie's house is entirely too visible from my kitchen. The last thing I want is more reminders of my epic fuck up.

Seems like I'm a masochist, though, because as the coffee brews, I can't help but stare out the window that faces her place. After zoning out, I hear the coffee maker beep, indicating that my life-saving fluid is ready for me. Grabbing my mug, I fill it with black coffee and inhale deeply. Second-best smell in the world.

As I turn to go back to my cave of work, I see movement out of the corner of my eye. Josie is leaving her apartment with Henry, who is holding a few of her bags. I'm rooted to the spot as I watch her nuzzle her nose into his chest while he holds her. I should be the one holding her. She should be here with *me*, not him. Fuck everything.

My eyes follow them to the car and watch as they climb in. I get a few glimpses of Josie's face, her eyes red from tears and something weighing her down. Our eyes meet for a long beat, and I can see how beat down she really is. I did that, I contributed to that. She breaks contact and looks down at her lap before Henry pulls out of the driveway and takes her away.

Self-loathing creeps in to reside nicely with the guilt in my gut. I need to suck it up and figure out how to get past my social issues... later, I'll do that later. Work is calling my name right now, so I go bury myself in code again, trying to figure out what needs fixing.

A couple of days later, my boss kicks me off my laptop at noon, threatening to take away all my access if I don't comply. I may have been working 14-hour days the last few days, so maybe he has a point. I've landed myself on the couch, watching daytime judge shows. Some of the judges are badass, and I find myself hooked more than I want to admit. The problem with this situation is that I can't ignore my Alpha instincts. They're loud and angry, making me more torn up inside than I was when I had work to focus on. Now I'm focused on keeping them contained, although my Alpha is not happy with that. There's a demand to wallow in pain and go into a rut to fight out the aggression and disappointment over missing our Match's first heat.

My phone rings next to me, and I look over, noting the time, surprised that so much of my day has gone by. Seeing her name on the phone sends a zip of anxiety through my body, but I can't keep hiding. Not if I really want to be in Josie's life, and I really do want to be. I watch the phone ring for another moment, picking it up at the last moment.

"Um, hi," I answer, eloquent as ever.

"Hey Jesse," her voice is soft and gentle, I wish I could listen to it all day.

I clear my throat, "What's... what's up?"

"I was hoping we could talk. Are you busy today?"

"No, day's wide open. Anything you need," I say, probably too eagerly.

"Okay, I'll be over to your place in a little bit. See you soon."

"Yeah, see you."

She hangs up, and I find myself a little bit thrown. The conversation wasn't pleasant, but it wasn't comfortable either. Is she going to cut me out? Why would she bother doing that in person? Either way, I realize I've left a lot of trash lying around, so I make a point to quickly pick up what I can and toss it in the trash bin. At least then my place doesn't look entirely like a slob lives here.

It only takes about ten minutes for the doorbell to ring. Quickly, I make my way to the door, opening it to see Josie standing there, waiting for me, and also glimpse Henry parked in her driveway. He catches my eye and holds up a hand in greeting. I do the same and step back so Josie can come in.

"Make yourself at home," I tell her, trying for casual.

She steps in with a small smile, but doesn't sit down. Instead, she paces around the living room, noting my sparse decorations and furniture set up. With the door closed, I take a seat on one of the chairs and wait for her to start. Finally, Josie turns, her hands on her hips.

"What the actual fuck, Jesse?" she asks.

I stare at her wide-eyed, trying to think if I just did something wrong, or if she's talking about her heat? Maybe something happened after? Shit, what did I do?

Josie paces, hands still on her hips, "I'm *furious* with you. I don't think I've been this mad in years. YEARS, Jesse!"

Hopefully, my choice to remain silent for the moment is a wise one, because I'm not sure I should interrupt her right now. Josie's eyes nailed me in place for a moment, narrowed and accusing.

"Did you, or did you not promise me that we were going to figure this shit out *together*? That we would talk about Pack stuff and work it out *together*."

"Um, yes, I did promise that," I admit, dreading whatever she has to say next.

She moves again, pacing as she talks, "Did I or did I *not* tell you I have trust issues? That I stop putting my trust in people too easily?"

"Yeah, Jojo, you did," I say, my voice tight with emotion.

"Then what the actual FUCK, Jesse?"

I lean forward and put my forearms on my knees, clasping my hands in front of me. My eyes stay locked on her, and I'm unwilling to look away. She needs me to see and hear this, so I will. Even though it feels like shit to hear how mad she is. My body tenses, ready for more of her verbal blows. The natural instinct to get defensive rises, and I try my best to tamp it down.

"I *needed* you, Jesse! Do you know how awful a heat is when you've met your Match and they leave you hanging? No, I suppose you don't," she waves me off, even though I haven't replied.

Her eyes look glossy, like she's holding tears back, but I don't think she would appreciate me trying to hug her right now. My hands clasp each other harder, and I refrain from attempting to comfort her. Josie needs to get this out and my dumb ass probably needs to hear it.

"I went through my heat disoriented and confused. Something was missing the entire time. It's like eating a chocolate chip cookie without any chocolate chips in it! Yeah, it's a cookie, but something isn't right. *Two* of my Alphas abandoned me the moment shit got serious. You guys were fine to watch the pre-show, but when we got to the main event, you both bailed.

"You have *no idea* how much that fucks with me. I've had enough flings to understand rejection. Do you think I wasn't scared to go through my heat? Do you think I wasn't nervous about bonding? OF COURSE I WAS! But I trusted my Matches, like you should have trusted me."

Josie has tears running down her face now, a slow, steady stream as she lays into me. Belatedly, I realize there are some on mine as well. As she talks, I try to open myself to her pain, and I can see it plain as day now. I'll never fully feel what she does, how could I? The full repercussions of my cowardice finally hitting me.

"Jos—" I start, but she cuts me off with a glare.

We stare at each other for a moment, and I tentatively restart.

"Jojo..." She looks more approving at the nickname. "Words will never be enough to make things right. If you give me half a chance, I'd love to be a servant to you. Do whatever you tell me to do, act however you want me to act."

Standing, I cautiously move the few feet between us and kneel down in front of her. In terms of dominance, Alphas are always at the top. It's just how we're made. Now, though, I'm giving her my subservience, kneeling and exposing my neck to her to show her that she's in charge here. Not me. It's a primal gesture, and based on the widening of her eyes, Josie understands it.

"Stop," she says softly.

I shake my head stubbornly, "No, I can't stop Jojo. I can't stop until I've made things right. Being part of a Pack fucking terrifies me, I'm so used to being alone that it sounds suffocating. Being without you, though? That's pure fucking torture and if there's any chance of getting you back, I will take it."

Her tears start fresh, running down her face, "You never lost me."

"I came too damn close to it. If you hadn't called today, I'm sure I would have been chasing you down sooner rather than later."

"What if I don't want you to? What if I want you to leave me be?" she challenges.

The words spear my chest with pain, but I know she needs to hear my answer. She needs my assurance, and I'm happy to give it to her. In her own style.

"I'm never gonna give you up," I tell her.

Her lips quirk.

"Never gonna let you down," I continue.

"Never gonna run around?"

I shake my head, "Or desert you. Not again."

She smiles, as I'd hoped she would, her love of 80s music shining through. Her face sobers, though, as another thought hits her.

"What if I'm not ready for a full bond any time soon? What if I'm too scared?" she asks.

"Then I will wait as long as it takes. I will support and love you from the side for as long as you let me, until you accept me or send me away. Even if you send me away, though, I'll still look out for you. You're it for me, Jojo."

She kneels down in front of me, placing her hands on either side of my face, "Never gonna make me cry?"

"Never gonna say goodbye," I continue, my hands resting on her hips, "Never gonna tell a lie or hurt you."

Grinning, her eyes still overflow with tears, and I start to get a little worried about her hydration levels.

"You're so cheesy," she accuses me.

Slowly, so she has plenty of time to pull away, I rest my forehead against hers, "Just for you, Jojo. Only you."

thirty-three

JOSIE

Reconnecting with Jesse is everything I hoped for. I was fully prepared to go nuclear on his ass, but, to my surprise, he just took my anger and held it. He didn't interrupt, he didn't try to deny anything. Did he already know how badly he'd fucked up? It sure seems like it. His forehead is on mine, and I draw comfort from the physical touch we have. I may not be able to feel the Match we have, but being able to freely touch him is healing for me.

"What now?" I ask him, "As sweet as this is, I need to know you plan to step up. I need you to tell me what you're going to do to fix this."

I feel a tad guilty putting it all on Jesse, but then I hear Ray in my head reminding me that he's the one who fucked up, not me. I get to be angry and make him work for it. Romance novel level groveling.

"Did you move in with Henry?" he asks softly.

He pulls back, helping me to stand and get more comfortable on the couch as we talk.

"A little. It was only going to be for a few days, but I want to make it permanent, just need to talk to him about it. I can't imagine he'll mind," I confess.

Jesse hums, "Okay then, I'll ask him if there's a place for me there. I don't think I'm ready to fully move in or bond yet, but you need to know I'm in this. So, I'm going to physically be in this."

"Really?" I ask, feeling *more* tears building in my eyes. I'm not sure how I have any left.

"Yes, I want to prove to you that I'm here, and I'm in this. Am I terrified? Yes. Am I going to let it hold me back? Not anymore."

I grin, "Okay."

"Let me text Henry and see about logistics," he offers.

"I should probably talk to Vic and let him know we talked. Henry knew we were going to talk, but I should probably update Vic," I say.

"Yeah, go for it, if you want to call, then you can do it here or go to another room, whichever you're more comfortable with," he offers.

I lean over and surprise him with a kiss on the cheek before pulling out my phone. When I glance up, Jesse is staring at me, slack-jawed and awestruck.

"Careful, you might catch a fly like that," I giggle.

He grins in response and grabs his own phone to start texting Henry. I pull up Vic's contact and hit the "call" button. While I won't put him on speakerphone, I also don't feel the need to go to a different room.

"Josie Girl!" he greets me.

"Hey you, how are you?" I can feel my grin stretching across my face.

"I'm better now that I get to hear your voice," he teases.

I giggle, "Such a charmer."

"What's up?"

"I wanted to check in with you and let you know Jesse and I talked," I tell him.

"Oh? Did it go well?" Vic asks gently.

"Yeah! I'm at his place now. He's actually texting Henry about moving in a little bit."

"That's awesome! I'm so glad he was willing to hear you and fix it. You'll have to let me know when he is thinking of moving in."

"Absolutely!" I reply, "Have you thought more about moving in, too? I know it's tricky with Si."

Vic grunts, "Hopefully soon, I might at least pick a day or two per week to stay there to start. I, uh, I don't want to leave Si right now, but I don't want to be away from you either."

"What's up with Si?" I ask, frowning at the tone of his voice.

Vic hesitates for a moment before responding, "He… he went into rut and while he's out of it, he's feeling pretty shitty about it."

"Is he there now?" Panic starts to settle in at the idea of Si suffering.

Vic hesitates, "Yeah, he took a couple of days off."

"I'm coming over," I tell him, hanging up before he can respond.

Jesse looks at me with concern, "Everything okay?"

I gather my phone and purse before sliding my shoes on.

"Si went into rut, and Vic said he's fine, but Vic sounded off, and I need to see him."

"Do you want me to come?" Jesse offers.

I shake my head, "No, I don't want to set him off more with another Alpha present. It means a lot, though, that you're willing to come help."

"May I hug you?" he asks, coming closer.

I hold my arms out, and he sweeps me up in his arms and we nuzzle each other for a moment before letting go. We're both smiling as we let go, and Jesse reaches up to caress my cheek.

"Good luck, call me if you need me, okay? Even if you just need something sugary to eat," he says.

My smile is stuck in place as I reply, "I will, promise."

Part of the reason I had Henry drop me off is so I can retrieve my own car. My keys are already in my purse, so I hop in the driver's seat and take off for Vic and Simon's house as quickly as I can. There's a distinct possibility that I push past the speed limit, but I admit to nothing. Quicker than usual, I pull into their driveway and park.

I want to just barge in and see what the hell is making Vic so nervous and on edge, but I pull the desire back and knock instead. Nobody answers in the first five seconds, so of course, I knock a second time, and harder than the first. The door opens, and my eyes land on Vic's face.

He looks like shit, a bruise showing on his cheekbone, one eye is black, and his lip is split and swollen. His eyes meet mine, sheepishly.

"Hey," he greets me.

"Vic! You said he went into rut not that he beat the shit out of you!" I cry, "Let me in."

He steps aside, hesitantly, and I glare at him, daring him to prevent me from checking on one of my Alphas. Is he officially my Alpha? Well, no, and I'm supposed to be mad at him. I'm still claiming him for the moment, though, until one of us formally rejects the other. My nostrils flare wide as I try to scent where he is, but I find him as soon as I turn the corner.

Simon is sitting on the couch, leaning forward with his head in his hands. I stride over to him and sink down to my knees in front of him. I need to see how bad off he is. He was the one in rut, but I'm sure Vic held his own. He would have wanted to end the fight as quickly as he could. Simon stays in his position, head down, hands covering his face. I can tell by the deep inhalation he takes that he's well aware I'm the one who rang the doorbell.

"Let me see," I say gently, grabbing his wrists.

He refuses to move, "No, I did this to myself, it's not your problem to deal with."

Now *that* pisses me off.

"Are you *fucking* kidding me, right now?" I seethe at him.

He tenses but doesn't move or speak.

"You know what, Simon? Fuck you. Fuck you for introducing yourself to me, fuck you for showing me your soft side, fuck you for making me think that you could be rational and discuss things with me, and *fuck you for loving Vic,*" the amount of venom in my voice surprises me, and I realize *this* is the anger that Ray was talking about.

Yeah, Jesse needed some sense talked into him, but he's shown me time and time again that he's willing to try. He owned his fuck up, and now he's taking immediate steps to show me he's trying.

Simon? He's sitting here wallowing in his own damn self-pity like he's a goddamn martyr. I fell for his fucking act too. He came in shy and reserved, Matched me, kissed me like I was his air, but didn't do anything more. We never went past kissing, and we never had individual time together.

Now, he's put Vic in between a rock and a hard place. He clearly loves Vic, and whatever he's done has made Vic love him too. I won't make Vic choose, he's bonded to me, and I can feel his turmoil. If he wants to split his time half and half, he can do that. I won't stop him. I won't allow Simon to play this game, though.

I stand and step away, glaring at Simon.

"I'm not going to beg you, I don't even want to. You don't consider anyone but yourself and Vic. That's fine, be with Vic. Know that you're putting him between a rock and a hard place, though, because I'm not going to make him choose. I'll just refuse to see you," I tell him.

Simon still hides his face when he clears his throat, "Are you rejecting me?"

His voice is tight, and I'm not sure if he's resisting tears or anger.

"No, Simon, I won't do that to you. If you want out, you have to make that choice. However, I don't have to see you or talk to you unless you're going to own your shit."

I pivot on my heel, not wanting to see if Simon finally looks up or not. My anger fades, giving way to a deep sorrow that I didn't know I was capable of. I want to mate bond him, so I won't reject him. Even now, in my anger, I know that we would be great together. I've done enough chasing him, though. He can choose to chase me and show me he wants this, or he can live in misery. I have two bonds who love me and a third who wants to show me.

As I storm out of the room, I run straight into Vic, who looks like he's going to murder Simon. I grab his hand and pull him out of the house with me. When we're outside, I turn and bury my face into his chest. Vic's arms immediately come around me, and my tears come fast and furious. I can feel his hand stroking my hair back as I cry out my frustration, my anger, and my sorrow.

Vic leads me to my car and bundles me into the passenger seat before walking around and settling in behind the wheel. He pulls out of the driveway and starts toward Henry's house. I stare out the window, my tears still going, my fingers interlocked with Vic's as he drives. I hadn't expected Simon to shut me out so thoroughly, and I responded with a vehemence that surprises even me.

Once Vic parks my car, he ushers me out of the passenger seat and into the house. It's quiet, and I'm sure Henry is in his office working. I turn to Vic once we step further into the house.

"Thanks for driving me to Henry's. I, uh, I can call you an Uber if you want. Or you can take my car and I'll pick it up later," I say through a stuffy nose.

Vic looks at me with fire in his eyes, "I'm not leaving you right now, Josie Girl. You need your mates to look after you, and that's exactly what we're going to do. Si and I had a breakthrough when his rut broke yesterday, so I have no idea what the fuck his problem is. You deserve better."

His hand cups my cheek, and our lips meet tenderly, Vic's reassurance flooding down our bond and my own desire threading through his. I send a tendril of desire through Henry's bond too, but based on the distant groan of "Fuck," I might have sent too much. My hands reach up and thread through Vic's hair, messing it up quite thoroughly. I moan in pleasure as Vic nips at my lips before moving down my chin to my neck, licking, sucking, biting any skin he can find.

Henry's scent hits me before I hear his footsteps. When he's close enough, I hear a pleased rumble come from his chest. His hands land on my hips and he pulls them back, my ass landing on his already hard cock. Henry dips his head to lick and nibble the other side of my neck before moving up to take my lips.

"What's the occasion for such a sweet return home?" he asks.

"Simon's being an asshole," Vic grumbles against my neck before he pulls back.

I can't see the look that passes between them, but I feel the tension between the three of us ramp up higher.

"I guess we'd better assure our Omega that her bonded mates are going to put her first," Henry suggests.

Vic hums in agreement, and I nod frantically, wanting their reassurance and love.

"Let's give our Omega the pleasure she deserves," Vic agrees.

thirty-four

VIC

Watching Simon refuse Josie's care incited an anger in me that I wasn't aware I possessed. After his rut, I thought things would smooth out; he would be able to surface with reasonable thought, knowing that he hadn't fully ruined anything. We talked everything out, assured each other that we still loved the other, but then he went and pulled today's bullshit. For now, though, Josie needs me more.

When Henry and I locked eyes, I could feel his intention down the bond we share. So, I pick Josie up and throw her over my shoulder as I follow Henry up to where she's staying. When we walk into the room, I realize it's the Pack suite. My eyes dart to Henry, and he nods with a little smile, confirming my thoughts about what the room is. I grin and plop Josie down on the bed mattress, which smells like the two of them already.

Henry looks at his phone for a moment before glancing at Josie and me. He nods to himself and sets the phone down after sending a message, and removes his shirt. Not about to be left behind, mine flies off as well, and I move to stand between Josie's legs.

She parts beautifully for me, and I lift her shirt inch by inch, kissing her skin as I go. I savor the soft texture of her skin and let out a slight rumble of appreciation for the rolls she carries. There's something so fucking sexy about a woman who carries extra weight, and I plan to make that clear to Josie as long as she'll have me.

Henry moves to her head and helps me to lift the shirt off her, fully exposing her torso to us, her breasts held in by a delicate, lacy bra. My hands move to her pants as Henry cups her, plucking at her nipples through the lace and making her moan in pleasure. He pinches her just right, and I can smell the rush of slick that escapes her. She smells like heaven, and I unashamedly place my nose directly between her legs and take a large inhale. My mouth waters at her scent, and the moment for subtlety and gentleness is gone. I yank her pants and her panties off, exposing her bare pussy to me.

"Fuck, you're so damn gorgeous," I tell her, tossing her pants to the side.

Her hips buck, seeking some friction to relieve the ache that Henry is expertly building with his talented tongue and fingers. I grab her hips with my hands and hold her down before swiping my tongue through her folds, from her hole to her clit. I thrust my tongue into her hole and try to lick up as much slick as I can while it continues to pour out of her. I use my forearm to hold her hips as I readjust, thrusting two fingers into her and sucking at her clit.

Josie cries out in pleasure and I can feel my cock starting to drip pre-cum at the sounds she's making. Her tight channel surrounding my fingers is heaven and I can't wait to feel her around my cock again. I slip a third finger in and begin to thrust in and out of her at a rough, rapid pace, alternating between sucking, biting, and licking at her clit. Her walls start to tighten, and I rumble in pleasure against her clit, wanting to feel her let go. Only a moment later, she detonates, squeezing the life out of my fingers and dripping slick down my hand. I ease her down from her high and rise so she can see me.

I have every intention of making her watch as I lick her off my fingers, but Henry surprises me by grabbing my wrist and sucking her juice off my fingers. Josie's breath catches in disbelief, and her eyes are riveted to where my fingers are in Henry's mouth.

"Holy fuck, that's so hot," she breathes.

Henry and I both grin before moving to remove the rest of her clothing. When his phone beeps on the nightstand, he takes a glance at it before smirking and returning his attention to Josie.

"How do you feel about one more, Josie?" he asks, mischief showing in his eyes.

Josie's eyes go wide as she looks at him. He lies on his back and encourages her to sit on him. Without preamble, he lines up his cock and slams into her, making Josie's head fly back and shout with pleasure. Henry looks at me and taps her ass, making me grin. I'll gladly take her ass. I hunt for lube as they continue the conversation.

"You didn't answer me, Omega," he growls, holding her tight against his pelvis as he grinds up into her.

She moans in pleasure, her eyes closed like she's savoring the moment. When I settle in behind her and pop the cap of the lube open with a soft *click*, she startles and tries to look. I reach around and grab her chin, keeping her face forward.

"Your Alpha is asking you a question, Omega," I rumble in her ear before I push her forward to dribble lube down her crack.

"What—what did you ask?" she asks Henry.

"I asked how you feel about one more joining us," he says, taking shallow thrusts now so that I can get my lubed fingers into her tight hole.

"Who?" she asks.

Henry smacks her ass gently before growling, "That's for your Alpha to know, and for you to find out. You just tell me 'Yes, Alpha' or 'No, Alpha' and tell me what you want. Trust me to give it to you if you want it."

I gently circle her back hole with one finger, loving the full body shiver she gives us, before starting to press in.

Josie gasps, "Yes, Alpha! Please Alpha! Oh, fuck, Vic that feels so good!"

"Good girl," Henry rumbles. Then he peers around me toward the door and nods.

To my surprise, I scent Jesse walk into the room. I refuse to lose concentration, though, and gently work my finger into Josie's back hole. We didn't take her here during her heat, but I'm wishing we had now. I don't want to wait, but I will for her. I refuse to cause her physical pain.

"Push against my fingers, Josie Girl," I encourage her.

She does just that, and my finger pops past her tight ring of muscle. I add a little more lube to my finger as I push it in and out, trying to keep things as smooth as possible. She gasps for more, so I ensure a second finger is lubed up and gently insert it alongside the first.

While I prep her, Jesse moves into her line of sight and gathers her hair into one hand, angling her head a little so they can see each other.

"Look at you, Jojo, taking your Alpha's cock while your Beta preps you. You're a dirty girl, aren't you?" he purrs at her.

She nods her head frantically, hoping he'll give her more. I'm surprised at his dirty talk as I slide a third finger into Josie. Her moans of pleasure only add to her frantic agreement. Jesse slams his lips against hers as Henry picks up the pace. I practice alternating thrusts with my fingers and his dick, before she feels good and loose.

I pull my fingers out of her and glance to the side when I see movement. Jesse is passing me a wipe from a small container in his hand before setting out hand sanitizer. I nod my thanks to him, quickly cleaning my fingers before dripping more lube down Josie's crack and ensuring my cock is fully coated. Henry slows his thrusts down and holds Josie still as I begin to push in. She tenses for a moment at the intrusion.

"Relax for me, Josie Girl," I encourage her softly.

She starts to relax, but I can tell she's stuck in her own head, unable to fully let go. Henry notices her hesitation and provides direction.

"Do you need a distraction, Omega? Would you like Jesse to distract you so your Beta can slide in?"

"Yes, please," she whimpers.

Henry swats her ass.

"Yes, Alpha!" she corrects.

Henry rumbles in appreciation of her correction, "Jesse, give her mouth something to do."

He hesitates only a moment before ripping his shirt off and unbuttoning his jeans. Josie reaches out and pulls him close, trying to help him pull his jeans down far enough that she can get his dick out. He gets his boxers and jeans low enough that they sit under his balls before she grabs his hardened cock and licks it like an ice cream cone.

The sight makes my own cock jump, thinking about how good her mouth will feel. She wraps her lips around his tip and sucks gently on it. The distraction works, and I make sure to add a little more lube before pushing in more. I'm a big proponent of lube, it should be used almost in excess when in someone's ass. She pushes against me like a pro, and I fully pop in past the ring of muscle. It's so tight already, then add Henry's cock into the mix and my own feels like it's going to be strangled in the best way.

We begin to find a rhythm, sawing in and out of her alternatively, the alternation only highlighting the feel of Henry's dick sliding against mine. I don't know if Henry and I will ever take that step together, but feeling him now is so erotic, I don't even care. Jesse has his head tipped back in pleasure, his mouth just about slack-jawed.

"Fuck, Jojo, your mouth feels so damn good. Can I fuck your throat? Only if you want, baby, god, your mouth is killing me," he rambles.

I'm not sure why I'm surprised, but Josie stops bobbing her head at the base of Jesse's cock and waits for him. Her eyes start to water, and I realize she's letting herself choke on him so he'll take over, and she doesn't have to stop. Jesse figures it out quickly and lets her stay there for another moment before pulling back so she can breathe again.

"Goddamn," Henry moans, beginning to pick up his pace.

All I can do is breathe and keep up with Henry's pace, trying not to blow first. The room is a symphony of moans and wet noises with skin slapping together. Josie's voice gets higher and higher as she gets closer to her release.

"Come for us, Josie Girl, let us see you shatter," I encourage her.

It's only a moment later that I feel her body spasm around my dick, and I'm betting she's choking Henry just as hard based on his face. The scream she lets out is muffled by Jesse's cock which sets him off. He groans as he comes, spilling out of her mouth, one hand on his knot, squeezing it to string out his pleasure.

My own pleasure sets off and I can feel the tingles start in my balls before it explodes across my body, my dick shooting hot cum into Josie's ass harder than I thought possible. Making choked noises, I finally finish and force myself to pull out faster than I want so Henry can knot her. Chances are, I could stay nestled in her ass, but for her first time, I didn't want to get myself stuck there and cause her panic.

Henry shoves his knot deep into her, locking them together with a roar of pleasure, sending Josie off on another orgasm. She cries out and then flops down on top of Henry as he holds their hips tightly together. He pulls her knees up just a tad and pulls her down on his chest to fully rest. Jesse and I get comfortable on either side of them, both of us ensuring we touch Josie.

It's a perfect moment, except for one missing person.

JESSE

It's been a couple of weeks since I moved into Henry's house part-time, but I'm surprised at how easy it's been. Vic has been here more than I have, but I'm beginning to feel like this is where I should be. These are the people I want to be around. So far, I only stay on the weekend, but I may extend that through Monday soon. Who am I kidding? I'll probably jump all the way in with my time.

Bonding still sounds like too much for me, but the idea gets easier and easier to digest each day. Once I move in full time, I'll sit down with the Pack and have a serious conversation about what bonding would look like. It wouldn't be fair of me to just bond Josie and not complete a Pack bond. I think Josie would always feel a bit off kilter, and I'm worried it will make me feel more alone than accepted.

Today is one of the rare days when I need to be in the office, and so far I've managed small greetings when people send one my way. Nobody is used to me actually recognizing their greetings, so it causes a bit of a stir when I start to do that. I still want to be alone more than the average person, but being forced to socialize with the Pack and Ray so much, it's becoming easier.

The morning of my day is spent at my desk, mostly avoiding

people, but also saying 'hi' if I'm spoken to. However, the afternoon finds me in a massive conference room, listening to one of our many directors and VPs talk about the upcoming projects we have. There were a couple of tries to let people dial in and listen, but it became too difficult to hear, and the system got overloaded. So, anyone within a certain radius was asked to come in, and the system was updated so those far away could still dial in.

My boss catches me after the meeting and pulls me to his office. I sit down in one of the chairs across from his desk and wait to see what he's going to say. We sit in silence for a moment while he figures out what he wants to say.

"Omega?" he asks.

I nod, "Yes, sir."

"Pack?"

"Not quite yet," I confess.

He nods and continues to think.

"Not my business, I just wanted to touch base with you. You had a frantic week a little bit ago, and now you're saying hi to people. Keep doing what you're doing. You seem happier."

"Thanks, boss, I feel it," I tell him with a smile.

He returns it with his own small one and waves me out of his office, grumbling about the month-end financials. He's a good guy, and if I had refused to tell him, he would have been okay with that. However, he's had my back for years, so I feel comfortable giving him the information because I know he won't pry.

When I get into my car to head home, I decide I want to spend the evening at Henry's. I send a quick message to the chat with him and Vic to ensure there are no other plans, and then head toward downtown. It's been a bit since I got Josie a present, and I want to bring her something. My Alpha is itching to provide for his Omega, to keep begging for the forgiveness we're trying to earn.

I'm tempted to go to the Omega shop and get her something soft, but I decide to go a different route. There's a small music shop a little way down from the Omega store, so I stop in there first. For a small shop, they have a huge variety of things to choose from. There's a section for CDs, one for tapes, one for records, and even a small merch section. I head there first, and after perusing the selection, I find the jackpot item.

Underneath a few other folded shirts, I see a Rick Astley shirt that she absolutely needs to have. The shirt is cream-colored, with neon lettering spelling his name, and his picture in black and white, framed by a colorful square and a blue squiggle line. It's a size XXL, but I don't think it will matter to Josie. If it's too big, she can wear it as pajamas or something.

"Is this actually vintage?" I ask the cashier as he processes my purchase.

He inspects the shirt, "I don't think so, but I'm not sure. I don't do the purchasing."

Fair enough. I give him my payment and leave the shop, walking down the sidewalk. Coffee is calling my name before I head home, so I amble down to Simon's coffee shop. I'm torn on the inside about whether or not I want to actually see him. The man has great taste in coffee, so I want to support his business; however, on the other hand, he hasn't reached out to Josie at all. He also hasn't outright rejected her, so it's hard to tell where he stands.

The shop is busy when I walk in, but the line moves quickly. I order and step to the side to wait, noting a distinct lack of Simon. I'm not sure if it's good or bad quite yet, but when my name is called, I step forward to grab my coffee regardless. As I'm about to turn and leave, I glance up and see Simon looking at me from just beyond the registers. He's standing in the back hallway to the offices, looking unsure and insecure. I gesture with my head for him to follow me, but I turn before waiting to see if he does.

I couldn't tell you why I invited him to follow me out. Maybe I'm a glutton for punishment, trying to socialize more. Maybe I saw something in his eyes that triggered compassion in me. I don't know, but I'm not trying to figure it out. I'm just going with the flow here. Once I exit the cafe, I glance behind me to see Simon not more than a few steps behind me. We take a few steps away from the doors and stop to look at each other.

"Well?" he asks.

"What?"

He frowns, "You motioned for me to follow you."

"True," I shrug.

"Do you need something?"

"Do *you*?" I counter, like a smartass.

He scoffs, "I don't have time for this."

"Seems like you have a lot of time, if you ask me," I tell him, raising a brow.

Simon pinches his nose between his eyes, "Stop with the games and say what you wanna say."

"You ever gonna call her?" I straight out ask.

"Why would I? She's too good for me," he counters.

I shrug like I don't care, when I actually care deeply about what he chooses to do.

"Then reject her," I tell him.

He blanches, "Absolutely not!"

"Right, so you won't go to her and try to fix anything, but you also won't let her go. You've got to choose, man, you don't get to have your cake and eat it too."

"It's not like you have room to talk," Simon retorts, "You left during her heat, too."

"I did. I left. Then she kicked my ass. She dressed me the fuck down, and I let her. Because I fucked up. Then I stopped feeling sorry for myself and started fixing things."

"You make it sound easy," he scoffs.

"Because it is!" I all but shout at him, "It is easy! You admit you fucked up, let her have whatever reaction and interaction she needs, then *be there for her.*"

Simon looks down at the ground, surprising me by breaking eye contact first. I step closer to him and force his eyes back on mine.

"If my anti-social, emotionally stunted ass can understand that and then be there for her, there's no reason you can't too. This act you're pulling is damaging and unattractive. I'm surprised Vic still puts up with it."

Simon's eyes flash with hurt, and he moves around me to go back into the cafe.

Was that a low blow? Hell yes, it was, but it's true. I am surprised Vic still puts up with this shit. How is he not over it? How has Josie not rejected him yet? It's not my place to question their relationships, so I don't. If Simon shows up for them, I'll happily include him going forward. The longer he does this, though, the closer I get to snapping. I can see the strain it's putting on Josie and Vic, and how Henry feels helpless to do anything.

On the way back to Henry's, I force myself to confront some shit. Henry is trying to keep the three of them balanced and together. Normally, they would all share the burden, but I can see the burnout happening in Josie and Vic as they try to battle the hole left by Simon in their lives while supporting the Pack. If there were more than three of them, they wouldn't have to work so hard. They could focus on healing their pain, and others could be the caretakers of the bonds.

To keep a bond strong, the Pack and its mates need to tend to each other, showering one another with love and physical contact. Help remind the ones who suffer that they're not alone in this world. That's a big burden for one person to do for two people, especially with one as a Match. It just increases the feelings that much more.

Maybe I should just jump in. The three of them have made it abundantly clear that if I need space, I have only to ask. More than once, they've left me to my own devices until I felt ready to engage again. The idea of sharing a bond with them is terrifying and comforting all at once. I'd never be truly alone again, but I also would understand the group better. Maybe there's a way to learn how to shut the bond down some, just stifle the emotional flow for a little bit if I get overwhelmed.

It's scary, but I know exactly what needs to happen, and I'm not going to put it off. When I get back to Henry's, I see everyone's car sitting there, and I know it's going to be an event. Especially since Ray is also home. She is one big personality, and I can't help but smile at her enthusiasm for life. Also, her sass. I need to pay attention and learn from her.

Everyone is in the kitchen, and Vic is cooking with some help from Ray while Josie and Henry observe with extremely unhelpful commentary.

"You call that chopping? My grandma chops faster than you!" Josie fires out in a fake angry voice.

"Hey! Don't forget who's cooking your food over there! I can easily burn it! I'm a Beta on the edge!" Vic replies.

"I need some popcorn for this show," I comment as I stand in the entryway to the kitchen.

Josie's head whips toward me, and she squeals, "Jesse!"

I meet her halfway as she hops down from her spot at the counter and runs to greet me. My arms wrap around her, holding her tightly as she holds me, my coffee abandoned on the counter so I can hold her. The bag from the music shop is still in my hand, and Josie notices it after a moment.

"What's this?" she pulls back to see.

I grin, "Couldn't resist getting my Omega a gift."

She lights up and grins, "Gimmie gimmie gimmie!"

Laughing, I hand it over to her, enjoying the pure joy she exudes from receiving a gift. She peeks in and gasps, yanking the shirt out and letting the bag fall to the floor. After a quick evaluation, she holds the shirt closely to her.

"Thank you!!" she squeals before attacking my mouth with hers.

I happily respond to her enthusiasm and put all of myself into the kiss, but I know dinner is going to happen soon, so we don't go further. Before I fully let her go, my eyes meet hers, and my voice is steady as I speak.

"I want to bond with you, Josie. I want to bond the Pack. I want to be in, fully and completely."

A coughing noise terribly hides Ray saying, "That's what she said," and the entire romantic declaration goes out the window.

Vic starts cracking up, Ray is giggling up a storm, Josie is trying not to laugh, and Henry is doing his best to remain firm. Spoiler alert: he's failing.

"Ray, really right now?" Henry chides.

Ray just shrugs, "You want a mature and romantic moment? Don't do it in a room with an immature teenager."

There's more laughter and banter, but before we sit, Josie turns back to me and leans in to whisper to me.

"Yes."

SIMON

Vic has been gone from the house more and more. I'm eating dinner alone again and wondering what the fuck is wrong with me. When Vic and I talked about Pack and relationships, I thought I had it worked out. I felt confident, like it was going to be okay.

When Josie found out about my rut, it all crumbled. There was so much shame in me, as if I'd failed her by being unable to control myself. When it was just Vic and me, it was easy to believe him, and I was planning to talk to Henry and Josie after both Vic and I were healed. Instead, Josie caught on to something in Vic's voice and came here before I was ready.

The horror in her voice still rings in my ears, and the only phrase that I can hear is "How could you do this?" I can't remember if she really said that, but it's her voice I hear when that question runs through my brain. How could I maim her best friend like that? How could I attack the man I'm in love with? What if I attack her next? Shame threatens to swallow me whole, and there are some moments when I want to let it.

My gourmet dinner of cold pizza that's been in the fridge too long settles like a rock in my stomach. I need some air. Grabbing a beer, I leave via the front door and head to my truck. While it's technically a truck, it's not full-size and it's not used for hauling anything. It was just the right price at the right time a few years ago.

There's a camping chair in the bed, so I open it and sit in the back of my truck on the chair, one foot resting on the side of the truck bed. It's a peaceful evening in a quiet neighborhood. The weather is beautiful, and by all rights, I should feel calm and relaxed. Too bad the only thing that can fix me is the woman I drove away. Pretty sure Vic is on the edge of leaving, too.

My head flops back and hangs off the back of the chair a bit, letting the wind blow gently through the curls on my head. Maybe I'm just meant to sabotage everything, be alone for the rest of my life because of one shitty experience that I'm letting dictate my fears. A car pulls up nearby, but I leave my head back, eyes locked on the darkening sky as clouds gently float by.

Footsteps get closer, then break apart. One set goes toward the house, and I hear the door open and shut. The other set turns into a body that's climbing into my truck bed. There's a shift in the balance of the truck as the person sits down on the other side of the bed. It's silent for longer than I anticipate it being, so I turn my head toward my companion.

Jesse's sitting with his forearms on his knees, looking at me. Frowning, I pull my head up and brace myself for the small head rush of having my head leaned back for so long. Neither of us says anything for a few moments, we just look each other over. Not quite sizing each other up, but assessing how the other is looking. I have a feeling Jesse wins in the battle of looking like he has his life together.

"What's up?" I finally ask.

"Vic needed to grab some stuff. We saw you sitting here, so I figured I'd come sit with you."

My brows draw into a frown. "You don't like interacting with people."

"I'm workin' on it," he shrugs, "it's getting easier with Pack."

"Must be nice," I mutter before taking a swig of beer.

Jesse whistles, like he's just seen something unexpected.

"That's some top-notch wallowing you got goin' on there," he comments.

I scoff, "Is it wallowing if it's your life? I fucked it all up again and there's nobody else to blame."

"Again? I thought your Pack trauma dumped you, not the other way around."

"They did, but there was clearly something wrong with me for them to do that," I sigh.

"Jesus, dude, you're more emo than My Chemical Romance back in the day."

I've never listened to the band, but his comment isn't wrong, and all I can think of now is pulling my hair over one eye and getting some black eyeliner. Which then triggers the laugh. Jesse chuckles a little before we both sober up again.

"Can I tell you something?" I ask.

"Yeah, sure, not like I got friends to gossip with. On purpose."

I look away for a moment before meeting his eyes again, "I feel like I already failed Josie and the Pack by going into rut. My dumb ass walked out on her heat, then went into rut and beat the shit out of Vic."

"From what I heard, he got a few licks in and took you down."

"Thankfully," I agree.

"Why do you feel like going into rut is bad?" Jesse asks with an open expression.

"I don't like feeling out of control, and I especially don't like *being* out of control. Since I wasn't there for her heat, I had no reason to go into rut. No real reason, and massive amounts of being out of control. What if I had seriously injured Vic? What if it happens again and I hurt Josie?"

Jesse smiles, "What if Josie lets you fuck it out of your system?"

I blink dumbly at him, startled into silence by the question.

"I mean it, what if she did? What if Vic did? What if you let the Pack be there for you instead of assuming you did anything wrong? Going into rut isn't shameful, Simon, it's biology," Jesse says.

"I pushed her away. What if she doesn't let me try again?" I try another argument.

Jesse smirks, "You know what I'm going to say, right?"

Sighing like a petulant child, I admit, "What if she does?"

"Exactly! Now before you can overthink shit again, get in that house and make up with your man. He's almost as mopey as your ass when he thinks nobody is looking. He misses you."

"You're surprisingly observant," I comment.

"If you tell anyone about that, I'll deny it," Jesse jokes.

Deciding that Jesse is right, I stand and face him with my hand out. He grasps it, and we do a bro hug before I hop down from the truck bed and go inside. Time to fix my shit for real this time.

Vic

Seeing Simon in the truck bed tears at my heart when Jesse and I pull up to the house. When I said I needed to grab a few things, he asked to come along for "bonding time," so I invited him along. We haven't talked much at all, except for him to shoo me into the house while he sits with Simon.

My office is the first stop. I need to grab a few more pads of sticky notes and some pens. Henry has extra monitors, so we set up a decent workspace for me already at his house. I've been spending Friday through Monday there, but lately Tuesdays have been creeping in as well. Everything feels so right with the Pack that it's hard to leave.

As I step into the bedroom, I'm faced with the physical reminder of why I came back here. I can smell Simon's Vanilla/Orange combination permeating the room we've been using. He never did move to a different one. My own Sandalwood weaves throughout Simon's scent; not as strong, but they complement each other well.

I grab a bag from my side of the closet space and add my office supplies to it. Then I rifle through my clothing, trying to pick a few more pieces to keep at Henry's. I will definitely need another pair of shoes, so those will get set in the back as well. The process takes a few minutes, and by the time I'm zipping up my bag, it's pretty damn full. Finally coaxing it to close, I turn to leave the room and see Simon standing in the doorway.

We stand and stare at each other for a moment, and he has a hard time meeting my eyes. I know he's been wallowing in shame since he denied Josie's care, but I haven't really tried to bring him out of it. The behavior was so unlike the Simon I know that I couldn't reconcile who I knew him to be with the cold version he presented to Josie. My heart feels like it's torn in two between the two of them. I just want to love them both; is that too much to ask? Lately, it seems like that.

"Hey," Simon finally breaks the silence.

"Hi," I refuse to give him an out.

Petty? Yes. Do I care? No.

He clears his throat, "I owe you a couple of apologies."

"Okay," I drag out the word, curious what he thinks he needs to apologize for.

"I'm sorry for how I treated Josie. I'm sorry for embarrassing you. I'm especially sorry that I went into rut and beat the shit out of you," he says.

That... was not what I was expecting.

"Si. I'm not mad at you. I miss you," I tell him.

He looks at me in surprise, "You do?"

"Of course I do! You're clearly torn up about how Josie learned about your rut, and I figured when you were ready to talk, you'd come to me. I just didn't want to push you after we'd had our last talk."

Simon runs a hand down his face, "God, I'm an idiot."

"But you're *my* idiot," I say with a small smile.

That earns me a short laugh in return, and I feel hopeful as a result.

"I'm embarrassed. I let things get out of control, beat the shit out of you, then took it out on Josie," he says.

Gently setting my bag on the ground, I walk over closer to him and grab his face gently in my hands.

"Baby, *I* beat the shit out of *you*. Nice try though, I knocked your ass out," I tell him.

He pushes me away playfully, grinning at my cheek.

"What brought all this on, anyway? I'm glad you're talking to me, but it's a bit of a surprise," I confess.

"Jesse."

"Jesse?"

"Yeah, he's a good guy," Simon confirms.

I nod in agreement, "He really is. It's been nice to get to know him, and he's happy to just exist in a room with people, no pressure to socialize."

Simon scuffs his shoe against the carpet.

"I need to apologize to Josie. She deserves that from me at minimum. Do you think she'll hear me out? Will Henry? Be brutally honest, man," Simon asks.

"They will. But I know Josie will want actions, not words. I also know Henry will follow Josie's lead, but he doesn't hold grudges."

Simon nods, taking in the information with care. His hand reaches out to grab mine.

"Thank you," he tells me.

I pull him in, wrapping my arms around him. He returns the gesture, and we hold each other for a few moments, just enjoying the feel of our bodies together again. My nose buries itself in Simon's neck, taking in a fresh hit of his scent. He pulls back and bends down to kiss me gently. I return it, hoping that this is the time he really does pull his shit together.

"Do you think I could swing by this evening?" he asks, and I can see his brain working on an idea.

"Probably, Jesse said he wants to bond in, but I'm not sure it'll be tonight. Plan to come over unless I text you, is that okay?"

"Yes, let's do that. I need to pack some shit and grab my car keys," he says, mostly to himself by the end.

I grab my bag and hoist it over my shoulder.

"Do you need directions?" I ask.

He waves me off from the closet, calling, "No, I got it."

I smile and head down the stairs, back out the front door. Jesse hears the door close and hops out of Simon's truck. Jesse ambles over as I put my bag into the backseat. When I close the door, I see Jesse standing at the front of the car, waiting for me before he walks around to the passenger side.

"Good talk?" he asks.

I raise an eyebrow at him, "You are a smooth talker, you know that? I'm keeping my eye on you."

Jesse smirks, "I don't know what you're talking about."

We get into the car, and I laugh as we drive back home to Henry's. I can't wait to bond him in and get Simon's ass in gear.

thirty-seven

JOSIE

Vic and Jesse walk into the house with very different expressions on their faces. Jesse looks smug, almost like he knows something the rest of us don't. Vic looks apprehensive but hopeful. I didn't think that going to get stuff from the house could be so eventful. Ray and I are chatting on the couch while she does homework, when we see them come in.

"What did you do?" she asks.

Vic looks at Jesse and back at Ray, "Me?"

"No," Ray waves him off, "lookin' at 'Mr. I'm too cool for people' over there."

Her impression of him, as she titles him, is actually pretty good. I can't help but give her some recognition for it.

"She's got you down, babe," I tell Jesse.

He shrugs, "She's gonna get one thing right eventually, I'm just glad it was about me."

Ray's response is to chuck a pillow at him. He catches it with a grin and walks further into the room, dropping a kiss on my head. Vic's apprehension is bleeding down the bond a bit, so I send a wave of love toward him, hoping to ease whatever is bothering him. He shoots a grateful smile my way before leaving the room to go put his stuff away.

"Do you need anything?" Jesse asks.

I try to think of something, but there's only one thing I want from him.

"Come cuddle me," I tell him, and he wastes no time in obliging me.

I burrow as close to his body as I can, and Ray's eyeroll is almost audible. She closes her textbooks and notebooks before standing.

"Whelp, that's my cue to get the hell outta dodge," she says, sweeping out of the room without waiting for a reply.

Jesse and I just look at each other and grin. I'm not sure if Ray really is grossed out by our PDA or if she just pretends to be. Either way, it's fun to poke at her. Jesse and I snuggle in silence, both of us content to just exist together. He's taken to spending more time around us, but not necessarily speaking up much. We don't force him either.

Henry and Vic have been surprised at how observant he is and the insight he can provide as they get to know him. I'm glad they are because I've seen it from the start.

"What happened at the house? Can you tell me?" I ask.

Jesse tilts his head in thought, "There were a couple of conversations that happened. Honestly, I'm not sure of the full outcome, but I'm hopeful."

"I'm not sure that I am." I bite my lip, assuming that Simon was the topic of conversation at the house.

"That's okay, Jojo, I can be hopeful for you."

I raise my eyebrows at him, "I'm not sure that's how it works."

"Sure it is."

"Do we need to talk about how brains and humans work?" I quip.

"No, but if we had our bond complete, I could definitely send my hope your way," he laughs.

I huff a small laugh before uncertainty sets in. Jesse catches it immediately because that's just who he is.

"Hey, I didn't mean to push. I was just making a joke. You know I'm ready, I know you accept me, the timing will figure itself out."

I tilt my head to give him a quick kiss. "You're amazing."

Before he can reply, the doorbell rings. I glance over with a frown but decide to go check it out. Henry's buried in his office, and Vic's putting stuff away. It's me or Jesse, and I usually make a point to answer the door when it's just the two of us. As soon as my hand touches the doorknob, I hear two sets of heavy feet coming toward me from within the house.

I glance over to see Henry and Vic doing their best to look nonchalant. At least they're trying. My brow furrows at them, and I make it very clear over the bond that I'm not falling for their shit. Surprisingly, they manage to hold their smiles in, although I do see a twitch of Henry's lips. When I swing the door open, I'm stunned into silence.

Simon is on the other side of the door, looking incredibly unsure of himself, but determined as hell in the same breath. He's holding two *massive* bouquets of flowers, one is all red roses and the other is a mix of a couple of different flowers, with petals that look fluffy and soft. I see a couple of orchids in the mix, but I'm not sure about the other two.

In front of Simon, there's a line of bags from various stores, including the Omega shop and his coffee shop downtown. My inner Omega is jumping up and down, shaking pom poms, and cheering for my last Alpha. She's easily won over by gifts, and I think he knows that. However, the rational part of me is not as easily swayed.

"I know this doesn't fix anything," he says before either of us says a greeting, "but I felt like I needed—no—wanted to bring offerings to try and get some of your time. There are no strings attached. If you want to take all of this and tell me to leave, I will."

My eyes roam over all the bags and the flowers, savoring the difference between the red roses of one bouquet and the pinks and purples in the other. Knowing I can't avoid it, I finally look up into his eyes. Their chocolate brown always sucks me in, trying to see what I can uncover within them. Today, all I see is remorse and a tendril of hope. I want to reply, but I feel frozen, unsure how to respond to the massive display before me.

Behind me, there's a cough that poorly disguises the words "let him in," and I turn to see the culprit. Weird, none of the three guys inside are looking this way, and the ceiling seems exceedingly interesting to them. My bratty side comes out in response, and I step out of the house and close the door behind me.

"That'll teach them," I mutter.

Simon must hear it because he laughs as I finish my grumbling. My eyes flash up to his with a small smile, and my fingers twist together in front of me as nerves threaten to overtake my brain.

"Um, hi," I finally say.

"Hey."

I reach timidly for the roses, and he happily hands them over, smiling the entirety of our interaction. My hands bring them to my nose so I can inhale the soft fragrance.

"They're gorgeous, thank you. What's in the other one?" I ask.

Simon scratches the back of his neck, "Um, orchids, peonies, and carnations. I told the florist I wanted two giant bouquets of love."

"L-love?" I choke out.

His eyes widen in slight panic, "Uh, more like intentions of love? She broke it all down for me, and none of them translate exactly, so I'm not trying to come over and force an emotion on you. Um, the roses are, like, romance, then the other flowers are refinement, beauty, and, uh, fascination."

"Wow, it sounds like you put a lot of thought into this," I comment.

"Not as much as I should have, but I hope that you like it."

My eyes flick down to the bags and back. They form a small wall between our feet, the handles ending around our knees. My feet shuffle back and forth as I try to figure out how to get my hands on the bags without looking greedy. Simon's mouth quirks into a smile, like he's well aware of the dilemma in my head.

"Would you like your presents?" he asks.

My hands clasp in front of my chest, "Is that okay? I don't want to just assume it's all for me."

"Angel, this is all for you, the very beginning of my penance if you'll allow it," Simon tells me, his voice low and earnest.

"Will you come in?" I ask, my words quick and hopeful.

"I'd be honored."

I reach behind me and push the door open before calling over my shoulder to the guys.

"Get over here and help with my bags!" I shout.

Vic appears, chuckling as he passes one to Henry, and I grab the last two. They follow me to the dining table where I set everything out, and Jesse appears a moment later with two vases filled with water. My eyes follow him, and he just smirks in response to my accusing look. Sneaky bastard knew there were flowers coming. Or he saw over my shoulder, but I am impressed either way with his preparedness.

I grab each bouquet from Simon and gently place them in their appointed vase. It occurs to me that I should remove the cellophane and any rubber bands that are holding them together, but Jesse just pulls out some scissors and carefully removes the wrappings around each bouquet. When he catches me watching, he offers a quick wink, and I smile before turning my attention to the bags. My eyes glance at Simon's quickly, and I'm a little unsure if there's an order here.

"Grab whichever one calls to you first. There's no wrong order," he encourages.

I grin and dig into each bag. There are about four bags, stuffed with items that are from whichever store is advertised, plus a few other small items. Every single bag has its own stash of chocolate, and I try to be subtle about piling all the chocolate together in one bag.

There are blankets and robes and even a super soft onesie from the Omega store downtown. I find coffee bags, cute mugs, slippers, soft headbands, puzzle books, coloring books, office supplies, and even a cute nameplate that says "Omega Boss" on it with flowers all over.

Everything is a perfect mix, and my words fail me as I look over everything a second and third time. He's nailed me down so well for only knowing each other for a couple of months. It's a perfect mix of soft and cozy, cute, chocolate, low-key activity, and encouragement in my business. My throat tightens up a bit, and I have to swallow a few times to get the ball of emotion down. I'm not sure I've ever felt so seen, not even with Vic.

"It's perfect," I whisper.

Simon just gazes at me, a soft smile on his face, while his eyes hungrily drink me in. My hands graze everything as I fidget under his stare. It's not uncomfortable, but I'm really not sure what to do. Is this enough to forgive him? Should I demand more gifts? No, that feels selfish. I'm not sure what the right response is. Someone in the room coughs, and my eyes look up, trying to find who made the noise.

"Right," Simon says softly, and I turn toward him as he kneels on the ground in front of me.

"What is it with Alphas and kneeling?" I mutter, thinking about how Jesse did a very similar gesture after I chewed him out. A snicker sounds from behind me, and I know Jesse caught my words.

"Josie. Angel. The words 'I fucked up' are not enough to convey how much I hurt you. How scared I was of our connection, and how terribly I handled it all. You deserve none of my anger or dismissal. You deserve every ounce of goodness and love there is in this world. I'm so, *so* sorry for how I dismissed you and abandoned you. These gifts are the start of a penance that I hope you'll let me earn. Never again will I let my fear and shame come between us. You and Vic are the best things that have ever happened to me, and I almost lost both of you in my idiocy.

"So, I'm taking my place at your feet, abandoning any Alpha dominance in front of you, to tell you that I want to be a part of your life. In any capacity that you'll have me. I have more to say to the Pack, but you're my first priority."

I stare at him, stunned into silence. There's not a single thought in my head at the moment. His words have wiped away any defense I had built up. It's way too soon to forgive him, though, isn't it? I pull out a chair behind me and plop down into it, grabbing a chocolate and stuffing it in my mouth. There's silence for a good few minutes, but he doesn't make any attempt to move.

"Tell them, talk to them, I need to think," I say distractedly, trying to work through my tangled reactions and desires. My hand waves at the guys as I speak.

A gut feeling appears, and I think that whatever he plans to say to them will make or break my decision.

thirty-eight

JOSIE

Simon turns away from me and stands when he faces the guys. Ha, suckers, they don't get kneeled for. My eyes stay glued to the four men as Simon approaches them. He stops a few feet away and clears his throat a few times before moving forward.

"I owe you three a large apology as well. I'm sorry that I backed out on Josie's heat when I was part of what started it. I'm sorry for avoiding Pack discussion and dismissing your thoughts. I'm sorry that you guys had to pick up the slack when I hurt Josie. I'm also incredibly sorry that I didn't trust you all more. If I had... if I had just been more open with you, this might not have happened. As much as I want to be back in Josie's good graces, I also need to be forgiven by you as well.

"My rut threw me into a shame spiral, but right as I was finally listening to Vic, Josie came back around to check on me, and my shame came full circle again. Instead of talking, I shut down. Jesse, I need you to hear how much I appreciate your pep talk earlier this evening. You didn't say anything new, I know, but what you *did* say pulled my head out of my ass," Simon tells them, his voice unwavering but full of emotion.

Vic steps forward first and pulls Simon into him. They speak in soft tones together before Vic pulls back and Simon lands a kiss on him. Smiling, Vic pulls back with a small blush so Henry and Jesse can chime in. Jesse takes a few steps forward before Henry can respond.

"You already know how I feel about doing all this. May as well support each other if everyone else is on board," Jesse says before holding his hand out.

Simon takes it, shakes it once, then pulls Jesse in for a quick hug. Jesse scratches at his neck as he steps back, a little overwhelmed by the touch. Henry is surprisingly less open than the other two. I think of Henry as my sunshine guy, but right now, he's all storm clouds as he looks at Simon.

They stare at each other for a moment before Simon breaks eye contact and looks at the ground. I honestly don't remember what they said to each other on the night of my heat, but based on the tension now, it definitely wasn't friendly.

"Why are you apologizing?" Henry asks.

I think the question surprises all of us, especially Simon, based on the level of bewilderment I see. Simon blinks at him, waiting to see if Henry is kidding or not, but when Simon figures out Henry's not kidding, he stands up a bit straighter and takes a deep breath. More chocolate finds its way into my mouth, and I make sure I have more ready to eat.

"I'm apologizing because Josie deserves better than I gave her. I'm apologizing because I let my fears guide my actions instead of working through them. I'm apologizing because we have a Pack pull, and instead of showing you that I understand how valuable that is, I ran. Every single person in this room deserves better than what I gave them, so I'm apologizing and hoping for a second chance," Simon tells him.

I feel Henry soften in the bond before his face relaxes. He puts his hand out there, and Simon grabs it. They don't hug, but I see Henry nod in acknowledgement of what Simon said.

"You know the end decision is Josie's, but I believe you want to be better and do better. If she says so, you're welcome here," Henry tells Simon.

As they all look toward me, I take a deep breath and let my lips flap together as I exhale. My head tips back, and I decide that the ceiling is very interesting at the moment. While I'm thrilled that they're all being so considerate of how I feel, it suddenly feels like there's a huge weight on my shoulders. The future of this Pack is in my hands, and while my Omega is telling me to stop being stupid and accept Simon, things feel more complicated than that.

The only other person in this room who knows and understands Simon on a deeper level is Vic. Since he happens to also be my best friend for life, I stand up and gesture for him to follow me. I find the empty den and pull Vic in with me, leaving the door cracked so I can see if anyone tries to eavesdrop.

"What do I do?" I ask him.

Vic just smiles, "I can't answer that for you, Josie Girl, you know that."

"It was worth a shot," I scoff.

"Ask me the question, the real one this time."

Our eyes meet, and I ask the question that really only Vic can answer.

"Is he capable of actually being here for all of us? Of staying instead of running?"

If Simon isn't capable of getting over his shit, then that's the end of things. I don't have the capacity to deal with him. It wouldn't be fair to me or the guys. Vic's face is soft but thoughtful as he considers what to say.

"Yes, I believe he is. He's a little slow to change, but once his mind is made up, he moves forward. When he would make changes at his last coffee shop, it took him forever to decide and implement what he was thinking. When he decided to open a new shop here, though? No hesitation, just determination."

"You callin' me a coffee shop?" I tease him.

Vic huffs a laugh, "No, it was just the best example I have. When he finally makes the decision, or when there's a need to make things happen, he's all in. If he hadn't talked to me at our place before coming here, I would be more skeptical. Since he did, though, it tells me that he's in. He wants this, and he wants to work for it."

"Okay," I nod my head.

"Okay?"

"Okay. Let's go back."

Vic reaches out to pull me into his body, hugging me tightly before kissing me silly. I lose myself to the feel of his mouth on mine, our tongues tangling in their own dance of passion. My scent rises as I perfume for him, freely letting my scent out with the safety he gives me. His hand slides down my body and instead of the sensual groping I anticipate, he pinches me and wiggles the skin on my butt. It tickles, and I push him away, laughing as I run out of the room.

I can hear Vic's feet chasing me the short distance to the kitchen and dining area as I slide in my socks. My laughter continues as adrenaline pumps through my body, the high from kissing Vic still thrums through me, anticipation from the chase, and excitement from our conversation all heighten my responses, leaving me giddy. The three guys in the kitchen watch with amused smiles as I slide past them, using the table to create space between Vic and me.

His steps slow to a stop as he reaches the table, grinning at me and breathing just about as hard as I am. We grin at each other, taunting as we scuttle back and forth on opposite sides of the table. There's movement in my peripheral vision, so I quickly glance in that direction, but don't let Vic escape my attention. The three other guys are watching us with a mix of amusement and concern.

"Are you guys just gonna let him chase me around like this?" I tease them.

"Looks like you're enjoying yourself," Henry comments.

I gasp in faux outrage, "Are my Alphas abandoning me in my moment of need?"

Vic chuckles low, "Your Alphas can't save you now, pretty Omega."

Grinning, I try to dart around the table and escape him, but a hard body blocks my way. I yelp in surprise and look up to see Simon blocking my way. He smiles at me, effectively blocking my way out, but not actively trapping me. There's space that I could squeeze through, and I doubt he would stop me. However, in the moment it takes me to stop and figure out Simon is blocking the way, Vic has caught up, and his hands grab me around the middle.

He pulls me in close and starts blowing raspberries on my neck. My squeals start up again, and now all my Alphas are laughing.

"I think that's the pitch used to call dogs," Jesse says.

I turn and glare at him playfully, "I will end you!"

"I'm already gone for you."

Of course, I melt at his words.

"Fine, I accept that. Come kiss me!"

Jesse laughs before ambling over and doing as I've demanded. Even though Jesse isn't overly dominant, he is an Alpha, so I'm surprised he's doing as I've asked with no backlash. He gets close to me, hand raising to caress my cheek before his fingers thread through my hair, and he pulls my head back, exposing my throat. He takes a deep inhale of my scent, causing a rush of slick to escape me, and pulls back to look in my eyes.

Why is it so damn hot when they scent me like that? It drives me crazy every time. Instead of landing a kiss on my lips as I had hoped, Jesse smirks and leaves a barely-there kiss on my temple before backing away.

"Tease," I accuse him playfully.

Jesse just smiles, completely unrepentant. Nobody moves after the interaction, and the reason for all of us being here slams back into my head. Everything feels so natural and easy, I've forgotten that we still have to talk. Vic still holds me around the middle as I look at Simon again.

"You have to work for it. Push me away a second time and we're done," I tell him.

He all but collapses at my feet and places one hand on my neck and the other hand on Vic's neck.

"I promise to do better by *both* of you," he swears.

Jesse clears his throat next to us and I turn to see Henry standing closer, but still letting the three of us work shit out. Jesse tells Henry to come closer with a jerk of his head, then looks back at me and Simon.

"Simon, Henry, and I talked while you guys were in the other room. We came up with a few ideas, depending on where your conversation went. Since you're giving Simon a chance, I'd like to wait to bond until he does. I don't want him to feel like an outsider in this Pack. You're the Omega, though, so if you want me to be bonded sooner, I'll do it."

My eyes look between Jesse and Simon, trying to figure out if there's anything they've left out. Neither of them looks overly nervous or concerned, just a normal amount of nerves. The fact that Jesse is willing to wait for Simon melts my heart, and it's exactly who I saw Jesse to be before he met the rest of the Pack. A little anti-social, but a huge heart for the ones in his life.

"Yeah, I think that's really amazing that you're willing to wait for him. I feel like you have each other's backs," I tell them, trying to hold my happy tears in.

"This is Pack," Henry comments from the side, "This is what Pack does, we support each other however is needed."

"Is it cheesy to ask for a group hug?" I ask.

Henry scoffs, "You're our Omega. Nothing you ask for is cheesy."

I giggle a bit before opening my arms to bring all of them as close to me as humanly possible. Simon moves so he can wrap his body around Vic and place his hands on my waist where Vic's are. Henry and Jesse happily come in close, not afraid to find a spot to grab me, and not afraid to touch each other in the hug.

"How did I get so lucky?" I ask softly.

"We're the lucky ones, Josie Girl, and we're all gonna work to make sure you feel as loved as you are," Vic answers.

thirty-nine

SIMON

It's been a few weeks since I apologized to Josie and the Pack, and it still feels like the best decision I've ever made. Josie gets a present from me almost daily, and I make a point to talk to all three of the other guys. Jesse is a gamble when it comes to how much he'll talk, but he's always nice about it. Sometimes he and I just greet each other, then hang out in silence.

Today I have a special treat for Josie. One of my new baristas' grandparents is Taiwanese, and she suggested adding boba tea to our shop. It's a popular location, and we've had success overall with coffee, so she said she'd help us with recipes if we wanted to try it out. The one in my hand is our first batch, and I'm excited for Josie to try it. So far, the samples have been great, so I'm hoping that she likes it.

When I step into the house, Jesse greets me and sees the tea in my hand. His eyes light up, and he moves closer to where I'm taking my shoes off.

"Honey, did you bring me a treat?" he asks.

I laugh and shake my head at him.

"Not today, this one's for Josie," I tell him.

He gets close and peers at the plastic cup in my hand. "It looks weird."

"Good thing it's not for you, then," I tell him primly, raising my nose at him before walking away.

He follows, chuckling, as I walk through the house to find our Omega sitting in one of her favorite places. Henry's study. She loves to grab blankets and cozy up on the small sofa in there, with a few books piled near her or her laptop ready to be used. Today, she's happily reading something that has a very buff torso on the cover.

"Angel, we can give you some muscles to look at. You don't need to read a book with them on the cover to experience it," I tease her.

Josie jumps a little and looks at us with a blush on her cheeks. A whiff of her scent hits the air, and I can smell her arousal in it. It's not a full perfume, but something she's reading that has gotten her worked up.

"Hey!" she greets us, her voice a little high with embarrassment.

I grin at her, unrepentant that we've interrupted her book time. My hand holding the boba tea comes forward, and I give it a slight shake. Her eyes go wide, and she puts the book down. Josie's hands reach out in a grabbing motion, eyes locked on the gift. My heart warms at how easily she accepts my gifts now.

She always loves them, but at first she was a little nervous to take them. She would tell me that she didn't want to come off as greedy, but after a few assurances that it would make me happy, too, she started embracing her Omega love of gifts. I oblige her excitement and step fully into the room to hand her the travel cup.

"This is one of our first attempts at boba tea over at the cafe. We've had a few samples with the employees, but this is one of our first fully made ones. It's a milk tea. We tried it with a few different tea blends, but this one is full sweetness, flavored with Taro, and has tapioca boba," I tell her proudly before fully releasing the drink to her.

"What kind of tea is in it? You said you tried a few different ones?" she asks, swirling the wide straw through the tapioca and ice.

I look at her blankly.

"Did you forget?" she smirks.

Hesitantly, I nod my head, grimacing. She giggles before wrapping those gorgeous lips around the straw and taking a first sip. I don't see any boba come through the clear tube, but Josie's eyes light up as she savors the flavor of the tea itself. She takes a second sip before talking, and I see one of the dark colored balls come up the straw with the tea. Her mouth moves slowly as she chews, and a smile grows on her face.

"This is delicious! It tastes like a fruity cereal! Jesse, you gotta try this. Did you already try it, Si? You need to try it too," she says excitedly.

"I have not tried these flavors yet, and I feel ridiculous that I can't remember the tea blend. Jesse can take the first sip, I'll wait," I tell them both.

Jesse takes his sip, and his face is a mixture of disgust and enjoyment. I hide my smirk, knowing that he doesn't want to disappoint Josie, but he is also not a fan. He hands me a drink, his mouth moving like he's chewing, but I'm not sure he actually took in any boba. Putting the big straw in my mouth, I take a mouthful of the tea and try to grab a boba as well.

"It's, um, very sweet," I comment as I slowly chew the boba.

"Definitely fruity," Jesse adds.

Josie happily takes another drink while smiling at us. She eyes us up and swallows her boba before talking.

"You hated it, Jesse, didn't you?" she asks.

Jesse rubs the back of his neck, "Hate is such a *strong* word..."

"It was definitely sweeter than I like, but I can see why you like it," I say.

She giggles sweetly, "It's okay, I love it so bring me one any time you feel like it."

"You got it, Angel."

Jesse and I then find seats in the den with her to just sit and exist. Jesse picks up a book at one point, but I alternate between watching Josie and closing my eyes to enjoy the peace. My body is craving hers more and more as we live together. Thankfully, Vic helps me take the edge off as much as he can, but I know he needs contact with Josie as well. Moreso really since they're bonded. So I try to balance my needs with everyone else.

We're basically operating like a Pack. That thought shocks me and snaps me out of my peace. Is this what Pack is? Balancing needs and ensuring everyone gets what they want? It must be, it *has* to be, because I refuse to believe that this happiness and peace are accidental. My eyes snap open, and I sit up straighter. Jesse notices the movement and raises an eyebrow at me.

"This is what it is, isn't it?" I ask him quietly.

He smirks and nods once. Seems like he's come to the same conclusion and is comfortable with it. Honestly, so am I. These last few weeks have been amazing, and the fear I once had seems silly now. When the right people are involved, Pack is great.

"What is it?" Josie asks.

"I was just thinking how happy I've been over the last few weeks. Getting to give you presents, interacting with the guys, and even just now as we all just existed together. Then it hit me that this is what it means to be Pack. Just being here for each other."

She grins, "I never thought of it that way before. You're right, though, it's all of that and more. I'm really happy that you're here, Simon, please know that."

"I do, I promise," I respond.

"What about me?" Jesse teases, a small smile on his face.

Josie giggles, "Yes, you too, my silent Alpha."

"Damn straight," he replies and settles back in.

There's a pause in the conversation, but it doesn't feel awkward. I know what I want to say, I just need to Alpha up and say it. My eyes glance between the two of them as I work up the courage to just say the damn thing.

"Guys... I'm ready. Whenever you want," I say.

Josie's face lights up in a wide smile, while Jesse's face is a mixture of happiness and relief. I'm not sure if the relief is because I'm finally ready so *he* can bond, or if it's just because I'm ready. Either way, it feels encouraging, and I'll take it. Josie snatches up her phone and sends out a text message in our group chat.

> **JOSIE**
>
> Vic, Henry, are you busy? The correct answer is "no."

HENRY

Lol, I'm never too busy for you, Omega.
What's up?

> **JOSIE**
>
> Simon wants to change his name. He's now going to be Bond, Simon Bond.

HENRY

… Babe, I love you, but that was terrible.

JESSE

Agreed. I'm sitting here listening to her giggle over it, too.

VIC

Lucky bastard. I'm free. Nest?

> **JOSIE**
>
> Nest

HENRY

Wait, why are we going to the nest?

VIC

Oh, honey…

HENRY

Shut up!

I'M CHUCKLING as I read over her shoulder, but when she puts the phone down and meets my eyes, the chemistry bursts between us, and my smile drops fast. I want to feast on her, taste every inch of her skin and lap up all her slick like a damn animal. My pheromones must be in overdrive because I can see her pupils widening as we stare at each other. Just as I'm about to lean closer, Jesse hauls Josie up and tosses her over his shoulder.

She squeals in protest, to which he answers with a slap on her ass as he hauls it to her nest. Grinning ferally, I follow them, hot on Jesse's heels. He drops her in the Pack suite, right at the doors that lead to her nest. I haven't been in there yet, and deservedly so. Last time I abandoned her, so I need to earn her permission. Josie disappears behind the doors to adjust her nest, and I look to Jesse.

"You good?" I ask.

He nods, "Been good, better now. Glad you got your head in the game."

"Me too," I admit.

Vic comes jogging into the suite a moment later and attacks me with his mouth. I grab his head and lower back before pulling him close to me. We kiss like we've been apart for years, and to some degree, it does feel that way. Everything is connecting today, and I can't wait to feel my bonds with Josie and the guys come to life. We break when we hear Henry enter, breathing heavily like he ran.

"You assholes could have clued me in better." He grins.

"What kind of Packmates would we be if we didn't encourage you to learn?" Vic asks.

Henry chuckles and flips him off, which sends Vic into joining the laughter. The doors to the nest crack open, and all four of us snap to attention. Josie peeks out, half her body in the nest and half out. She looks over all of us, nods, and grabs Jesse. She reappears a moment later, beckoning me closer before grabbing me wordlessly.

Her nest is perfect, filled with soft blankets and fuzzy pillows. She has a few body pillows thrown in as well, each of them covered in a plush microfiber case. The fairy lights strung along the ceiling blink in three different colors. There are two strands of white with a strand of green and a strand of blue woven in. The walls are a muted blue, with hand-drawn ivy crawling around them haphazardly.

When I turn, Vic and Henry are in the room, looking amused, but not stepping a toe past where Josie points. She turns and looks from me to Jesse, assessing the situation. As I watch her, I'm not sure if she's fully here at the moment. It looks like her Omega has taken over entirely, and she's running on pure instinct. It's hot as hell.

Grabbing at my shirt, she tries to pull it off me without words. I give her a smile.

"You want my clothes off?" I ask her, my voice low and husky.

She nods, a small whine escaping her.

"Whatever my Omega wants, she gets," I say, pulling my shirt fully off my body.

A glance at Jesse and I can see he's not waiting for Josie to manhandle his clothes. When she turns to him, she purrs at the sight of him getting undressed. Then she grabs both our shirts and weaves them into the support area of the nest. She fusses for a moment before turning toward Vic and Henry with an eyebrow raised. They abandon their shirts and toss them her way. Only once her nest is exactly how she wants it does she relax and come back to herself a little bit.

Sitting primly on her heels, she folds her hands in her lap.

"My non-bonded Alphas, please come into my nest and bond the fuck out of me."

JESSE

I'm standing fully naked on the edge of Josie's nest when she purrs for us to bond her. This time, I'm not running. Well, I'm not running away. I plan to run toward her for the rest of our lives. Two steps into the nest and I'm on my knees next to her, my nose against her neck and inhaling her addictive scent.

Simon hesitates only a second before abandoning any hesitations he had. I know he's all in, so I don't worry about the hesitation being bad. He hasn't said if he's ever been in a group dynamic, so I'm guessing that he's trying to figure out how to make it all work. Honestly, I chose not to be part of the group sex dynamic until bonded, so I don't know either, but I want Josie too much to give any fucks.

While I'm lost in her scent, Simon is slowly pulling at her clothes, exposing her body inch by inch. I pull back and help him remove Josie's clothes. She should just walk around naked all the time. Her body is too beautiful to hide. My inner Alpha purrs his agreement in my head. Unable to resist, my mouth latches on to one of her nipples, sucking the tight little bud into my mouth and teasing it with my tongue and teeth. She moans in delight, arching her back to push more of herself into my mouth. Simon's rough breathing is close enough to me that I know he's on her other nipple, helping to drive her pleasure higher.

Male groans in the background tell me that watching this is equal parts pleasure and torture for Henry and Vic. Too bad for them that our Omega hasn't called them in yet. Simon and I take our time mapping her body with our tongues, mouths, and hands. At one point, we bump hands as we both try to feel how soaked she is, and instead of pulling away, we silently work it out so we both push into her.

"Goddammit," I groan, feeling how hot and wet she is.

"I cannot wait to get my dick in there, Angel. You're going to feel amazing," Simon rumbles against her skin.

Josie whines again, arching to try and take our fingers deeper.

"Need..." She loses her voice as we pull out and push back in at the same time.

Letting Simon have her pussy, I trail my finger down, lower, circling around her back entrance. She gasps, but doesn't pull away. Instead, she spreads her legs wider, maneuvering so one of them is propped behind me. My fingers push a little more, adding pressure to the small circles I'm making.

"Have you taken anyone here yet?" I ask her.

She nods her head wildly, scrabbling to try and find an anchor while Simon ramps up his teasing. "Just once."

He alternates between circling her clit and diving deep to stroke her G spot. The teasing is driving her nuts, and she finally snaps, pushing us both away from her holes and pushing me down on my back. Her legs straddle me, and she sinks down on me slowly. Her head dips back in pleasure, and I growl with how good it feels.

I grip her hips as she explores this angle more, slowly alternating between rising up and down and griding around on my cock. There's no way I'm bonding her in this position, but I *will* let her have her fun. She starts to look a bit frustrated, but I'm not done watching her pleasure herself.

"Need more, Omega?" I ask her.

"Yessss..." she all but hisses.

I drive up into her suddenly, making her gasp and bounce hard.

My hands hold her steady as I begin to pump in and out of her, making her moan and pant with her pleasure. She begins to babble nonsensically, repeating "please" over and over again. My hips stop moving, and I sit up, grabbing her hair to pull her head back.

"Please, what, Omega?" I growl.

"Bond. Bite. Fuck," she says.

"You want my bite? You want me to fuck you senseless and bond you?" I ask her.

"Yes, please. Bond. Bite. Please."

I flip her over as smoothly as I can and drive in as deep as I can. My knot is swelling as I go, and I know it won't be long before I have to lock us together. Changing the angle, I pull one of her legs up over my shoulder as I drive deeper and harder. Her swollen clit needs attention, but I don't want to compromise the position of how I'm holding myself up.

"Si," I call out.

With no further communication, he shuffles over and starts to play with her clit, completely unbothered by my cock and knot so close to his fingers. He alternates between circles and rapid, random movements. I can hear her breathing getting faster, breathier, higher. My mouth starts to water at the thought of biting her, and I can't wait any longer. The swollen knot on my dick is bumping her entrance with every thrust and catching Simon's finger too.

"Come for me, Omega, come so I can knot you and lock us together. Gonna knot you for days, sink my teeth into you. Make you *mine*," I groan as I slam into her.

On the final thrust, my knot pops all the way in, and she detonates. Her walls clamp down on my cock and my knot before milking them repeatedly. The pressure and the movement of her muscles draw me over the edge with her. Pleasure zaps through my body as I feel my cock pump out streams of cum, filling her as much as I can.

Before we can come down from the high, I lunge forward and bite down on her neck, opposite side of her first two bites. Her orgasm starts over, and my legs almost go weak with how much pleasure she's giving me. I've never felt anything so hot and soft pulsating around me like this. It's the best feeling I've ever had. She tries to thrash in her pleasure, but I hold her tight to me, not letting go of my bite.

After a moment, I let go and lick the wound. I want it to heal well, and licking it helps that process. Pulling back, I try to look in her eyes, but she surprises me by surging up and digging her teeth into my neck, her little growl of possession catching me by surprise. The bond fully connects, and I lose my breath for a moment. If I thought my world changed its axis when I first touched Josie, that was nothing compared to this. My entire universe is wrapped up in her.

I can feel her in my chest, a feeling of energy, light, love, and devotion. There's a hint of the bonds she has with Vic and Henry, but primarily it's her and me. We stare at each other, reveling in the feeling of closeness the bond brings us. Our emotions flow freely between us, and I know we can't have it be that way all the time, but right now it's perfect.

We snuggle in the nest for a bit, Josie taking just a moment to indicate that Vic and Henry can join the nest. Both strip down and crawl in, Vic wrapping himself around Simon from behind. My knot finally pops free, and I know it's time for us to fully Pack up. Henry appears with a soft cleaning cloth and gently cleans up Josie. Part of me feels like I should be doing that, but my time with Henry has told me he likes the care duties. So I let him.

Josie smiles at him gently before turning her head to look at Vic and Simon. They're tangled together, Vic murmuring in Simon's ear while he strokes him gently. Simon's eyes are half closed, and he's breathing heavily, almost slack in Vic's hold. The dynamic strikes me as beautiful. An Alpha letting their Beta take full control like that. It's a huge sign of trust. However, the second Josie whines, they both snap their eyes to her, and Simon nods.

Vic grins as Simon moves closer to Josie, bringing his lips to hers. They share a passionate kiss, tongues tangling and hands roaming. I reposition myself out of the way, sitting up by Josie's head so Simon and Vic can access what they need. Henry sits next to me as we watch our Packmates bring pleasure to our Omega.

Simon breaks away from Josie and locks eyes with her. "Can Vic join?"

She grins, "Yes!"

"Good Omega," Simon purrs, causing Josie's toes to curl in.

He sits up fully, checking on Vic, who has a bottle of lube at the ready. Simon then turns back to Josie and gives her a soft smile before snapping into Alpha mode.

"Present, Omega," all but snaps at her.

She greedily flips around, her head by my hip and her ass thrust high into the air. Her hand starts to wander on my leg as she anticipates Simon's next move. He gives her a light smack on the ass, causing her to moan.

"I'm going to fuck you. Then I'm going to knot you. Then I'm going to bite you. You will be my Omega, and I will always be your Alpha. You want me to knot this tight pussy?"

"Yes, please, knot, bite, please!" Josie babbles.

"Fuck, yes," he rumbles, his teeth clenched together, "Vic's going to slide into my ass, making sure we're all connected as you and I bond."

Josie lets out a guttural moan, "God, yes!"

Simon doesn't waste another second before positioning himself and sliding into Josie's tight heat. He gives her a few thrusts before halting while buried to the hilt. As Vic gets ready to join, Simon reaches around Josie and begins to play with her clit. Watching the three of them together is more erotic than I would have expected.

There's a tenderness between them that I've not taken the time to really notice. Once the bond is fully in place, I fully expect the three of them to take full advantage. Vic slides into Simon slowly but steadily, causing pleased moans to escape both men. Simon pulls back a little from Josie, and Vic moves with him, pausing in place as Simon thrusts into Josie again. Vic stays in that same spot, his face a mixture of torture from staying still and pleasure from their actions.

Simon fucks himself on Vic as he drives into Josie. He starts a rapid tempo, and Josie begins to moan in small, unintelligible words. Vic is almost growling like an Alpha with pleasure, even though he's the Beta who holds us all together. Simon doesn't last long with pleasure on either side of him. His finger flies over Josie's clit building her higher and higher before he slams all the way in, popping his knot inside of her.

Josie screams her pleasure, head thrown back, eyes closed in ecstasy. Simon grunts as he empties himself inside of her. Behind Simon, Vic begins to pound into both of them, not caring about what state either of them is in. As Vic chases his release, Simon moves Josie's hair and bites right next to my mark, so her neck matches on each side. Another orgasm drags out of Josie with the bite, and Vic stutters his temple before shouting his release, his body plastered to Simon's. The three of them breathe together before Josie turns her head and pulls at Simon. He turns and gives her access to cement their bond.

They revel in their bond just as Josie and I did. A smile spreads over my face as I watch the three of them regain their breath. Vic pulls out first, then goes to get some cloths to clean them all up with. He can't get to Josie yet, but he lays a soft kiss on her forehead while they stay knotted together. She's so blissed out that I imagine she'll take a nap before Henry can have his turn.

When I turn to look, he's sheepishly cleaning himself up. Looks like he couldn't wait. I'm surprised I didn't hear him, but my focus was solely on the show in front of me.

"Couldn't wait," he says softly with a small chuckle.

"Not judging, bro, I get it," I reply.

Henry tosses the cloth out of the nets before looking back over at me.

"Pack bond?" he asks.

I could say I want to wait. Now that I've bonded with Josie, I would be okay for a few weeks before the imbalance starts to set in, but Simon and I agreed that we're all in.

I hold my wrist out to Henry, and he returns the favor with his unmarked wrist. We bite down simultaneously. This bond is like finding my family. It's not as all-encompassing as Josie's is, but it's the support I didn't know I was missing. However, there is one missing link. I nod over to Simon, and Henry winks at me before moving.

"Pack bond?" he asks Simon.

Simon shoots him a sleepy grin and holds his wrist out. Henry holds out the one I just bit, and they repeat the action of simultaneous bites. When Simon enters into the Pack bond, there's a sense of peace that I never would have been able to find on my own. It's a love that spans beyond my understanding, but now that I've had it, I can't understand why I was so hesitant.

Grabbing blankets, we all dog pile in the nest around Josie and Simon, not caring who is lying or touching who. We keep our dicks covered, not quite wanting to go there, but beyond that, it's all good. Everything feels right now.

There's a smile on my face as I drift off for our Pack nap, and I feel a tear of joy slip down from the corner of my eye. I'm finally home.

epilogue - 6 months later

JOSIE

My brain feels like mush as I look over the tutorial *again*. Buying a new staff management software shouldn't be this difficult. I'm pretty sure the words are blurring into a different language as I try to make sense of all these steps. I sigh to myself, realizing I need to admit defeat.

I need help.

Not a moment later, Jesse pops his head into the room that I've overtaken as a small office.

"You rang?" he asks.

"I'm admitting defeat. Can you help me?"

He smiles and comes to sit near me as he explains, in English, how things should work in the system and gets everything set up. Being bonded is nothing like I thought it would be. I figured it would be wonderful, but it's so much more than that. Jesse and I talked about it shortly after bonding and agreed that it's like coming home. I'm home with these men, and they with me.

The emotional connection was tricky to figure out, but we got it down. Then the mental communication came. That threw all of us for a loop. Henry went into research mode and found that it's something that can happen with Mate Matches, but it's not widely talked about.

Thus our surprise. We tackled it together, though, just like we do with everything in our lives now.

Even though it took me a few months to stop assuming the other shoe is going to drop, the guys were so patient with me, and now there's no fear. We've all been able to talk through and push past our issues. There have been a few therapy sessions, but nothing insurmountable when we support each other.

"That's all you gotta do," Jesse says.

"I'm telling you, the instruction manual made things way more complicated. I'm pretty sure it's written in Cantonese."

"It's in English, my silly Omega. You're just impatient," Jesse tells me with a grin.

I let out a fake scoff of outrage. He just laughs before placing a kiss on my nose and walking downstairs again. When I glance at the clock, I see that I've still got an hour before dinner. We've made it a policy to eat at least one meal a day together. It's typically dinner but sometimes we have to switch to breakfast. All this to say, I need to get some shit done.

Going into the program, I follow the steps Jesse explained and add all my employees now. After I bonded with the guys, I finally had enough energy and support to start growing Touch Helpers. I'm fully in management mode, and I have seven touch helpers, including Georgie and James. They've been steadfast at my side and extremely helpful in training new employees.

Next, I add all our clients and start assigning each Touch Helper to their clients. We have a definite backlog that I need to make time to tackle. Later, I'll tackle it later. For now, I need to get existing information shored up in this system. I focus on the task at hand, working as quickly as I can so my Pack doesn't have to call me down to dinner. Again.

Josie Girl, food's done.

Shit, Vic caught me, I'm officially late.

Be right down! I reply to him.

Quickly, I lock my laptop and scamper down the stairs, excited to see what we're eating today. Ray graduated from high school four months ago and has been taking summer classes at the local trade school, learning how to cook. She's been cooking dinner for us more frequently, and it's fun to see what she comes up with.

Is all of it good? Fuck, no. She admits it when it's a miss, though, and we order out. All of us want to see her succeed in whatever she chooses, so when mistakes happen, she doesn't seem to worry. She does throw food at Simon sometimes for cooing at her about how proud we are, but he's trying to get that reaction.

Seeing Simon's fun side come out as we continue to grow as a Pack has been the best thing. He's the kid in class who likes to poke at people to get a reaction, but he's smart enough not to take it too far. He and Jesse get into some trouble sometimes. When I make it to the kitchen, I see those two conspiring in their chairs, and I give them a look so they know I'm on to them. Henry's at the head of the table, and I haven't seen him all day, so I plop myself right on his lap.

"Mmmmm, I missed you today," he says in his low rumble.

"Same," I say softly, resting my head on his shoulder.

A gagging noise comes from the other end of the table.

"Get a room!" Ray says dramatically.

I look over at her, feigning wide-eyed innocence, "Oh, are you unhappy that we're in love? Does it bother you to see us snuggling? I'm so sorry. I'll come snuggle you instead. You definitely need more love."

Standing up, I start to move toward Ray when she flings a vegetable at me from the serving dish.

"Keep your cooties to yourself!" She grins.

Grinning back, I hold my arms out, "But Ray... I just want to love you! Let me love you!"

We start laughing as we joke around before Vic finally speaks up.

"Josie Girl, there's a ton of love at this table. Now sit down so we can eat."

I blow out a breath, "bossy."

"Sassy Omega," he mutters.

I point at Henry, "You're a bad influence."

Henry just shrugs, "He's not wrong."

We grin and dig into the food. Tonight, Ray made some kind of lamb chop with fancy vegetables and rice. Look at us eating healthy and shit. The first bite has everyone fawning over how good the food is. Ray really has a knack for cooking and is serving up fewer flops the longer she works at the skill.

My heart feels so full, I worry it will burst at times. Seeing Simon and Jesse bond brings me more peace than I could have imagined. Vic is the Pack's voice of reason, and Henry leads us the best he knows how. Mostly, he loves us all and takes care of us. All four guys dote on me, but also remind me that I'm a strong Omega who is fully capable of taking care of myself.

Honestly, I don't know what would have happened if I'd never taken the job to see Ray. She kind of kick-started everything. Vic and Simon may still have happened, but it wouldn't be this perfect existence we've carved out for ourselves.

I look over at Ray, "Thank you."

"For what?" she asks.

"For allowing me to meet you and be your Touch Helper. If I hadn't taken you on, I wouldn't have bumped into Jesse. I never would have met Henry, and I don't know what would have happened with Vic and Si. I just wanted you to know that I'm so thankful to have you as part of this life."

She gives me a wobbly smile, "Sappy."

"You love it."

"True," she admits.

I look around the table and let the moment seep into my bones. Life might not be perfect, but this Pack is as close as I could imagine.

I won't give them up for anything.

acknowledgments

I cannot explain or say how extremely grateful I am to everyone who has read this book. Omegaverse isn't something I expected to write, but it was so much fun and I can't wait to write more of them. The support I have received from each of you is amazing, and I'm so grateful to you all.

Extra special thanks to my husband who is steadfastly and sarcastically supportive of my writing. He knows how to make me laugh and always gives me great humor ideas with his sarcasm. You're the best, babe.

Writing these characters was a stretch for me, because I had to figure out how to balance the anti-social with humor, and the tenderness with hardship and just the right amount of designation behavior. These characters definitely challenged me as an author and gave me some new insight on how to continue to improve my writing. I hope that you love them as much as I do.

about the author

Eliza Jonas is a red-head Michigan author who loves coffee, her children, her husband, and words. Not necessarily in that order. She has dreamed of being an author since the fourth grade, and is extremely grateful she is now able to share her words with the world. Her biggest hope is that someone feels seen, finds comfort, and/or finds some good ideas from her books.

also by eliza jonas

Brainstorm Series

Let It Go

Here In Your Arms

Hold On

Stand Alones

Back To December

Matchverse

Knot Gonna Give You Up

Matchverse Book 2 - TBD